30p

CW00556108

CHILDREN
of the
VOID

"I think I should give you a small sample of what you will receive if I find you slacking in your practice." (p.149)

CHILDREN
of the
VOID

By

Miss Regina Snow

With Pictures by
Giacomella Dagui

CITY & COUNTY OF SWANSEA LIBRARIES

WILDFIRE
A Wildfire Club Edition

© MCMXCVI The Wildfire Club
B.M. Elegance, London, W.C.1.

All rights reserved.
No paragraph of this book may
be reproduced without written
permission from the publishers.

Approved for distribution in
the Celestial Empire and all
Imperial Dependencies.

Set in Monotype Bembo
at the Imperial Press

CITY & COUNTY OF SWANSEA LIBRARIES	
Cl. NOV	
Au.	Pr.
Date 4/97	Loc. SKET
No. 0000164809	

First edition
Printed and bound in Great Britain by Antony Rowe Ltd., Chippenham, Wiltshire
on 21-lb Felsted Cream Wove : Demy 8vo (8½" x 5½")

CONTENTS

LIST OF ILLUSTRATIONS

INTRODUCTION

To my Readers in the 22nd Century

I T IS no doubt an impertinence for a writer to suppose that she may be read a hundred years and more beyond her days. And yet, if civilisation should reassert itself, as I fancy it will do—for it is not quite so frail a thing as might appear at this time of writing—there will be little indeed that you, my dear reader, will care to peruse from the last quarter of the 20th century.

It will be well known to you that that period was a sordid and benighted time ; a time whose works of fiction were of so indecent a character—even works of no particularly licentious nature being replete with a shocking grossness of language and assumptions—that I cannot imagine you will find them in bookshops or libraries open to the general public. It may be that this book too will fall under the general ban, or will, owing to certain of its themes, be taken for something it is not and tactfully forgotten.

For it is a curious irony that, even in its own day, this book was regarded as somewhat 'controversial', despite the fact that no impure language or gross carnality mars its pages, in vivid contrast to almost everything issued by the 'main-stream' publishers of its day.

Ironically, a certain appeal to 'forbidden' areas of sensuality had to be made in the book, partly because by no other means could it make its way in a market utterly hostile to decency of every sort. And curiously too, it appeals to *nuances* of sensuality which, even in that age of 'polymorphous perversity' were virtually unknown. This is part of the subtle irony of the life lived by the protagonists of this book, who, like their real-life counterparts, were utterly alien to the age in which they lived.

For what will be of especial interest to the reader of the 22nd century, is that in many respects this book thinks as you do. It is more Bohemian, no doubt, but a sort of Bohemianism has been thrust upon us by our strange and unnatural circumstances. But this book demonstrates that not *every one* in the late 20th century was taken in by the saturation-propaganda of the 'mass-media' of the period. Not every one viewed the outlandish life and thought foisted upon the age as 'normal'. A few people there were who could see the position in perspective, and to whom that strange psychotic age looked as grotesque and aberrant from within as it seems to any observer—such as yourself—looking at it from without.

What, you may perhaps ask yourself, would *you* have done if you had found yourself born into such a dark and twisted age ? The truth, we fear, is that you would almost certainly have *accepted* it, and, however much you inwardly disliked it, treated it as normal. That is what the overwhelming majority did at the time, and although you can now see the age for the monstrosity it was, had you been born into it, you would probably have been no different from its millions of other victims.

But suppose you *had* been different. Suppose, despite being born into that age, you had retained the power to see it objectively, as if from without. Suppose you had looked at the ridiculous clothes, the clown-ish advertisements, the inverted morality; the fragmented, soul-disrupt-ing character of everything from popular music to the design of every-day objects; the entire disjointed, atomised, neurotic mess of a civilisa-tion in a phase of unadulterated decadence. What would you have *done*?

This book tells the story of what one group of women did under these circumstances; and although the account is, in the strictest sense, fictional, it is a very exact account of the manner of life they chose and pursued. It has not been dramatised. It shows the everyday events of such a life.

It is, by any standards, a curious life, because, having been cut loose (along with the whole society) from all civilised norms, these girls felt themselves free to reconstruct their world in any form that suited them. And what *did* suit them was a world without men. In most other re-spects, their life and culture was drawn from the decades immediately preceding the great cultural collapse of the 1960s: though they were not, as their contemporaries tended to imagine, attempting to 'live in the past'. Their aim was rather to pick up the threads of civilisation at the point where they had broken and develop them onward from there. They were hampered, of course, by lack of numbers and resources, and therefore had to lean more heavily on the already-existing culture—artefacts, films, magazines, clothes, music—of the pre-Eclipse decades than would otherwise have been the case.

Partly in response to their lack of numbers, and partly owing to their own particular character—and perhaps to something in the nature of the Feminine itself—each girl developed more than one *persona,* greatly ex-panding the number of 'characters' present in the District. This they sometimes referred to as Life Theatre, although they regarded the differ-ent *personæ* as genuine and separate individuals, which, to a very sur-prising extent, they seemed to be.

The use of discipline within this group may, or may not (depending upon exactly how civilisation has developed by your time) seem curi-ous. What must be understood is that these girls lived in an age where all normal social discipline had broken down, and while the tyranny of governments and financial powers over the life of the individual was growing rapidly and alarmingly, the average person was encouraged into a cult of 'personal independence' that left her entirely stripped of the healthy and strengthening constraints of ordinary social discipline. One might say that all the *middle* levels of discipline were being broken down—family, sexual morality, local loyalties, ordinary decorum—leaving nothing between the atomised individual and the centralised financial/commercial/political power-structure.

The need to replace these middle levels, to put structures and 'hard edges' into their lives was intuitively grasped by these girls. They grasped the essential fact that if they were to attain psychic and social autonomy and develop a strong group-morale of independence and self-rule, then the rules and forms that governed their lives—the 'hard edges'—must be of their own making, not of the Enemy's.

One more aspect of this life which may seem remarkable is its division into two sexes: blonde and brunette. It should be understood that this division had nothing to do with the colour of a girl's hair. The brunette sex was feminine—a strange thing in itself in an age that had jettisoned the very notion of femininity—while the blonde sex was ultra-feminine. In those days, the ideal of masculinity was dominant everywhere. Women were persuaded that they must adopt the same values, aggressiveness (or 'defensive hardness') and work-ethic as men and that this was what they desired and was a 'liberation'. The Aristasians embraced the idea of femininity as an eternal reality and a principle superior to the masculine.

The two feminine sexes, fanciful as the idea must surely seem to any one unfamiliar with it, seems quite definitely to answer to a reality within the feminine soul. Girls quickly discover whether they are blonde or brunette and react to other girls within Aristasia accordingly. It is quite common (though not universal) for a girl to have both blonde and brunette *personæ*, but even so a girl tends to be *fundamentally* blonde or brunette and to know which she is and to see life through the eyes of her sex.

All the remarkable characteristics of Aristasia, as shown in this book through the microcosm of the semi-imaginary District of Maryhill, came about in the late 20th century owing to the breakdown of legitimate civilisation. Without necessarily leaving the cities of the time (for rural districts were no less a part of the Pit), these girls *seceded* from the entire collapsed culture of their time. They did not belong to the society that surrounded them. It was not, as far as they were concerned, a voluntary decision. Nor was it a thing that could have been done under 'normal circumstances'. They were both *forced* and *mandated* to create their own civilisation by the collapse of the world about them.

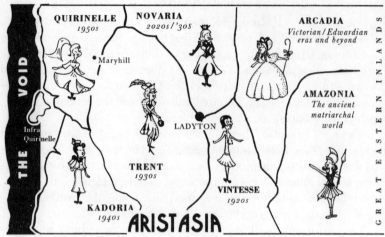

QUIRINELLE *1950s*

Maryhill

NOVARIA *2020s/'30s*

ARCADIA *Victorian/Edwardian eras and beyond*

AMAZONIA *The ancient matriarchal world*

LADYTON

Infra Quirinelle

TRENT *1930s*

VINTESSE *1920s*

KADORIA *1940s*

ARISTASIA

THE VOID

GREAT EASTERN INLANDS

Please note: *correspondences of provinces with periods of historical time are for general guidance only and should not be taken too literally.*

Morally and culturally, civilisation had ended; just as completely as it would *physically* have ended if it had been obliterated by atomic bombs. As they were wont to say at the time, any one who had fallen asleep in 1950 and woken up in the Fourth Decade of Darkness (the 1990s) could have been in no doubt that civilisation had passed away and been replaced by a clownish, sub-standard parody. The gradual nature of the inculcation of this parody, together with the constant saturation-propaganda of the mass-media of the time had inched most people into the successive, unconscious acceptance of each progressive stage of the madness. These girls could not be so deceived. They saw the obliteration of civilisation for what it was, and saw that they were standing not in a world but a void: and just as if everything had been *physically* destroyed by atom-bombs, the only world there could be, *culturally* and *psychically*, was the one they created for themselves.

And thus they were the Children of the Void.

MISS REGINA SNOW
SPRINGFIELD, QUIRINELLE

GLOSSARY
of the Aristasian Language

Amazonia: Eastern province of Aristasia corresponding to the ancient matriarchal civilisations.

Arcadia: Eastern province of Aristasia corresponding (primarily) to the Victorian and Edwardian Eras.

Art Neo: Broadly this term may be translated as *Art Deco*, but only those parts of Art Deco that are theatrical, feminine and *sound*. The bleak-and-barren blockish styles that are sometimes included in Art Deco are not Art Neo. Art Neo is considered primarily the art of Novaria (q.v.) which has spread to other provinces. The philosophical reasons for this, and for the use of the term are too complex to enter into here.

Bongo: 1. *noun* a dweller in the Pit (q.v.): particularly one deeply affected by the ethos of the Pit. 2. *adjective* having the qualities of the Pit.

Colony: An Aristasian household (or 'settlement of Aristasians') which fulfils public functions within the District (q.v.)—such as that of a cinema, a library, a restaurant, a night-club, a school etc. The colony is the fundamental building-block of the Empire. See page 37 for a diagram of the Honeyset Colony in Maryhill.

Decades of Darkness: The decades following the Eclipse (q.v.) are considered too offensive to name in Aristasian company. Under certain circumstances the First Decade of darkness may be referred to as the 1960s (because the earlier part of the 1960s, in certain aspects, corresponding to the Aristasian sub-province of Infraquirinelle), the following decades are only ever referred to as the Second, Third and Fourth Decades of Darkness (or one might just say "the Third Decade" for short). Where a specific year must be referred to, the form is e.g. 2D3 meaning the third year of the Second Decade of Darkness.

District: Administrative area consisting of colonies (q.v.) and households, controlled by the District Governess. Usually a group of

Aristasians in regular social contact will form a District. *Children of the Void* is a story of the daily life of the semi-fictional District of Maryhill.

Eclipse, the: The cultural and spiritual collapse of the early 1960s. Civilisation proper ended at this time and the Void (or the Pit) took its place. The process, obviously, was not instantaneous, and some elements of civilised life remained throughout the First Decade of Darkness and even into the Second, among the population at large, as opposed to the mass-media. Some hold that a second Eclipse took place at about the turn of the Second and Third Decades, after which deformism and moral inversion were complete and spread rapidly to every level of the populace, leaving very little intact.

England, London, New York, etc. It goes without saying that when an Aristasian mentions these places, or any others, she is referring to them as they are in the real world (q.v.), not to their Pit-parodies. These are termed Pit-england, Pit-london etc.

Fleem: Abbreviation of *flea-market*; usually a euphemism for 'car boot sale' (a term not used in Aristasia). Sometimes used as a verb: "They've been fleeming this afternoon." Fleems are a cheap source of up-to-date (q.v.) articles.

Golem: A bongo (q.v.), especially in his aspect as an unnatural being: an artificial creation of the Pit.

Her: Aristasians tend to use 'her' and 'she' for unspecified persons in the same way that pre-Eclipse speakers and writers use 'him' and 'he'— e.g. "Any one breaking the rules will have her licence revoked". In Aristasian contexts, of course, all unspecified persons must be female, but even when speaking of real-world (q.v.) history or literature, this form will be used. When speaking of bongos (q.v.) one often uses 'him' and 'he' since the Archetypal bongo is masculine just as the Archetypal human being is (from the Aristasian perspective) feminine; and also because no true bongo of either sex is actually feminine (though some of them are female). Sometimes when a patriarchal real-world context seems to require it the 'he' form is used. What is not used in any case is the awkward and ultra-bongo 'he or she' ("any one breaking the rules will have his or her licence revoked"), or the semi-literate 'they' ("any one breaking the rules will have their licence revoked").

Infra: Abbreviation of Infraquirinelle (q.v.), but sometimes used pejoratively for things whose realness (q.v.) is dubious: " Is this [film, song, car etc] all right?"—"Well, just about, but it's a bit Infra."

Infraquirinelle: Sub-province consisting of an island off Quirinelle, and containing those elements of the first decade (see **Decades of Darkness**) that are still-human.

Iron Curtain, the: the barrier separating ourselves from the rest of the Real World (q.v.). Essentially the Iron Curtain is the Pit itself seen in its aspect as a barrier, cutting us off from normal civilisation. So, if one sees an advertisement for photographs of film stars in a Trentish Picturegoer magazine, one might say. " Look at these lovely pictures they are selling in England (q.v.). I wonder if we could get any through the Iron Curtain". In the Aristasian world-outlook, Real-World Trent (q.v.) is contemporary, and separated from us not by time but by the Pit and the War therewith. The ravages of time are translated into the ravages of that War. A friend recently received a delightful clockwork doll from Quirinelle, England, and, noting how even the box was in almost-new condition, said, " Look how beautifully she has come through the Iron Curtain."

"*J'agroo*" for "I agree": This is schoolgirl dog-French combined with a " yeeth-and-byeety" joke. See page 134 for such jokes and pages 115–117 for the ideas behind them. It is at first difficult for one surrounded by the bongo-English accent to hear that *oo* is actually pronounced as *ee*, but careful listening and comparison to pre-Eclipse English soon makes the phenomenon hilariously unmistakable. The idea behind *j'agroo* is that if the word had actually been *agroo*, bongos would necessarily pronounce it *agree*. The Aristasian speaker is deliberately over-correcting. Such over-corrections were not uncommon in the speech of the semi-educated in the days when the semi-educated still aspired to improve themselves and had not been persuaded, to their lasting harm, that their ignorance is just as good as any one's knowledge. An example of over-correction is the sergeant-major's, " I h'ain't standin' for it " —he is over-correcting his own tendency to drop the aspirate by placing one where it does not belong. More analogous to the present case is the local pronunciation of *Missouri* as *Missoura*, which derives, apparently from an over-correction of the local rustic tendency to modify final *a* to *y*, (e.g. *Americky*). The Aristasian, of course performs such over-correction consciously and humorously, usually in association with some other joke, as when she calls the Bongo-B.B.C.

the Booby-soo* or refers to a first-decade singing group who made a seminal contribution to the decay of popular music as *the Bootles* (so named, legend has it, because they came from somewhere near Bootle). In this latter case, and to some extent in the one before, the joke helps to maintain the Aristasian taboo on pronouncing Names of Darkness.

Kadoria: Province of Aristasia corresponding to the 1940s.

Maid: May mean a maidservant, but is also used as the generic term for blondes and brunettes, or even for human beings in general (c.f. the pre-Eclipse real-world use of 'man' and see **Her** above). So: "Let every maid rally to the defence of the Empire", "Maid is not an evolved animal but a fallen angel", "Maid is the only creature on Earth that uses language." The two uses of the word are not ambiguous or even really separate. One refers to "My maid Mary" in exactly the way that Wooster refers to "My man Jeeves." A maid in this sense is distinguished by the fact that she is *only* a maid, rather than a lady (though she may be a 'lady's lady').

Maiden: Sometimes used for an individual maid without any particular implication that she is young or unmarried—as in: "Let every maiden read for herself what I have written". This is regarded as a dignified or Old Aristasian usage.

Novaria: Province of Aristasia corresponding to a projected future which has recovered from the Eclipse (q.v.) and returned to sanity. The 'futuristic' tendencies of Aristasia tend to cluster about this Province and Vintesse (q.v.).

Pette: A girl. Originally short for 'chapette', although this shade of meaning is probably less present in its usage than the pun on 'pet'. Its *nuance*, at once jaunty and ultra-feminine, is unique and purely Aristasian. A 'pette', like a '20s 'flapper' or a '60s 'dolly bird' is a phenomenon specific to her time and place. The word also, with its overtones of ownership and obedience, stresses the ethos of ferocious group-independence and equally ferocious revolt against the false divide-and-rule Pit-cult of 'personal independence'.

---

* Some one has suggested that this should logically have been "Boo-boo-soo", but we see no reason that it should. The southern Pit-english bongo would pronounce *Booby-soo* and *Boo-boo-soo* alike as *Bee-bee-see*.

Pit: The psychotic, anti-feminine world created by the Eclipse (q.v.). See **Void** for a fuller definition of this term.

Provintal: Pertaining to a Province. To say that the Quirinelle Pathe News is "very provintal" means that it encapsulates the spirit and essence of the Province. "You look very provintal", means that one looks very real (q.v.) and very much of the Provinces. This can be used even when no *particular* Province is meant.

Quirinelle: Province of Aristasia corresponding to the 1950s. While in terms of earthly chronology the 1950s are the latest historical period covered by a Province, in Aristasia Quirinelle is considered somewhat old-fashioned as compared to Trent (q.v.) or Vintesse (q.v.). Maryhill, the District in which this book is set, is in Quirinelle, very close to the Trentish border.

Quirrie: Short for Quirinelle, but only in its adjectival sense. One talks of Quirrie music or Quirrie respectability, but to say "I live in Quirrie" would be unidiomatic.

Real: Authentic, not mutated by the Pit. So real cars and real films are what bongos (q.v.) would call *old* cars and films. To call them 'old' in Aristasia would be a great gaffe. They are contemporary, while the Pit equivalents should be referred to in the past tense, as something which, for *us* at least, is dead and done with. One would also say of people in up-to-date (q.v.) films: "they look so *real*". As one comes to understand the complete inauthenticity of the Pit and all its manifestations, this expression takes on deeper and more *piquant* meaning.

Real World, the: Essentially this expression encompasses everything outside the Pit—not only Aristasia, but the world before the Eclipse (q.v.). It could also include any group of people who, for whatever reason, remained outside the Pit (the Pennsylvania Amish, for example). Of older people who still retained all the attitudes and values of their youth, did not watch television and were scarcely aware of the condition of the late 20th century, one might say: "They are still living in the real world." Or one might say "No one in the real world would even think such things", meaning that only in the Pit were such assumptions possible. Generally the Real World means the world before the Eclipse, so the Real World is where we find England (q.v.), London, New York etc., as opposed to Pit-england, Pit-london, Pit-new york.

Silly Monkey(s): S/M.

Slave: Usually a bongo (q.v.), i.e. a mind-slave of the Pit (q.v.); but there are rumoured to be actual slave-girls in parts of Aristasia. If they exist, they do not come into this book.

Trent or Trintitia: Province of Aristasia corresponding to the 1930s. Trent is the largest of the five Western Provinces and is looked upon as a centre of fashion and sophistication, especially by the more 'home-like' Quirinelle (q.v.).

Up-to-date: From the Western provinces, but especially from Trent, Vintesse and Novaria. So we speak of up-to-date cars, songs or films. Arcadian ones would be 'old-fashioned', bongo ones 'outdated' or 'obsolete'. Things from Quirinelle can be up-to-date, but never quite ultra-modern or up-to-the-minute as things from Vintesse might be.

Vintesse: Province of Aristasia corresponding to the 1920s. Although chronologically the 1920s are the earliest of the decades represented by the Western Provinces, Vintesse is actually considered the second most modern of them and is closely allied with futuristic Novaria (q.v.).

Void, the: The Pit (q.v.) is also called the Void, but the two terms are not interchangeable. 'Pit' refers to the distorted, hell-like *contents* of the post-Eclipse world, while 'Void' refers to its utter emptiness of anything of value or interest—just as the sea is void of fresh water or the desert void of everything but sand. The Void is the Pit as seen from within Aristasia—simply a yawning nothingness, defined not by what it *is*, but by what it is *not*. It is in this sense that Aristasians are Children of the Void. Bongos (q.v.) are Children of the Pit because they are shaped by the specific contents of the Pit, by its distortions and neuroses—by its attempts to escape its own ugliness through 'alternative' uglinesses, or its attempts to find rest in conformity to the 'standard' ugliness, or any of the thousand mix-and-match permutations of Pit-poisoning. Aristasians are Children of the Void because they are shaped not by the specific contents of the Pit, but by the experience of living surrounded by a wholly rejected nothingness and having to re-create the psychic world in order to have a world in which to exist at all.

Cast of Characters

The characters are arranged in groups. Each group represents characters that manifest in the same body (and which therefore cannot appear at the same time). Within each group the characters are listed in order of appearance in the novel. The sex of each character is indicated in parentheses.

Miss Quint *(brunette)*
Annalinde Milchford *(blonde)*
Miss Nightwind *(blonde)*

Miss Milchford *(blonde)*
Hostess at The Constant Nymph *(blonde)*
Maria *(brunette)*
Aunt Alice *(brunette)*
Miss Blue *(blonde)*

Lehnya *(brunette)*
Wendy *(blonde)*

Odeon usherette *(brunette)*
Sinta Serendra *(brunette)*
Susan *(brunette)*

Emma Kadrina *(brunette)*
Jane *(blonde)*
Miss Maybridge *(brunette)*
District Inspector *(brunette)*

Alice Trent *(blonde)*
Miss Baines *(brunette)*
Miss Worth *(brunette)*

Betty/Charmian *(brunette)*
(Senior waitress at the Soda Fountain)

Angeline Southern *(blonde)*
(Junior waitress at the Soda Fountain)

"It is not that they are bad men. They are not men at all. Stepping outside the Tao, they have stepped into the void. Nor are their subjects necessarily unhappy men. They are not men at all: they are artefacts. Man's final conquest has proved to be the abolition of Man."

C.S.Lewis—*The Abolition of Man*

EX IMPERIAM NIHIL EST

Outside the Empire there is nothing.

September
WEDNESDAY
1. The District Visitor

HIGH HEELS clicked along the front path. The door was knocked in the correct pattern—for few would care to open to a Pit-crawler. The door was opened.

On the doorstep stood a woman in a cream mackintosh with belt and epaulettes. A print headscarf covered her perm. Her lips were pillar-box red and one guessed, though they were covered with close-fitting leather gloves, that her fingernails matched her lips, even as her bag matched her shoes. She was *very* Quirinelle. Even her stockings were authentic 1950s from a wrapper that had come unopened through the Iron Curtain, with its Quirrie cover-girl still caressing her calves on the front.

Not that one could imagine this austere young lady caressing her calves and gazing wide-eyed and kittenish from the front of a stocking-wrapper. That quality which the girls called 'Quirrie respectability' breathed from every pore. Quirrie respectability and brunette authority and District seriousness. She was from the District, of course.

"Good afternoon, Miss Milchford. My name is Miss Quint. I am from the District Governess's office."

Miss Milchford smiled. She was nervous, of course, but she was a hostess. That always comes first with a blonde. Before official business, before nerves, before everything. The house, the hearth, the Hestia, and she the priestess thereof: the help of travellers; the comfort of those within; the creatrix and sustainer of that first building-block of reality— the home, whereon rest all things: the District, the Province, the Queen, the Empress, everything. Without you, dear blonde, there would be nothing. The District Governess herself, and all above her, would be but empty names. But that is why we must protect you and discipline you; ensure both your safety and your soundness.

And Miss Milchford *was* blonde. Very blonde. Not in point of hair-colour—her Vintesse bob was on the dark side of chestnut—but in every important respect, a soft-eyed, glowing-hearted doe-blonde.

"Do please come in, Miss Quint."

Miss Quint entered. She noted the Art-Neo lamp on the hall table in the form of a slender girl holding a white globe of light. Her quizzical look perhaps indicated a slight Quirinelle disapproval of the *risqué* Trentish nubility. As they passed into the drawing room she noted with approval the delicate plastic lace cloth on the trolley. Possibly upon her a *nuance* of gentle humour was lost. Possibly she took the Quirrie-respectability of such a cloth entirely at its face value, not noticing the delicate juncture at which Suburban Respectability shades off into Quirrie Bad Taste and both are sources of sophisticated pleasure to the more modern minds of the Home Provinces.

She was not a sophisticate, this Assistant Governess. Her vowels were flat—not of course with the classless drabness of the Void, but with a respectable, suburban flatness by no means wholly unaffected by the sterling enunciation of the up-to-date B.B.C.. A careful, upward-aspiring but not pretentious diction as crisp as the click of her high-but-not-too-high heels.

"You have a very nice home, Miss Milchford." She was noticing the Art-Neo looking glass, the dozen photographs of glamourous Trentish film stars, blonde and brunette, dotted about bookshelf, sideboard and mantel in silver and wooden Art-Neo frames. It was all a touch Trentish and modern for her more homely Quirinelle taste, but she could not deny it was charming.

"Thank you. I do try." Miss Milchford's crystalline vowels shone against the flatness of Miss Quint's like jewels in a dull-silver setting.

"I am sure you do, Miss Milchford. Do you feel ready for inspection today?"

"Not quite, I must confess, miss." The schoolgirlish 'miss' expressed her nervous humility before this suburban brunette and the whole order she represented, up to the shining Empress herself.

"Well, I am afraid we cannot delay further. Show me the bedroom."

They went up the stairs with more film-star pictures on the wall. Miss Milchford tapped the barometer in nervous reflex as she passed it and noticed the glass was falling. A considerable collection of clothes were thrown over the banister at the top, though she had been trying to get them put away in time. Fine furs were jumbled with short Infra dresses, coats, skirts, scarves and stockings. It was something of a contrast to the cool Art-Neo order below but only a taste of the disorder of the bedroom where clothes, papers and every manner of thing was strewn to a depth of several layers. "You have to be Sir Flinders Petrie to find a matching pair of stockings in this house," Annalinde had said last week.

Miss Quint pursed her pillar-box red lips. "Not much of an improvement, is it, Miss Milchford?"

"It *is* an improvement," said the distressed house-blonde, "though perhaps it does not show much. You'd be surprised how I have worked on it."

"I take it you have a cane in the house."

"Yes, of course, miss."

"Would you be so kind as to fetch it?"

"Certainly."

Miss Milchford opened the wardrobe and, reaching in among the clothes unhooked from the rail a crook-handled disciplinary cane of the type used in schools. It was long and moderately heavy—of the senior rather than the junior variety. She handed it to the Assistant Governess who felt its weight, flexed it, straightened a slight curvature in a very professional manner and said: "This should serve quite acceptably. Shall we return to the lounge?"

They descended the stairs and Miss Quint instructed her hostess to take up an attitude facing one of her deep green Art-Neo armchairs and to bend over until the palms of her hands were resting on the seat. Miss Milchford had on a very charming Trentish dress, figure-hugging from waist to thigh and then flowing outward in those lovely undulating folds that only a bias-cut skirt can achieve. As she bent down the material stretched tight across her thighs and her small but comfortably-upholstered seat until one could see the line of her knickers and the trace of her suspender.

Despite her charming blonde passivity and her long acquaintance with the laws and authorities of her country, Miss Milchford could not but feel that there was a touch of indignity, even of incongruity, in the fact of herself, a grown woman and a responsible householder, bending over her own chair in her own exquisitely-furnished drawing room, to be caned like a child:—and caned furthermore by a woman with flat *a*'s who called the room a *lounge*. A part of her—a very small part—rose up in protest; wanted to revolt against the whole absurd procedure. To that part of herself she replied, very reasonably, that it was equally absurd for a lady of her standing to have such a hatefully untidy bedroomand that she deserved all she received—and that, in any case she was bound in obedience to the representatives of proper authority, that to revolt against a punishment like this were to revolt against the Golden Order itself—to cast oneself on the side of the Void where immediate chaos is the perfect servant of ultimate tyranny.

Some colouring perhaps also drifted through her mind regarding the body in which this Miss Quint was incarnate: and if it did it would in one way have reconciled her more fully to the punishment and in another stiffened her against it. But that colouring, if it was there, was so slight as hardly to be noticeable. Miss Quint was Miss Quint. Her authority was that of the Empire and of the Golden Order. The mechanics of this particular manifestation were of no relevance to anything—especially when the manifestation was in any case so consummate.

But Miss Quint was speaking. Her mundanely authoritative Quirrie-respectable brunette voice was forming words to which it would be shameful not to attend.

"First let me commend you, Miss Milchford, upon the excellent appearance of your home. The hall and lounge—all the places that your guests see are quite lovely, and you have *perfect marks*, Miss Milchford, perfect marks for Wholeness. There is not one thing on view that carries the infection of the Void. Not a carrier-bag, not a book or paper, not anything. So I want you to understand that I shall be carrying a high Commendation to the District Governess. I do not want you to feel that the fact that you are about to be quite sharply disciplined is a wholesale condemnation of your very fine Hestia. Nothing could be further from the truth, Miss Milchford. You are in many respects—in the most important respects—a credit and an asset to the District."

"Thank you, miss," said Miss Milchford from her somewhat ungainly position.

"But you understand, don't you, why it is my unavoidable duty to cane you?"

"Yes, miss."

"A little untidiness, Miss Milchford, may be overlooked upon occasion. But chronic mess and chaos of the sort I have seen today cannot be allowed in any colony of this District, even behind the scenes. You do understand that, don't you?"

"Yes, miss."

"It is not respectable, Miss Milchford. It smacks of the—if I may say it—the hippified consciousness of the Void."

"I do understand," said Miss Milchford. "I do realise. I just can't seem to improve."

"Well, we are here to help you improve. I am going to give you three strokes of the cane, Miss Milchford. If there is not a considerable improvement by the time of my next inspection you may expect a rather more severe chastisement."

Miss Quint lay the cane across her hostess's seat, just above the line of the knickers. She let it rest for a moment, tapped it once or twice against the chosen spot, watching the firm flesh give slightly beneath the tight dress and then raised the cane high and brought it down in a perfect stroke. Miss Milchford's breath hissed backwards through her lovely white teeth. One forgot, one always forgot, quite how hard it was to bear. The pain surged through her, increasing to a climax some seconds after the stroke, commanding her with the imperiousness of brute nature to stand up and desert her obedient post. With quiet determination she refused. She felt the firm pile of the upholstery comfortingly

*"You understand, don't you, why it is my
unavoidable duty to cane you?"*

counter-irritant beneath her palms and braced herself grimly for the second stroke.

The cane whistled once more through the air, cutting the cloth-prisoned globes a little higher on their circumference with a satisfying report. A faint moan was forced from the lips of the stoic little blonde whose hands pressed so firmly and determinedly on the chair-cushion. She looked so utterly delightful in her suffering. How many fine shades of feminine loveliness would be lost to the world completely if blondes were not punished occasionally?

One stroke only now. It must be an effective one. A little lower, perhaps. On the thighs, just below that subtle ridge of knicker—no, almost *on* the ridge, in that delectable crease where thigh becomes bottom, a tender but perfectly lawful place for punishment. Miss Quint cut in the singing stroke almost horizontal through the air. The blonde let no cry escape her, but the shuddering exhalation that followed a moment after impact was tribute enough to the effectiveness of the stroke.

"You may rise, Miss Milchford," said Miss Quint, fingering the sturdy cane with satisfaction.

Miss Milchford rose and faced her. "Thank you, miss," she said sincerely. How little she had desired that caning. How much she had hated it as she endured the three cruel strokes—and now, not a minute afterwards, she could feel how much good it had done her; how warmly quiet her heart was, how tremblingly thankful her soul.

"I should also be grateful, Miss Milchford, if you would prepare for me, in your fairest hand, three hundred lines: 'I must endeavour to keep my home in such harmony and order as befits an Aristasian lady.'"

"May I write it down?"

"I will dictate it before I leave."

Miss Milchford served tea and scones. She noticed, with a gentle glow, that the tea one enjoys after a caning is subtly unlike any other.

"It *is* hard for you, isn't it, Miss Milchford?"

"I am afraid it is. We are rather Bohemian, you see. Very much in the realm of ideas. I find it hard to control earth-like things—material objects. It isn't just laziness or lack of time, though I am sure it is a bit of both. But—well, the earth-element of life just does not respond well to me or I to it. Does that sound absurdly pretentious?" She felt sure that this all-too-earthly brunette would find it pretentious, but surprisingly she did not.

"I do understand, my dear, but that, I am afraid, cannot excuse you from your duty. You do understand that?"

"Oh, of course."

"But you must not think that we are only here to criticise and punish you. Our job is to help your household and households like it—which are, after all, the very fabric of the Empire—to become all that they should be within the Golden Order. So I have come to you with more than words of encouragement, strokes of the rod and impositions. I have come to you with a suggestion which, I think, may help to solve your problem, though it will certainly add to your responsibilities."

"I am all attention."

"Last week a girl was sentenced by the Provintal Court to a six-month period of Punitive Service. Obviously it is necessary to find a household in which to place her and a mistress to care for and discipline her. My suggestion is that you should be that mistress. Of course you would have to organise and control her, but she could devote her time to all the things you find so difficult."

"Would she live in?"

"Yes, that would be necessary."

"And would she—how shall I put it—would *she*—qua maidservant—be here all the time?"

"You mean is she a plenary slavey or do other *personæ* manifest through her? No, she is not a plenary. That means that she has other *personæ* and it would be normal for them to be permitted some expression, though this need not occur in the early stages. How much expression will be ultimately your decision. She may be kept in her bonded *persona* twenty-four hours in a day if you wish it, either as punishment or simply because it is her mistress's will. One of her *personæ* is a child, to whom you will be *in loco parentis*, another is, I believe, quite a sophisticated young lady. You may deal with her as you see fit. She can be suppressed altogether if that seems best. Her status can be changed to plenary if her mistress requires it, though it is not at present recommended."

"So I shall have to take in a child and a Pippsie and no doubt a few others from time to time."

"Yes."

"And shall I have to whip her regularly as part of my duty?"

"She will have to report to the District Governess each month for a caning. You will not be required to carry out scheduled whippings as part of her punishment, except for one at the beginning of her service, but you are expected to treat her quite strictly. You will be given a Punishment Book in which to record her discipline. We shall inspect it each fortnight and will expect to see a reasonable number of entries—though if there are too many she will be summoned before the District Governess. You will be given a set of regulations for the discipline of a

Punitive girl and will be issued with a General Disciplinary Strap, though you are welcome, of course, to cane her with your own excellent implement whenever you choose. You have experience of administering discipline, I assume."

"I do cane my daughter occasionally—not nearly as often as I should, I fear—and give spankings from time to time."

"I am sure that is an excellent foundation. Remember that you are not on your own. We are never further away than your telephone. If you wish to have her disciplined by an Assistant Governess, that can be done at any time. If you require advice we can give it. I think it might be advisable for you to have an assessment and lesson in the administration of corporal punishment—but we can arrange that later. These are all details. What do you think, in principle, of the suggestion I have made to you?"

"I am not quite sure——"

"If I may be frank, Miss Milchford, it is not fitting for a lady of your standing to be completely without a maid—do you not think so?"

"Yes, that is true——"

"You have been in Quirinelle and in this District for some time now. You are very well acclimatised. It is time that you accepted more both of the benefits and the duties of your position."

"You are right, Miss Quint. I shall do it."

"Splendid. The necessary arrangements will be made presently. In the meantime I shall make a note of your line" She wrote some words in her little Quirrie notebook, tore off the page and handed it to Miss Milchford "Three hundred by tomorrow morning, please."

"By tomorrow morning, but——"

"By tomorrow morning. Good day, Miss Milchford."

Miss Milchford saw her guest out and closed the door. Miss Quint stood facing down the path, seeing for a moment the garden gate and the Void beyond—an uncommon sight, for the front curtains were always closed against the unpleasing vision of bongo-cars and pit-dwellers. She seemed at first to walk toward the Void, but turned quickly sideways, crossing the front of the house and turning again beside it, through the side gate and into the street known as Bottle Alley where brunettes of the younger and faster sort kissed blondes against the wall after the Odeon had closed. It was daytime now, and no one was there. She opened the kitchen door and slipped quietly upstairs to the bedroom. There she removed her mackintosh and hung it in the wardrobe, and, sitting before the dressing table, took off her headsquare and put it in a drawer, slipped off her Quirinelle perm and placed it on a wigstand, blotted the pillar-box red lip-rouge severely and went over it with the darker shade that belonged to Annalinde, put on Annalinde's scent, and in general effected the transformation of herself into the younger, more sophisticated Trentish girl who spent much of her time in the house.

Satisfied, she left the room, and then recalled herself and returned. She quickly slipped off Miss Quint's rather staid white cotton knickers with tiny floral perforations that looked almost as if they should match a vest and slipped on some lacy nylon semi-transparent ones of her own. Knickers were not seen, of course, but they contained a very deep and subtle magic for *personæ*. One should never forget them. If it should chance that one's skirt was lifted for a punishment, one would very properly receive double the allotted chastisement or more if one were discovered to be wearing some one else's underclothes. She dropped Miss Quint's knickers in the washing basket and proceeded downstairs.

She found her mother in the drawing room, beginning her lines.

"Hello, Mummie," she said, listening to herself to ensure that her vowels were as pure as usual. They were.

"Hello, dear."

"What are you doing?"

"Just something the District Governess's office asked me to do."

"Red tape."

"Don't talk like that dear. The District looks after all of us. It helps to create the reality of the Real World. You must not talk like a bongo, as if the authorities of *our* world were alien and exterior like theirs. Any more of that and I shall punish you severely."

"I am sorry, Mummie. Have you seen one of them?"

"Yes, dear, an Assistant Governess called Miss Quint."

"What was she like?" One could not help being curious about how the performance had looked from the outside. Of course, Miss Quint was nothing *really* to do with her. She had no illusions about that. Still one had been the *midwife* in the operation, had one not?

"Neat. Attractive in a dullish way. Very respectable. Very strongly manifested. I was quite afraid of her. She is the very essence of Quirrie respectability, I should say. She made one feel quite enclosed in the District. She wants us to take a Punitive girl."

"Are we going to?"

"Yes."

"Rather exciting, isn't it? Will she bring any relations?"

"A child and a Pippsie. Possibly some others."

"Do we know any of them?"

"I am not sure."

Annalinde slid into one of the Art-Neo armchairs. It was delightful to know that Miss Quint had been so strong, and so exactly what she should have been. It made the world feel rounder. She closed her eyes and contemplated the confining thrill of Quirrie respectability.

"Do you know what's on this week?" she asked after a little while.

"I am afraid not, and I am not sure I shall be able to come."

"Why not?"

"Miss Quint has given me three hundred lines. They are quite long ones and she wants them by tomorrow morning."

"But couldn't you have told her that tonight was Odeon night?"

"I half-tried but she would not hear any excuses. I expect anything one has to miss is considered part of the punishment."

"Oh, the beast."

"Now, Annalinde, would you like to stay in and write three hundred lines with me?"

"No, Mummie." There was really little danger of such an imposition. Her mother was far too soft in general for that, though it was wise not to provoke her directly. But really. Miss Quint *was* a beast. She *did* know about Odeon night and her smug little sense of duty told her to ignore it. She had felt that tingle in the white, pinprick-patterned fastness of her secret, most enclosing place, that her lines should have that enclosing, spoiling effect. Not that she was a bit sensual except with the dry sensuality of Quirrie matter-of-factness. Not that she had been fully conscious, in her own *persona*, of Odeon night, but insofar as she half-felt it from Annalinde's consciousness she was glad rather than otherwise. And insofar as Annalinde had protested from within, she was pleased to frustrate her. And now that the sentence had been given there was nothing that Annalinde or her mother or any one else could do about it. Miss Milchford must grind out her lines and Annalinde must go to the cinema without her or not at all. Both their evenings must be spoilt. but more Annalinde's than her mother's, for Miss Milchford was mature and accepting, while Annalinde was passionately self-willed and always felt strange and unprotected going anywhere without Miss Milchford or one of her *personæ*.

"Why don't you ring Lehnya and ask her to take you?"

"A blonde ask a brunette? Wouldn't that look very forward and undignified?"

"I don't think so, dear. She knows you always go with me or Maria or Hilary or—well, one of *us*. I am sure that is why she has never asked you. I think she would like to take you."

"Won't you ring her, Mummie?"

"I do not think I should. You should not always put me between yourself and the world. Of course I have stood between you and the

Void, and that was proper, and I always shall. But now that there *is* a world and not just the Void, you must make a little of your own way in it."

"Isn't that the bongo cult of 'personal independence'?"

"No, dear. I am not expecting you to be independent in that stupid, atomised way. Of course you will always be cared for and protected. What I want is for life to become fuller for you. For you to have relations with persons other than—well, *us*."

"I find you quite sufficient."

"Suppose I were to die?"

"You won't."

"Please God I shan't, though only She knows. But these exclusive relations with one person only—they are the stuff of the Pit. A part of atomisation. In a real world a girl has many relations to many people. Love takes a dozen different forms. That is normal and proper. You are not truly happy as you are. The world should be giving you more, fulfilling you more. And you should be giving more to *it*. That is your duty, dear. You have such a lot to give, my wonderful child.

"Now go and telephone Lehnya."

"I *can't*."

"But you must, dear. Don't you see that your agonised, adolescent embarrassment is a fine and precious thing? It is the very centre-piece of this particular *tableau*. Be grateful for it, cherish it. It would not come at your bidding, but here it is unasked, in all its hot intensity. Considering that your chronological adolescence was lost in the Void, are you not fortunate to find it here, complete even in its most excruciating moments? And is it not a gift not given to others, even in the real world before the Eclipse, that we can not only suffer these things, but appreciate them in all their delicacy at the same moment? What the Void has stolen from us we can, perhaps, never quite recapture, but we can capture *nuances* we could never otherwise have enjoyed. We are in a world that would never have existed but for the Void, despite the fact, and because of the fact, that we have seceded from it and rejected it utterly."

"What a curious thought. Yes, in a way we *are* the children of the Void."

"The only spawn it has that are not monsters."

"Are they *all* monsters down there?"

"Not entirely, poor things. All of them have held out—preserved themselves—to some degree, and none of them entirely. But insofar as they *have* preserved themselves unpoisoned, they are to that degree what they would have been if the Eclipse had not happened. Insofar as they are not monsters they are not yet wholly children of the Pit.

"We are the only *pure* children of the Void. It is a very strange and yet a very lovely state. We are mining curious facets of sensibility that could not quite have been before: perhaps the final fruits of this world-cycle."

"But perhaps not."

"No. There may be a Restitution. But in either case you will telephone Lehnya."

It was not her mother who spoke to her now: it was the sage who spoke. She went obediently to the telephone, cherishing as the precious thing it was her adolescent agony. It did not make it easier; but then would it not have weakened the spell if it had? She picked up the heavy bakelite receiver and slipped her varnished finger tip into one after another of the holes in the silver dial. KALinsie 0474.* She had a sick feeling high in her chest as the ringing tone sounded again and again. Perhaps she will not answer, she thought half-hopefully."

"Hello, KALinsie Oh-four-seven-four."

"Hello, is that Lehnya?"

"Yes, who—I say, is that Annalinde?"

"Yes." How surprising to be recognised like that. Perhaps Mummie was right. Perhaps Lehnya did take an interest in her.

"How nice to hear from you, dear blonde. To what do I owe the pleash?"

"Well, it's nothing really, only——"

"Only what?" asked Lehnya with competent brunette kindness.

"Only, well Mummie is busy and she can't take me to the Odeon and, well——"

"I say, Miss Annalinde, I hope you won't think me forward, but, that being the case, may I make so bold as to request the pleasure of your company in the one-and-ninepennies?"

"Saved by the belle," thought Annalinde. "What utter tact." Aloud, she said "Well, I don't quite know. This is rather unexpected. I shall have to ask my mother, of course."

"Go and ask her then."

Annalinde pattered to the drawing-room door, wondered whether her mother would approve of all this blondeish temporising and pattered back to the telephone.

"Mummie says yes, but you must have me back by half-past ten."

---

* Each Aristasian subject is assigned a Provintal Telephone Exchange based on the alphabetic equivalents of the area code of her bongo telephone number. The number can then be dialled in its correct form, beginning with the first three letters of the exchange on any up-to-date letters-and-numbers dial telephone. Aristasian telephones, of course, *ring* and do not bleep.

"No sooner said than done—well, four-and-a-half hours sooner to be exact, since it is just about six now, but what are four-and-a-half hours between friends? Shall I pick you up at seven?"

"Oh, yes—if you really want me." Immediately she wished she could swallow the words back. What an awful, *gauche* betrayal of the blonde unavailability she had been so carefully projecting. She felt herself redden from her neck to the roots of her hair. Thank Heaven she was talking on the telephone and could not be seen.

"Seven o'clock, then," said Lehnya, who apparently had not noticed the offending phrase.

Apparently, but of course she had. What could she make of it? Did the clever, fascinating Annalinde feel about Lehnya as Lehnya had felt about her these many weeks? One could hardly imagine so. She just wanted some one to take her to the cinema when her mother was unavailable. Blessed mother!

2. The Odeon, Park Place

LEHNYA was young. As a matter of fact, she had never taken a blonde to the cinema before. She knew very little about blondes, except that they were a wholly different order of humanity; so frail, some said, that one might break their bones by holding them too roughly. Certainly frail of heart and delicate of limb; swept by unpredictable moods and tempestuous passions; beautiful, sensitive, thrilling, mysterious and utterly, utterly different from oneself.

Lehnya lived in a tiny flat on the hovering edge of the Void. Pit-cries came to her at night from the darklands below. Pit-reverberations from the centralised electronic mind of the Octopus echoed at times through her very walls. The denizens below her door seemed harsher and more desperate than the common run of barbarians, and though one knew it was a matter of degree rather than of kind, and that their very lowness in the scale of being doubtless protected them from the worst intellectual perversions of their barbarian 'betters', that did not make it any easier to pass through them; nor did a bicycle afford the enclosure and protection of a motor-carriage.

At times Lehnya felt fear unbecoming a brunette. She felt it more now than when she had been outside the pale—or rather she could no longer pretend to herself that she did not feel it: no longer pretend that the ugliness and nastiness were somehow not what they were, and that she did not loathe them. She did not simply fear personal insult or attack. She feared the hateful, slickly-offensive advertising hoardings, the soulless telephone booths, the nasty clothes and empty, hardened faces. Assault was but the teeth and claws of the Beast—a very small part, proportionately, of its body. The hateful propaganda that screamed from its walls and its loudspeakers, flashed from its screens and its shop windows and hung upon the bodies of its victims, were the blood and bone and muscle. She feared the power of the Beast, economic and psychic as well as physical, to rend her, spoil her and poison her.

But these considerations were far from her mind this evening as she pencilled her slender eyebrows with a Marlene-Dietrich flick-up at the ends, pulled up the metal zip of her black velvet dress, pinned on her hat, buttoned her lovely, real coat and tucked her fox-fur in her basket—it was far too likely to fly off if one wore it on the bicycle.

She was wildly overdressed for her age, she knew, and it certainly did not make her feel any less her age. She felt more adolescent and nervous and dressed-up than she had ever felt in the grey, electronically-conditioned limbo of her chronological adolescence. She dabbed her imitation Chanel no. 5 inside her wrists and behind her ears and found herself humming a popular air;

All my troubles are mended,
She's my needle and thread :
She's got me walking on the tip of my toes
And my hat's on the side of my head.

"Tip of my toes,"—she slipped her highest heels into her bicycle basket. She should tower over Annalinde if possible. Blondes liked to be towered over.

She mounted Granya, her trusty steed, and sped off over the Sea of Shadows. One did not need to feel *that* unprotected, after all. Granya was a *real* bicycle, and as much an extension of the Empire as the armoured interior of any Bentley or Austin. Certainly one would not wish to traverse that place on foot. Granya was a swift-winged charger and Lehnya an Amazon Knight, or perhaps a dark-eyed enchantress who, with a bolt of light from her fingertips could wither any pit-crawler where she stood and in her place would grow the true human being that she had been if the Eclipse had not happened.

She tried it as she sped along. A deracinated granny in a pink track-suit crumpled to the ground beneath the blinding shaft, and in her place stood a silver-haired lady, humble but dignified, in a respectable coat and skirt. A grotesque white-and-fluorescent-orange bongo police car went up in flames as lurid as its clown-stripe, and out from the inferno drove a real black police Wolseley with its bell ringing. How contemptible that the bongo police should drive cars that, instead of reflecting the grandeur and majesty of the Law, were even more garishly mad than the ordinary bongo-tin—and made a noise like a particularly idiotic space-toy. No wonder Imperial law was recognised as the only Law. Justice must not only be sane but be seen to be sane. Bongo-law looked as mad as it was—as mad as the inverted order it enforced. Three straggle-haired, ragged-trousered tattooed lumps of post-femininity lumbered along the street cackling obscenities and oozing slut-ugliness from every pore. Three dazzling shafts transfixed them, froze them, disintegrated them ; and from the dust rose three wide-skirted, pony-tailed teens, silly and common but virgin-bright. Not idealised nor raised to a higher plane, but simply what they should have been had the cathode-grip of the Beast not twisted and tortured them out of form.

Hoardings went down, shop fronts went up, consumed in the purifying flame. Aluminium telephone kiosks melted to slag and red ones arose in their stead. Gibbering mind-slaves were mown down in hordes and replaced by the equivalent human beings. Beams of avenging light flashed from the charging wheel-steed until the evening sky pulsated with their refulgence. She would bomb this town silly—no, she would bomb it sane, bomb it whole, bomb it healthy : burn it with kindness and flood it with gentle light; put it to the refining fire and the healing sword; lay unwaste the wasteland.

She passed into the quieter streets near to the colony. Less aggressively hateful, but still the awful cars, still the same awful clothes, which, on better-off slaves, who should have been civilised and had no possible excuse for them, seemed more wilfully nasty than on the helpless-minded denizens of lower reaches of the Pit. But they were all equally helpless, equally devoid of mental defences, of overall vision or the means for analysis of their own position. Their honest revulsion against one tentacle of the Octopus always drove them more firmly into the suckers of another. It was absurd to blame any of them in one way; yet in another way they were all—even the stupidest—conscious collaborators in the betrayal and desecration of their own humanity. No one could wear such clothes and not, in her heart, *feel* what she was doing.

Like an island in a sea of darkness stood the colony. An ordinary house, indistinguishable from those about it, except for the real car parked outside, and yet to Lehnya's eyes, and not only to hers, an aura seemed to spread about it. The very leaves on the path, dropped from the overhanging magnolia tree seemed to have a different quality from the leaves in the Pit. They were *real* leaves, somehow, glistening with the heart-gold of their celestial prototypes. She had felt it from the beginning, before she knew anything of the invisible golden dome that surrounded the house, or of the golden thread that connected one colony to another. She dismounted and knocked on the door. An ordinary house, indeed. The *only* ordinary house in a street of madhouses all linked to their dark centre by the cathode ray. But the house was not in that street, now, nor in that town, nor on that plane of being. From within the dome it stood on a high promontory, with nothing about it and only the Void below; and in another respect, it stood in a little square with a few other houses, which, in Pit-terms were miles or half-miles away, yet since there was nothing but Nothingness between them, were they not side by side?

The door was opened, and there was Annalinde, wonderfully, heart-wrenchingly blonde—so very young, so very nervous. She looked shyly downward and glanced up into the brunette's face.

"Come in, please. I am not *quite* ready." She was charmingly painted and sweetly scented. She looked ready enough to Lehnya. "Ready to eat," the inconsequential phrase passed through her mind, but she could think of nothing to say aloud. Nothing clever or gallant. She felt almost giddy with nerves and shyness.

"Would you—no, would you sit here?" Annalinde had almost shown her into the drawing room and then had changed her mind and put her on the little chair by the telephone. Why? But of course! Rooms had *personæ* too. One could not go into the drawing room on this night of the week, nor the dining room either. Annalinde had almost forgotten too. One did. It seemed almost as absurd to associate the drawing room with the Constant Nymph as to associate Annalinde with Miss Quint. Indeed one never did associate them with each other, but for certain reasons of vulgar mechanics *they* could not associate one with another either, nor could one see Annalinde when Miss Quint was carrying out her duties, or the drawing room on Odeon night. In a perfect world such things could happen, but beneath the moon we are subject to the Limitations of Matter. Trifling limitations enough, providing one remembers them and steps the dance of life neatly about them. One can even see virtue in them, adding, as they may, to the elegant economy of the dance.

"You don't mind waiting a moment, do you?" asked Annalinde.

"If I had been asked to wait for a fortune in gold I might have shown some impatience, but to wait for you, Miss Annalinde, I count among the rare pleasures of life."

"My, how you do run on." Annalinde's Southern Belle was extremely well-turned, and Lehnya could tell that the compliment had impressed her. She was so glad to have prepared it for the occasion, because at present all inspiration had deserted her.

Annalinde disappeared upstairs. Lehnya looked about the hall. She had never called at the house like this on Odeon night before. She had always left her bicycle in Bottle Alley and walked round to the great French windows of the cinema. It was a delightful hall, with a wonderful Art-Neo lamp in the form of a girl holding an incandescent globe. There were up-to-date magazines on the hall table—*Mother and Home, Woman's Own* and a county magazine, all belonging to the present month and with smiling Quirinelle pettes on the covers. She picked one up, flicked through it, and put it down again. The contents were charming, especially the advertisements, but she could no more read a magazine here and now than she could at the dentist's.

Annalinde took some little time, whether because she was really quite behind in her preparations or because she thought it the thing to make a brunette wait a little we cannot say. Lehnya felt that she might be being deliberately kept waiting and did not really mind in principle, although in practice it felt uncomfortable. Annalinde seemed very protected, very hemmed in by Aristasia. Largely unaware of the problems of surviving on the edge of the Void—cosseted and a little selfish. Lehnya rather liked those aspects of her. A blonde *ought* to be just a little spoilt. She ought to have little notion of life-in-the-raw. To be self-centred could be the most charming thing in the world, provided it was done charmingly—but, of course, to do it charmingly one could not be wholly self-centred. Bongo self-centredness is charmless because it is gross and greedy. It is a crass placing of the self before all in obedience to the propaganda of atomisation which wants a world where no one can trust another and only the Octopus is constant in their lives. Blonde self-centredness is genuine self-centredness, but it is also a pose, and like all poses, it involves seeing oneself from without. It is the self-centredness of a winning child, not that of a bawling, brainwashed baby.

And there was the strap, of course. Blondes were brought up with the strap. However petted they might be they were also whipped in a way that brunettes, on the whole, were not. They learned to be very careful and delicate; very demure and obedient, slightly timid and yielding. The counterpoint of Annalinde's frill-trimmed self-centredness with her chastised maidenliness was to Lehnya as overwhelming as a sweetly narcotic scent.

Annalinde reappeared, her circular skirt rustling with half a dozen layers of paper-nylon petticoat. She selected a waist-length fur coat from the stand and allowed Lehnya to help her on with it. She put on her white gloves and her beret. She would have liked to wear a more elaborate hat belonging to some one older, but decided that discretion was the better part. She picked up her pink Quirrie bag and Lehnya opened the door for her, ushered her out and offered her arm. It was delightful, if rather unnerving, to feel the furry blonde arm in hers.

"To the one-and-ninepennies," said Annalinde.

"You know there aren't any one-and-ninepennies really," said Lehnya.

"I don't know any such thing. I have never paid for myself. Money is too gross a substance for a high-born blonde to handle."

"I am sorry, my lady."

"You should be, but you are forgiven. Shall we have the best seats in the house, whatever their price may be?"

"We shall, if they are not all taken."

"Oh dear, have I delayed us too much?"

"Probably not. Do you know what is on?"

"No, don't you?"

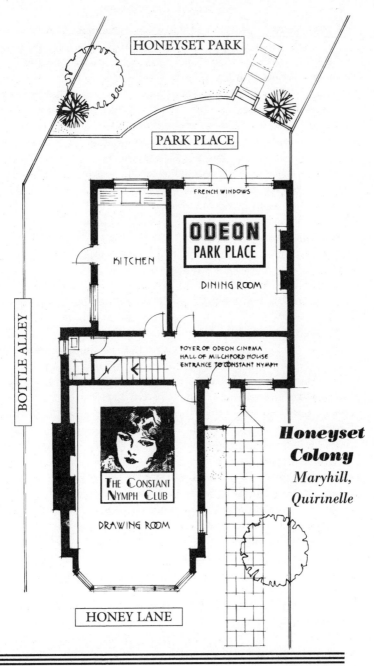

HONEYSET PARK

PARK PLACE

FRENCH WINDOWS

KITCHEN

ODEON
PARK PLACE

DINING ROOM

BOTTLE ALLEY

FOYER OF ODEON CINEMA
HALL OF MILCHFORD HOUSE
ENTRANCE TO CONSTANT NYMPH

THE CONSTANT
NYMPH CLUB

DRAWING ROOM

*Honeyset
Colony*
*Maryhill,
Quirinelle*

HONEY LANE

T H E   V O I D

CITY & COUNTY OF SWANSEA LIBRARIES

"No. We can look at the poster in Bottle Alley."

There was always a poster in Bottle Alley advertising the week's programme at the Odeon. Katherine Hepburn was starring in Little Women—a new film from Trent. They looked at the poster briefly. They *were* a bit late. How delightful it was to be conducted by so tall and so competent a brunette. How fright-making to be without Mummie and not even to have her near—and yet how exciting. *Will she try to kiss me? Should I let her? Could I stop her? Brunettes are so very strong, one has heard. I wonder how strong Miss Quint is. I know I am putty in the hands of a brunette from the times I have tried to prevent my brunette cousin from pinching or spanking me. She can hold me with one hand and punish me with the other, and I really want to stop her. And yet Surique is a brunette and she shares my body. She might be stronger than Lehnya. Could one resist the magic if one really tried? I am not sure one could unless one stepped into the Pit—and then what? Punitive Service, terrible whippings. How dreadful. How much better to obey and be a delicate blonde.*

Lehnya felt Annalinde's arm tighten on hers as if calling on the brunette's strength to support her. She looked at her elegant little up-to-date Timex watch.

"They've already begun. Can you run a few steps?"

Blonde horror—"I had really rather not." Lehnya was relieved. She had realised as soon as she said it that she was not safe to run in those heels. They reached the big glass doors with their velvet curtains behind them. The usherette was seated at her desk with a tin box of change neatly divided into compartments with different coins of the Realm and her strap placed neatly before her.

"You're late," she said reprovingly. It was not the usual usherette. The news was already showing on the crystal screen. Something dull about the English Prime Minister, Mr. Winston Churchill. Pity they could not show Aristasian news. They looked apprehensively at the usherette. Neither of the girls knew her or had any idea how strict she might be. She touched her strap. Annalinde looked nervous. Lehnya was not immune from punishment, of course, but blondes were so much more likely to be disciplined.

"The blonde's fault, I shouldn't wonder," said the usherette in her mildly Cockney accent.

"Yes, miss," murmured Annalinde, scarcely audibly in response to her fixed stare.

"Well, we shall see." Suddenly her cat-green eyebeams were turned from Annalinde and played more matter-of-factly upon Lehnya. "Stalls or circle, miss?"

"Stalls, please."

"That'll be one and six."

Lehnya took her purse from her bag and extracted a shilling and a six-penny piece. She still had a half-crown and quite a bit of smaller change. She had come well-financed for this outing. They went to the Art-Neo armchairs at the front rather than the upright chairs at the back. The sofa was already occupied by a couple who had taken care to arrive early. By the time they were settled the news was covering a fashion show and the quality of attention from the audience was much richer than it had been for Mr. Churchill. Wonderful, wide-skirted ball dresses, silver lamé, sophisticated short hair and glossy lips, women at once more elegantly mature and more innocent than any mind-slave woman could be; lush Quirinelle music; civilised, well-modulated commentary; a mingling of rich and delicate scents—but of course, those did not belong to the film: they belonged to the girls about one. The two worlds merged into an inseparable whole—the real world, the civilised world, the world of enchantment. She had glanced toward the two girls on the sofa, following the line of her thoughts from screen to auditorium. The blonde gave her a cute, nose-wrinkling smile. The brunette opened her fingers in an elegant little half-wave, at once delightfully patrician and warmly inclusive.

On two occasions during the film, Annalinde asked questions about who was who—a thing which often seemed to puzzle her—both times a little louder than strictly necessary, for she was an excitable girl. On the first occasion the usherette shone her torch on her, isolating her in a pool of exposed light in the midst of the warm sea of darkness. On the second occasion she did it again, but this time with the admonition: "Report to me after the showing please." Annalinde clasped her hands and looked, wide-eyed, at Lehnya. Lehnya wanted to squeeze her hand in comfort but could not quite pluck up the courage to do it.

To say that the rest of the showing passed without incident would be absurd. The incidents were plentiful and enthralling, but all of them took place on the crystal screen. In the interval Lehnya spent 5d on two choc-ices and Annalinde chatted in an undertone, even though there was no restriction on conversation in intervals.

"Oh, how dreadful, do you think it will hurt?" she said to her escort.

"I suppose it will," said Lehnya. "Haven't you had it before?"

"Not from this usherette. She *does* look strict."

The blonde on the sofa leaned toward them. "Poor Lindie," she said.

"Yes, poor Lindie," said Annalinde with an intonation of 'poor pussy'.

"But *silly* Lindie," said the blonde.

"Can't help it," said Annalinde with mock petulance.

"Do you the world of good," said the brunette. "I expect you did it on purpose."

"Are you going to sit there and hear this brunette talk like that about me?" said Annalinde to Lehnya in her wonderful Southern Belle accent, widening her eyes to Bette Davis proportions.

"Oh, you wicked trouble-maker," said Lehnya.

"Gel like that ought to be flogged," said the brunette.

These people, dear reader, are not going to introduce themselves. They know each other already. It falls to us, then, to tell you that the brunette is Emma Kadrina and the blonde Alice Trent.

The film recommenced and an hour sped by in renewed enchantment. Annalinde did not venture any further questions, even in the most subdued of voices. The National Anthem played and every one stood up for Queen Elspeth. Bags were sought, gloves drawn on. Emma Kadrina held a fur-collared coat as Alice slipped her slender arms into it with exquisite grace, and the couple, with a jaunty wave at Lehnya and Annalinde disappeared through the velvet curtain into the night.

"See you at the Constant Nymph?" called back Alice.

"Posso," replied Lehnya.

The usherette was doing something with the cash, taking no notice as yet of her two remaining customers. She cannot really have had much to do in so small a cinema, but she found something. She knew that Annalinde could not leave until she had been seen to. At last she called the girls over to the cash desk, her lips pursed in primly lower-middle-class severity. She looked at the neatly dressed-to-go-out blonde.

"Right. We'd better deal with you, hadn't we?"

"Yes, miss."

"Name?"

"Annalinde Milchford, miss."

The usherette opened the Odeon Punishment Book and looked leisurely through it. "Been disciplined a few times in 'ere, haven't you, Miss Milchford?"

"Once or twice, yes, miss."

"Bit of a trouble maker, are we?"

"Oh, hardly that, miss, just——"

"High spirited?"

"Perhaps."

"Perhaps, *what*?"

"Perhaps, miss."

"That's another stroke."

"Thank you, miss."

The usherette continued her perusal of the book. "*Talking, talking, late arrival, talking, screeching*—screeching, Miss Milchford?"

"Yes, well, you see——"

"I don't want to know. *Talking, talking, throwing sweet papers*——"

"It wasn't just me—you see the others were——"

"Thank you, Miss Milchford. I see you were reported to the District Office for that as well as strapped."

"Yes, miss."

"What did you get?"

"The Number Three District Strap."

The usherette whistled. "Must have hurt."

"It did."

"How many?"

"One hand, two seat."

"Quietened down for a couple of weeks after that, I see."

"Yes, miss."

"Perhaps you need it again. You can be reported for being down in here too often, you know."

"Yes, miss."

"Right. Talking twice and late arrival. Let's get started." She turned to Lehnya. "Would you care to wait in the foyer, miss?"

"Yes, thank you."

Lehnya went through the inside door into a panelled foyer, quite similar in some respects to the Milchfords' hall, but, of course, quite different too.

The Cinema Strap was short and softish. A stitched affair with round-ended tails. It was nowhere near as hard and penetrating as, say, the Classroom Strap, but it had a keen sting, especially when used with determination for several strokes. There were sounds of preparation. Lehnya guessed Annalinde was being bent over rather than having it on the hands. Curiously, the heavier and harder straps were *much* worse on the hands, but many girls thought that a strap like this one was worse on the thighs, especially if the usherette 'cheated' and lifted one's petticoat as well as one's skirt.

There was a sharp slap and a tiny squeal. Another slap, harder than before. Lehnya felt her temperature rising. Just that. Not an obvious heat of passion, but a very marked rising of her temperature, of whose exact cause she could not be sure, except that it was obviously associated with the strapping. The strap fell a third and a fourth time. She could hear Annalinde gasp. A fifth and a sixth. There was a cry of blonde half-protest silenced by some words from the usherette which Lehnya could not quite catch. A seventh and an eighth stroke. A pause. The usherette spoke again. This time Lehnya made out: "and one more for forgetting to call me 'miss'." A slap rang out even louder than the others. Annalinde cried out. There was a buzz of words from the usherette. Brief, submissive replies from Annalinde, and then the door was opened.

"You can come in now," said the usherette.

It was Annalinde who had been instructed to open the door. The usherette was in her seat again, beginning very carefully to make her entry in the Punishment Book.

"Well, you can take her away now, miss. Try to see she behaves herself on the way home."

"Thank you, goodbye."

"Goodbye."

"Goodbye."

Through the velvet curtain into the night, closing the glass door behind them. The little lawn and shrubberies of Honeyset Park were pale grey-green in the moonlight and fresh with an evening-grassy scent. Lehnya would have liked to suggest a walk in the park, but she dared not. She felt warm still, really quite hot. Some one had told her that it was a biological fact that blondes are more than usually attractive to brunettes when they have just been whipped; certainly there was a curious *aura* about Annalinde now. She seemed more than usually soft and warm—quiet in a way that was terribly fragile and inviting. As they walked into Bottle Alley, Lehnya wanted to seize her shoulders and press her against the wall and kiss her mouth the way she had heard brunettes did to blondes in Bottle Alley. She simply could not. She respected Annalinde too much; she feared losing her regard—and yet, would she not enjoy it? She was really *very* blonde. Her just-whipped state suited her so terribly. *Had* she provoked the usherette on purpose? Perhaps half on purpose was more likely. Would she actually lose respect for Lehnya if she did *not* kiss her? Would not Lehnya be demonstrating her brunette strength and resolution and dash and fire by doing so? Might she even seem a little feeble simply walking demurely through Bottle Alley? Well, better feeble than *vulgar* and in any case she was too shy to take such a daring initiative.

"Was it painful?" she asked gently, showing that she was a brunette of taste and delicacy if not one of pushful intrepidity.

"*Terrible*," said Annalinde actressily, but with feeling.

"Do you want to go to the Constant Nymph, or shall I take you straight home?"

"Oh, the Constant Nymph, *please*," said Annalinde.

3. The Constant Nymph

THEY TURNED left and came presently to the door of the Constant Nymph. It was one of those 'knock three times' sort of places—an ordinary front door, not unlike the Milchfords'. You knocked and a girl opened it. You were ushered past a table with an Art-Neo lamp in the form of a girl holding an incandescent globe into a room with tables and a wind-up gramophone. The girl was tall and glittering with a short Infra skirt. She looked, curiously, just a touch like Miss Milchford senior, but it was purely a family resemblance, of course, for she was much younger and sophisticated in a rather flighty way.

"Come in, darlings," she said, and then with a look at Annalinde: "Are you sure you're not under age?"

She really *should* have worn that hat. "Oh no, I am much older than I look."

The hostess went to a sideboard and picked up an ivory dice. She rolled it and looked quizzically at Annalinde. Annalinde's heart pounded. It was a dreadful moment. The decision of Fate would have to be obeyed.

"Yes, you probably are. Come in then. What will you have?"

"What cocktail is on?" asked Annalinde.

"Fountain of Youth."

"Good, I'll have that."

"Just coffee," said Lehnya. They sat down on deep green Art-Neo chairs near to where Emma Kadrina and Alice Trent were sitting. The gramophone was playing *T'aint no sin to take off your skin and dance around in your bones*. As the singer had not yet taken up the refrain, Alice did so, in a high, jinky voice, and Annalinde joined her. The brunettes applauded. The blondes sang cleverly together. They often did so. A waitress brought the drinks for the new arrivals. She was actually Alice Trent's maid, Betty, a near-to-plenary maid by her own nature—that is, one who manifested but a single *persona* with only the slightest of variants. When she came to the Constant Nymph as a waitress, she was really only Betty doing a part-time job, although they called her Charmian here. Such a quiet, courteous plenary girl could be half a dozen maids, waitresses and shop-girls, as her very unobtrusiveness lent her a versatility of her own. She was innocent and pure-sighted enough to see the *personæ* of her mistress and her mistress's friends each as a separate girl in her own right, and, within the limits of her quiet and unassuming nature, had her own relationship with each of them.

Annalinde took the bubbly, just-shaken cocktail from the silver tray, holding the triangular, Art-Neo glass up to the pink light. Lehnya took her coffee in the orange and black Art-Neo demi-tasse, a chromium Art-Neo coffee-spoon resting in the saucer. She put fivepence ha'penny on the silver tray—tuppence for the coffee and threepence ha'penny for the Fountain of Youth.

"Coffee?" said Emma Kadrina. "Not undifferentiated, I trust."

"Yes, I fear so," said Lehnya.

"Well, I don't know, I'm sure. I remember when the Aristasiani were hard-drinking pettes to a pette. Now half the new-bunnies seem to come into a perfectly respectable club like this and ask for a drop of the soft stuff—quite openly. What do you think of it, Lindie Milchford, sitting there drinking yourself jinky when you're hardly old enough for mother's milk and watching your elders and betters sober themselves up on coffee from the binge they haven't been having? Is it *sound*, do you think? Or is it a touch of Pit-pimminyism?"

"Oh, I don't think it's *that*," said Annalinde. "Do you know, I think it is a certain *delicacy* often enough. Some of the pettes these days are so finely-strung that such stimulants as alcohol are almost too gross for them. We are advancing, perhaps, into a rarer state of femininity."

"What a fascinating thought. I wonder if it can be true. I notice it does not affect you, Miss Lindie."

"Oh, I am not sure, perfectly. I don't tip it back the way I once did, you know, and I have heard that our cocktails are getting just a shade more *ætherial* than once they were."

"Weaker, you mean?"

"Well, depending more upon subtler influences than mere alcohol for their plenary effect."

"Annalinde Milchford, I hope you will forgive me for the suggestion that you are blathering. There's a drop or two of alcohol, I think you'll find, in that Fountain."

Annalinde sipped it meditatively. "Yes, I think you are right, but perhaps we are moving slowly toward the time when spirits are purely non-material."

Alice Trent felt moved to declaim.

" ' *Tea, although an Oriental, is a gentleman at least ;*
    Cocoa is a cad and coward, cocoa is a vulgar beast.' "

"I don't think any one has ordered *cocoa*, even in these rarefied times, sweet Alice."

"But you used to have Ovaltine in the Silver Swan ; you told me so."

"Yes, but only late at night, and then laced with a healthy jigger of rum. Rum and Ovaltine is a marriage made in heaven. I wonder if we could persuade them to make some here."

There was a knock on the door and the hostess left the room. There was an atmosphere of expectancy. During the foregoing conversation Sinta had arrived: a sophisticated and well-spoken young lady who, in build, but in almost no other respect, resembled the usherette who had been 'on' at the Odeon this evening. With Sinta present the Constant Nymph was, as the girls were wont to put it, quorate. No one else was expected and there was an excited speculation as to who the new girl might be—she *was* an Aristasian, certainly, for the knock had been correct—but the excitement was repressed from any too obvious outward manifestation in the name of good form. After all, this was a public place. There was no reason why any of a thousand residents of this fair city might not call in at any point in the evening. No reason outside the vulgar mechanics of manifestation which one, of course, did not acknowledge. Nevertheless——

"I wonder who that can be," said Alice Trent.

"Just a customer," said Emma Kadrina. "We haven't a monopoly on the place, you know."

The club door opened and the hostess ushered in a tallish girl with short mid-brown hair. She was wearing a mackintosh of rather schooly appearance, and rather less make-up than was usual in Trent-Quirinelle circles, indeed in Aristasian circles generally. She looked shy and awkward and very much as if she had rather be at home with mother. She had left a battered brown suitcase and a travelling bag in the hall containing, if not all her worldly belongings, certainly all that she was to possess for the next several months.

Annalinde had a vision of her travelling on an up-to-date bus through drizzling rain to get here. She could see the bus with its lights on in the dreary night. She could see the girl standing in the bus queue, lanky and displaced, among people standing with their overcoat collars turned up against a night wind, not very cold but damply penetrating. A melancholy Kadorian scene, it was, like something out of a film at the Gaumont—a somewhat seedier cinema than the Odeon. She could see a man trying to light his pipe, a coarse woman repeatedly looking at her watch. It was not Aristasia, of course, but not the Pit either—some shadowy corner of the real world that hovered always in the æther beside the solidified nightmare of the Pit. The little crowd was not hateful and poisoned like the golem-crowds of the Pit; dressed in drab respectability rather than loose-faced lunacy, but nonetheless alien, caring nothing—how could they know or care?—for the isolation of the too-tall schoolgirl rent from all that was familiar, though that was little enough, and sent into an unknown place of punishment.

It seemed like a scene from a film, and no doubt the films had helped to build it as they had helped to build so many things. Nevertheless the scene was not, Annalinde knew, directly from any film, but from the inner world of this girl standing inside the door, looking into the warmth and light and jinky music of the Constant Nymph like a barefoot child with her face pressed to the pane from outside, even though she was within.

No one had seen this girl before, and, more unusually, no one had seen any one remotely like her. The hostess, having ushered her in, had left her, and she wandered hesitantly toward the bar.

"Can I help you, miss?" asked Charmian in a neutral sort of voice. She was always neutral with strangers, a manifestation of her shyness.

"Do you serve tea, please?"

"Tea? No, miss. We've got coffee if you like."

"Thank you. May I have some coffee, please?"

"Very good, miss. It's tuppence."

Charmian's attitude was entirely natural. She was not a sophisticated girl, she was simply what she seemed; therein lay her genius. The restraint of the others was, to a certain extent, a piece of theatre. It would be normal for a newcomer in such a public place as this to be welcomed with the golden warmth of Aristasia, for places in Aristasia are not quite 'public' in the sense that they may be in other countries. Yet here and now, the Constant Nymph must be a public place in exactly the sense which that expression bears in those other countries, and the delicate drama of the girl walking alone and friendless into a strange city must not be shattered by any too easy and obvious club-acceptance.

Was the girl aware of this? Probably not. To her the drama was entirely real, as it ought to be, and to the others it was not so very far from that. One allowed the natural inhibition one feels in the face of some one quite new to be gently heightened. The hostess had not, in any case, introduced her. Introductions are important in Aristasia. One hesitates to move forward without them. And if not introduced, then why not? Was she entirely *persona grata*, or did some dark shadow hang over her? She could not be a true alien or she had not gained admittance.

Emma Kadrina, above all was nonplussed, for nothing of this had been breathed to her, and surely, whatever happened in Maryhill, the Guvie should know of it. Not that Emma Kadrina *was* the District Governess, of course, but—well—what the Guvie knew she tended to know also. Was this colony acting without authority? No, hardly that. Then some other authority must have arranged this without consulting her—a very considerable step for the Milchfords and an interesting evolution of the reality of her own ambience, not to be 'behind the scenes' of every development in Maryhill, but to be confronted by some

as simple *events*. It is axiomatic that in the Theatre of Life there can be
no distinction between players and audience, but Emma Kadrina and
her immediate relations had not been so wholly 'audience' as this for a
long time. One welcomed it. It was, after all, the aim of the entire operation. All barriers must melt and life become inseparable from the
Game. Only when a few more became wholly trustworthy could this be
achieved, and strides were clearly being made and yet—and yet one
would hardly have been human had one not felt with the least hint of a
qualm the diminution of personal power that must necessarily be en-
tailed. In all of us who have seen the Pit, there must be the hint of a
distrust of all power outside the control of the self; yet that, Emma
Kadrina knew only too well, is but the base instinct of the natural
maid—for what self is there truly, but the suprapersonal Self—the
Spirit? One must not slip into the erroneous notion of a 'real self' behind the *personae*, which certainly exists as a causal thread, but not as an
entity. One might fear a de-centring, a lurch into chaos, a loosing of
the reigns of Order—but that, too, was absurd. The Golden Order
would be maintained from the Centre, as always. None would ever
dispute that, but no one could hold the reigns of Fate. Fate must be dis-
persed into the Game itself as the Game becomes ever realler.

There was a certain voluptuousness of submission in accepting this, a
tremulous joy in abnegating one's own will; the same joy that must be
felt by the humblest slavey and the Empress herself if the Golden Order
is to prevail. In every traditional order it must have been felt, but was it
ever felt with such strange, chaste sensuality as in this feminine realm
that hovered above the Void? Perhaps, she conjectured, perhaps only in
the Golden Age—only in the very first and dawning times and in the last
times toward the sunset of civilisation. For the last times are in certain
ways the mirror of the first.

Meantime, if there was a certain unregenerate coldness in her, living
beside the submissive warmth, toward this new turn of events, she
should let it transmute itself into the coldness necessary to this moment
of the Game. She ignored the newcomer, as did the others. She had
not even heard the question to which Charmian was replying.

"Oh, I don't know about things like that, miss. You'll have to try
asking one of the customers."

The girl came hesitantly over. Emma Kadrina looked unapproachably
sophisticated and rather cold. Alice Trent was too perfect and too
blondely attached to Emma. Lehnya shyly avoided her eye and Sinta was
deep in conversation with the hostess. Annalinde seemed the only possibility.

"Excuse me——"

Annalinde smiled kindly. She could not have avoided smiling kindly but by the most Herculean of efforts, for nothing else was in her nature. She did not imagine that she was called upon to play a rôle quite alien to Annalinde, so she smiled kindly and the girl was much encouraged, though still in the highest state of nervousness.

"Excuse me, miss, but I've to go to Honey Lane and am told this is the nearest I can get until later. I suppose there is a bus or something. Can you possibly help me."

Annalinde smiled more kindly than ever. "No, there isn't a bus, but it is true, to paraphrase the Irishman, that if you want to go there you can't start from now. You'll have to start a little later—but don't worry, I am going there myself. You can come with me."

Lehnya cursed in silence—a mild, Aristasian curse, of course, but the feeling behind it was less mild. One should never place one's trust in the future. She had funked taking Annalinde into the park and had funked kissing her in Bottle Alley, but she had made up her mind quite firmly to kiss her on the way home, or at least on the doorstep. But Honey Lane was where the Milchfords lived, and there was—in a manner of speaking—only one house in Honey Lane. This *gauche* and gawky child would be with them now every step of the way, and who could tell when or whether she would get the chance to take Annalinde out again?

"Would you care to join us?" asked Annalinde.

"Thank you, I should," said the girl. Everything she said was very careful. A foreigner would perhaps be surprised how much an Aristasian can tell about a *persona*. This girl looked about fourteen. An oldish twelve or a youngish sixteen were the outer limits of interpretation and not a single girl in the room, in her private estimate, was that far wide of the mark in either direction. Her chronological age was rather different, no doubt, but it is hard to convey how very little thought was ever given to such banalities as chronological ages—things almost as ridiculously *bourgeois* as the concept of 'real names'.

"What is your name?"

"Angeline Southern."

"Are you a long way from home, Angeline?"

"I have no home, but I am a long way from all that I know."

"Why have you come here?"

The girl's voice dropped almost to a whisper, scarcely audible above the music. "To take up a situation."

"How interesting. What sort of a situation."

Her voice dropped even lower. "As a maid—punitive."

"How exciting."

"Is it exciting? Is it not shameful?"

Annalinde blushed. It really was dreadful of her to call it exciting, but she did find it so. Her family had never had a maid before, and the idea that this curious child must be treated with considerable severity interested her deeply.

"Did you come on a bus?"

"Yes, how did you know?" In terms of vulgar mechanics the girl could not say with absolute certainty *how* she had come, for she had been blindfold from the very outset until her unveiling on the steps of this place; but the idea of the bus had been impressed upon her very firmly and, anxious to begin her new life of penitence properly and to atone from her previous wanderings she had concentrated very dutifully upon the bus, picturing it in her mind with great vividness and drawing upon all she had seen in up-to-date films of real buses. Whether Annalinde had picked up the bus journey from the intensity of the girl's thoughts or whether she had been informed of it by a third party we cannot state; we shall say only that the former is far from impossible, and many things like it happen every day in Aristasia, while the latter is also very likely, and some combination of the two most probable of all.

"I felt you coming on the bus very strongly as soon as you arrived. I had the scent and sound of it. An unhappy journey, I thought, but it had a certain wistful charm."

"Yes, you are right. How wonderfully you put things." Angeline began to realise that what she had done was not merely to submit, but to abandon herself to the romance of her position; all romance can be attained only by self-abandonment, and it had taken this extremity to bring her to it. How wonderful to find at once so magical a soul to share and deepen her feelings. "Shall I ever see you, do you think, during my time of service?"

"Who is your mistress to be?"

"A Miss Milchford."

"I am her daughter. I shall be, I suppose, your young mistress."

"Oh, miss. Should I stand?"

"Not tonight, I think. Tonight you have not taken up your situation. Tonight we shall be just girls together, shall we?"

"You are very kind. What is your mother like? Will she beat me?"

"She is quite a dolly really. She will beat you when you need it, of course, but she is not terrifying. I've an aunt, though—Aunt Alice—and she is *ferocious*. She is not there all the time, but you had better be careful of her."

"Thank you, I shall, miss."

The two girls had been talking quietly while the others made exuberant conversation. Even Lehnya had been drawn away from Annalinde by the amusing discourse of Emma Kadrina. Now that young lady turned to Annalinde.

"You two seem to have found something in common."

"Oh yes, Emma Kadrina," said Annalinde. "This is Angeline Southern and I have discovered that she is come to be our maid,"

"How delightful. You will be rich now."

"Oh, I don't suppose it will make any difference to our financial state."

"But has your financial state anything to do with whether you are rich or not?"

"I had always thought so—was I wrong?"

"Well, how would you define being rich?"

"Having a lot of money, I suppose."

"That is a very modern definition. But how, in any case, would you define money?"

"Isn't that obvious?"

"Not entirely. There are different sorts of money. In America one sometimes finds hoards of Confederate money—that is, money issued by the Confederate States of America before they lost their War of Independence and were overrun by the wage-slavers of the North. One might find a million dollars of such money and it would be worth next to nothing. In Weimar Germany inflation reached such extremities that one could have millions of marks and they would buy, perhaps, a loaf of bread. In either case one could be said to have a great deal of money, but would one be rich?"

"Certainly not."

"So having a lot of money cannot be the definition of being rich?"

"So it would seem.

"It may perhaps depend, then, on what *sort* of money we have. On what that money has the power to do—and perhaps upon whether we have the power to do those things regardless of whether we have what is called 'money' or not."

"That seems probable."

"I recently had occasion—lawful and unavoidable occasion, I assure you—to peruse a barbarian magazine. I was struck by an expression used by one of the writers. He asked 'What is the good of being rich if you have to clean your own shoes?' He spoke of other things that all but the richest of the 'rich' slaves have to do—they have to answer their own doors, wait at their own tables, get out of their own cars in the rain to fill their own petrol tanks. In fact they have to live in a manner that an unpretentious middle-class suburban family less than a hundred years ago would have considered positively squalid. I have never had to do *any* of those things, and I hope I never shall. Now the fact is that these people command vastly more bongo-money than I do or ever shall, but can they be considered rich in comparison to me? After all, it is not as if they were rich eccentrics who *choose* to live as proletarians. They live in the way they do because they have not the *power*—the *economic* power—to live in any other way—whereas I have that power. And now so have you.

"The question 'what is the good of being rich if one has to clean one's own shoes?' might have been better and more philosophically phrased: '*is* one rich if one has to clean one's own shoes?'

"Another way of approaching the problem might be to suggest that while Confederate money is *dead* money—money which can do nothing—bongo-money is *crippled* money—money which can do certain things, but is incapable of doing other things: things which money has always been expected to do throughout history—or if it can do them it can only do them by quite excessive and disproportionate expenditure of itself, wholly inaccessible to the well-off or the ordinary 'rich'. Like a crippled person, crippled money cannot do many important things that healthy money can do, or can only do them with far greater effort than healthy money can do them.

"Now *why* is bongo-money crippled? Is it an accident, or a deliberate policy? Let us first ask: what is the function of money? The function of money is essentially to organise people to do things for us—to bake us a loaf of bread, to build us a house or a motor car and so forth. We induce them to give us the use of their bodies, their minds and their property. When we buy a motor-car, we are indirectly employing people to tap rubber-trees, ship the rubber to another place where tyres are made, extract iron ore from the ground and turn it into steel and a thousand other operations.

"There is nothing inherently wrong with this system, but it is one in which centralised control and tyranny can become increasingly potent. The individual, and the community, are ever more remote from the actual function of control. An essentially totalitarian system like that of the Pit is anxious to ensure that, this is accentuated—that while an individual's money can still organise *through* the controlled economic system, it loses the power of direct control. It wishes to ensure that no individual can employ other individuals except through businesses which are part of the pyramid of financial control. An estate, employing fifty servants is a little world, independent of the system. This is the independence the Octopus has worked so hard to destroy. The 'person of independent means' is intolerable—especially if her position is hereditary, meaning that, she has never had to grub for it in the economic system and therefore is wholly independent, mentally as well as practically, from that system. Everything has been done to destroy such independent means and the possibility of inheriting them. Every individual must be a proletarian, dependent for her livelihood upon employment, or at least on the good will of the financial structure.

"A 'liberal education' in the traditional sense means a *free* education, that is, the education of a lady or gentleman who is free from the economic necessity of 'making a living' and can study for non-utilitarian, purely cultural, reasons. This is the education that the Octopus cannot allow, because it cannot allow the personal independence from the financial structure that goes with it. Every one in the Pit, from the road-sweeper to the Prime Minister or the chairman of the largest international company, is a proletarian. All are wage-slaves except a tiny few, and those few can be made and broken by the system at will. The independent gentleman cannot exist, and therefore liberal education cannot exist, and since liberal education is the foundation of culture, culture cannot exist. It is supplanted by a proletarian pop-culture, the only alternative to which is a distorted and dying remnant of traditional culture supported by committees and growing more grotesque and perverted with every passing year, having lost its roots in a free, educated caste. It is pointless for a wage-slave culture to try to imitate its betters."

"So are we the only rich?" asked the hostess.

"In a manner of speaking, yes," replied Emma Kadrina. "Certainly, we are the only free souls; the only true aristocrats. The only people capable of building a culture."

"What of our money," asked Alice Trent, "is that more powerful than bongo-money?"

"I think we can hardly argue that," said Emma Kadrina.

"Yet there might be a case—a partial case——" said the hostess.

"Please tell us," said Emma Kadrina.

The hostess perched herself daintily on the arm of Miss Kadrina's chair. Her short Infra skirt rode high up her legs as she sat down and she must keep her knees pressed neatly together and not cross her legs. Her stockings must be pulled tight on the shortest of suspenders, one realised, for no shadow of darkening stocking to be visible even where the hem curved upwards at the sides of her thighs. It seemed somehow a curious attire in which to be speaking philosophy, and the Savoy Orpheans' wonderful rendering of *On the Air* a curious background; but of such delightful contrasts is Aristasia made.

"Bongo-money has a very obvious potency," said the hostess. "It controls, for the most part, the distribution of property. I could not buy a country estate with validated Aristasian shillings even if there were enough of them in existence, which there probably aren't. But consider what a few pennies have bought tonight—at the Odeon, where many of you have been, they have bought the services of some of the finest players in the world, to entertain but a small house. Cameramen, cartoonists, writers, dressmakers, wardrobe mistresses and hundreds of others have spent literally thousands of hours preparing two hours' entertainment for you. Only the greatest potentates of antiquity commanded such dazzling luxury.

"It is true that any bongo can have these things for nothing, but what of that? The worth of a thing is surely the value one appreciates. A priceless manuscript is worth nothing to an illiterate nomad. In London in the sixteenth century apprentices went on strike because they were given fresh salmon every day. In the last century oysters were cheap and plentiful and were considered fit only for the poor. The value of a thing is largely conventional. Make anything good scarce enough—say chocolate or tea—and it will become a magnificent luxury, a wonderful indulgence, a symbol for millionaires and potentates. Now, we in Aristasia have the power, through our Order and discipline, to restrict anything we choose and so to make it a luxury. What happens when a thing is restricted? Its true qualities are appreciated to the full. Chocolate *is* a wonderful gift of God. What happens when it is too plentiful? We despise it and become complacent about it and do not value it at its true worth. One might actually suggest that up-to-date children who are given chocolate as a rare treat are actually *richer* in the matter of chocolate than bongo-brats who are fed the stuff day and night to keep them quiet. One might even say that the bongo-brat has never really *had* chocolate as the real child has.

"Do you see what I mean? Baudelaire replies to the 'utilitarian' idiots who separate 'practical common sense' from 'pointless luxury and æstheticism'. He points out that all we actually *need* is some crude shelter from the elements, some rough food and some water. That is all that is necessary to sustain life. *Everything* beyond that is a luxury and a superfluity. The most hard-nosed practical man in the world is spending all his life pursuing unnecessary fripperies. All the solid, no-nonsense, down-to-earth, anti-romantic daily grind of grey 'realism' has never been anything more than the wild chase for fashionable fads and fancies. Or to put it otherwise, nearly all the time people think they are serving the necessities of the body they are actually feeding the inclinations of the soul. In the Pit they have been taught to feed their souls on poison—on a culture that makes them cynical and discontented, that cheapens and dirties everything, most of all themselves. It is not only the obvious things labelled 'culture'—films, music, advertising posters—but the design of everything from motor-cars to telephone boxes to kettles. 'In an ugly world the richest man can buy nothing but ugliness'. But, as Emma Kadrina has just taught us to ask—is the man who can buy nothing but ugliness really rich? And is the girl who sees even an up-to-date film through poisoned Pit-eyes really seeing the film?

"Through purifying our sensibility, through placing new boundaries in our lives, through manipulating scarcity and value back to normal proportions, we can become the only rich; our money can be the only money which buys anything worthy of the name of luxury—because only we have the perception that makes it such—only we appreciate the countless luxuries available to us as the luxuries they truly are. Only we have un-poisoned our souls to the point where they can *be* rich. In terms of mere physical provision, the late 20th century provides material riches beyond the dreams of most ages to every one; yet Pit-dwellers are more profoundly impoverished and more discontented than any people before them. The problem is not a physical one but a psychological and spiritual one, and only we have the power to solve it."

"And is discipline part of the solution?" asked Annalinde.

"It is absolutely crucial," replied the hostess. "Discipline, that is, in the broadest sense—in which, of course, the narrower is also included. The Pit is essentially a *psychological* tyranny. It controls people through the mental states it creates and through its manipulation of their desires and aspirations—by the creation of an electronically-controlled mental environment. Our job is to create our own environment under our own control—that is, under the control of the Golden Order. If we do not live under the discipline of our own Order, then the *hard edges* of our world—the ultimate dictates as to what we can and cannot do, what we can and cannot have—come from the 'outside', that is, from the Pit. But if our own world sets those limits before we get to the physical or Pit-financial limits, then we place ourselves under our own discipline rather than that of the Enemy and his world. We are not more or less free as individuals, but as a nation we are free, and as individuals we are submitting ourselves not to hostile alien forces, but to an Empire we love and respect. Do you see?"

"Not *qui-ite*," confessed Annalinde. "It seems a touch abstract."

"It *is* rather abstract, I fear, but let me give some concrete examples by way of illustration. Take the arcade games you play. In the Pit they are available in great profusion and once you have one you can play it as often as you wish. Here they are only available occasionally and cost quite a lot of a girl's pocket money. Consequently they are luxuries, rare and special treats which add a thrill to life. The 'limits' which make them rare and valuable are not those of how many games one can afford in bongo-money, but of how their use is regulated both financially—in Aristasian money—and in terms of opportunity, and, of course, on which games—a small minority of those available in the Pit—are authorised for use in the Empire. The limits, the scarcity-value, the control, you see, are all *ours* not the enemy's—we inhabit a world bounded by *our* regulation, not that of his world.

"The same is true with other things—films, for example: they come to us regulated through the Imperial cinemas. We cannot simply see them at will. And then we have to obey various regulations, such as keeping our houses in a proper state and following standards of dress. The keeping of maidservants—an economic dimension almost eradicated from the Void—is regulated by the Imperial System. One could give a hundred other examples. Most of the *hard edges*, the practical realities of our lives are created by our world, not by the exigencies of the underlying Void. Many of the rules we live by may seem governessy and restrictive, but without them we should not be defining our own reality. We should be allowing it to be defined by limits forced on us from below. All of this is sustained by discipline. Without discipline we should simply drift downward to the point where the limits which enclosed us were not our own, but those of the Pit."

The new girl spoke hesitantly, half-raising her hand as if she was not sure whether or not to behave like a schoolgirl. "If you please, miss, may I ask a question?"

The hostess smiled. "But certainly."

"I hope you won't think me impertinent or that I am playing Devil's advocate."

"By all means play Devil's advocate if you wish. It is the only way to clear our minds of uncertainties."

A bell rang, and Charmian's matter of fact voice cut into the rarefied ether of conversation. "Time. please, ladies."

"Go on," said the hostess encouragingly to Angeline.

"Well, it is just that when you say that the late 20th century provides great riches, might it not be argued that in accepting and using those riches but rejecting the late 20th century you are being hypocritical?"

"Ah, *hypocritical*," said the hostess, smiling impishly. "The Octopus's favourite word. It means so much and so little. But what does it mean on this occasion? May I take it to mean that in accepting the produce of the Pit, while declaring ourselves the eternal enemies of the Pit, we put ourselves in a false position? We acknowledge the virtue of the Pit by our very acceptance and give ourselves the lie? Is that what our hypothetical critic is saying?"

"Yes, I think so," said Angeline nervously. The hostess's tone had been somewhat ironical, but it was clear that the irony was not directed personally at Angeline—only at the Devil she was advocating.

"Very well, then let us answer this hoary old objection once for all. The argument is based on the false assumption that the riches of the Pit *belong* to the Pit. They do not. They are the inherited merits of civilisation—the very civilisation that the Pit is cheapening and destroying day by day. The 'science' of which the Pit-golems boast is but the inherited wisdom of their betters, and the forward momentum of a movement started long before their time. Telephones and motor cars were in operation in the last century, wireless in the early years of this. Television was broadcasting decent programmes to a select audience in the 1930s. Personal computers, medical advances and all the other technical developments that have happened since the Eclipse would have happened just the same if the culture had not collapsed in the First decade of Darkness. The riches of the Pit do not belong to the Pit, they belong to the Real World which the Pit has destroyed. They are not the Octopus's, they are ours. They are the fruits of that culture which we preserve and he destroys.

"There is no necessary connexion between technical advance and cultural decay. On the contrary, when cultural decay goes far enough technical advance will decay with it. If the Enemy of civilisation has seized the fruits of civilisation, that does not mean that the fruits are his in any sense except mere brute possession. In taking the fruits of civilisation from the Pit for our own use, we are reclaiming what is ours and only ours; for we are the sole remaining representatives of that civilisation which has made them possible."

"And what," asked Angeline, "of the people who now make those things?"

"They are our people!" said Lehnya, suddenly and bravely venturing into the conversation. "We call them bongos, slaves and golems because that is what they have become. They have been transmuted by the Octopus. But that is not what they truly are. They should be whole and real and healthy like the people in the films. Perhaps one day they will be whole again, or perhaps they will never be, but in any case, it is right that they should be working for us. Whenever they make or sell something that helps Aristasia to go forward, they are striking, though they know nothing of it, a blow against the slavers who have mutated them and who keep their souls in chains."

"Oh, bravo, Lehnya," cried Emma Kadrina. "I believe that is your maiden speech."

"To Lehnya!" cried Annalinde springing to her feet and holding her glass aloft. At once the company were all on their feet, clinking glasses in an intricate pattern and echoing: "To Lehnya!" Angeline, not wishing to be discourteous, but wondering whether she was really welcome as a participant in this strange impromptu ceremony, stood awkwardly, clinking her small coffee-cup gingerly with each glass that approached her. Lehnya flushed deeply and tried to look brunette.

The bell rang again. "Empty your glasses, please, it's well after time."

As all places were resumed, the hostess turned kindly to Angeline. "Does that answer your questions, dear, or was there something else that troubles your enquiring mind?"

"No, miss. There is nothing else."

"Yes there is, I can see it in your eyes. Come along Angeline, out with all your Devil's advocacy. You are among friends here."

"I am not really *advocating* these views, I just want to know what the answers are."

"Of course, and so you should."

"Well, you say, and Lehnya says, that we are the continuation of the civilisation which created the riches, that the descendants of that civilisation are really *our* people—and yet we are a Feminine Empire. We have ways and laws that they have never known, we do things that the old civilisation—even just before the Eclipse—would not understand. *Are* we the continuation of that civilisation?"

"Yes and no," said the hostess. "We are the Children of the Void. Our world could only have come about under the strange circumstances of the collapse of civilisation. That collapse is a terrible disaster, and yet from our point of view, it opens possibilities that could not otherwise have been opened—allowed us to found an Empire that could not otherwise have been born and explore new areas of sensibility that would otherwise have remained in the bud."

"What a wonderful phrase," said Emma Kadrina, "'Children of the Void'."

Charmian rolled a dice. Several eyes turned uneasily toward her. In this country customers and not merely licensees were held responsible for after-hours drinking and it was entirely possible for the whole party to be soundly chastised. Charmian, however, continued with her tidying and cleaning of glasses.

"So has the Pit done some good?" asked Angeline, unaware of the danger that had passed.

"No," said Annalinde, "not the Pit. From the Pit we have taken nothing, or if we have we are working hard to cleanse ourselves of it. We are not children of the Pit. The poisoned consciousness of the Pit has contributed nothing to our world. We are not formed by what the Pit *is* but by what it is *not*—by the emptiness that it has left where a world should be. In that emptiness we have to build our own world, and in the curious nature of that founding of a civilisation upon the remains of a civilisation still warm, as it were, new and delicate possibilities can be realised that might perhaps have been realised in no other way. If we were children of the Pit, there would be nothing strange or delicate about our world: we should be just another species of golem, trying to be 'different' just like the rest and being just the same as all of them. We are not children of the Pit, we are Children of the Void."

Charmian picked up the dice. "Come along, please, ladies. You don't want us all to get in trouble, now do you?"

"Perhaps we'd better go," said Lehnya.

"Yes, perhaps," agreed Emma Kadrina reluctantly.

The hostess fetched coats and brunettes helped blondes into them before putting on their own, all prolonging the last few moments in the golden glow of the Constant Nymph.

"I suppose this is part of what is meant by creating our own boundaries and our own 'hard edges'," said Alice Trent. "None of us wants to go and we all have to."

"But I think I can begin to understand for the first time how important it is that we have to," said Lehnya as she courteously helped Angeline on with her mackintosh. Angeline smiled at her gratefully.

"You'd better go out the back way," said the hostess, "just in case."

They passed through the hall and through a darkened room with tall French windows at the back. They passed through a velvet curtain and issued out by Honeyset park, still silent and strange in the moonlight.

"It is right about independent incomes being necessary for culture," said Lehnya. "I was reading the introduction to a Kadorian book of Tennyson's poems and it said that if modern inheritance taxes and other methods of destroying private incomes had then been in force we should probably never have had the poems of Tennyson or Milton or Shelley or Byron or the Brownings or Swinburne or many others."

"It is Virginia Woolf's requisite of 'a room of one's own'. One must have a degree of privacy and independence to create freely."

"Wasn't Tennyson a rich lord?"

"No, he just had a small private income."

"But is it fair?" asked Angeline, "after all, most people can't have one."

"More did than you'd think. Certainly a large-ish proportion of intelligent people. After all intelligence *is* hereditary, whatever Johnny Golem has been trained to think."

"Funny how they ignore the findings of their own beloved science, as soon as it conflicts with their notions."

" *Their* notions! The Octopus's notions."

"Do you think the Octopus really believes them?"

"Anyway, don't you see how it works? The Octopus doesn't want any one to be independent, so he says to Johnny Golem—'look Johnny, not every one can have this, so no one shall have it. That's fair isn't it, Johnny?' and Johnny says: 'Duh, yes, Occie, dat's fair all right.'"

"But then *we* haven't private incomes," said Alice Trent, "we live the most precarious lives financially, so why are we free?"

Emma Kadrina pondered. "It isn't just a matter of the income itself, I fancy. Take academics. For a long while before the Eclipse they *were* wage-earners, but they still thought and acted as free gentlemen. Later they became wholly proletarianised and thought of themselves as wage-slaves. They even started calling themselves 'teachers' as if they had been working in comprehensive schools. Their whole attitude changed and their minds were no longer free. Why? Not, I think, because of any objective change in their circumstances (it is true that their security of tenure was much reduced, but the change in attitude predated that) but because they had been mutated. They changed from having the *sensibility* of independent minds to having that of proletarians. We, on the other hand have the sensibility of free gentilmaids. Only a world with gentlemen in it could sustain the academic in his free spirit, Destroy that world and you destroy the *sensibility* that goes with it. To take independence from the 'privileged few' destroys—and was always intended to destroy—the mental independence of a much greater number—indeed of all who ever had it. Now *our* independence can survive because it is supported by a world with its own *morale*."

"And its own regulations and hard edges."

"Precisely. It could not attain psychological reality without them."

"And the District Governess and the Number Two District Strap."

"Not to mention the Number Three Strap."

"And the cane."

"And the fact that if one of us falls into difficulties she knows her sisters will always support her."

"One for all!" cried Lehnya.

"And all for one!" replied the others in concert.

They had gathered now by the gate at the end of Bottle Alley, fortified by furs and strong drink against the wind that was blowing up in the East. Not fortified enough in all cases.

"I'm cold," said Annalinde rather petulantly.

"Beast!" said Sinta.

"I am sorry," said Lehnya, "I shall take you home."

"Thank you. Come with us, Angeline."

As they walked to the front door the conversation still continued behind them. Some one has said that Aristasia is one long conversation that never stops; only pauses from time to time for sleep and business and other dull necessities.

"Will you come in for a moment?" asked Annalinde, feeling in her neat little bag for her keys.

"Shall I be allowed to?"

"I—I don't know, I hope so." She opened the door gently.

Mummie was there, putting a finger to her lips. "Aunt Alice is here," she whispered, "please be quiet."

Annalinde stepped in quietly and beckoned the other two.

"This is our new maid, Angeline," she whispered.

"Hello, dear," said Mummie, taking the girl's hands. "Come with me. I shall show you where you sleep."

Lehnya and Annalinde were alone in the hall. It was Lehnya's moment. Could she seize it?

"What do you think of Angeline," she asked weakly.

"I don't know," whispered Annalinde. "She asked her Devil's questions demurely enough, but I wasn't *wholly* impressed by her manner. I fancy she has some dreadful nonsense stuffed into her. She is a Punie, you know. Perhaps she has come to have it knocked out of her. Anyway, she's come so she must *want* it to be knocked out at heart."

"Good for her, then. That's the important thing, isn't it? Do you think your mother can do it?" Lehnya knew Annalinde's mother as a mildish person whose bouts of authority were tempered with much kindly indulgence.

"I *think* so," said Annalinde. "Anyway, there's always Aunt Alice."

Lehnya had never seen Annalinde's Aunt Alice. In fact no one outside the household seemed to have seen Annalinde's Aunt Alice. Lehnya had even been materialistic enough to doubt on occasion whether Annalinde *had* an Aunt Alice—but now she had heard Miss Milchford speak of her, so she must have.

"Does she beat you?" asked the brunette.

"Oh, dreadfully."

"Really, or are you acting?"

"No, really. I'll show you the traces one day after she's done it perhaps, or would that be indelicate?"

Lehnya felt that strange warmth rising inside her. One must not *think* about it: that was the thing. One must just *do* it.

She did.

Annalinde was pressed firmly against the oak panelling. Lehnya's mouth sought hers and found it. For a long minute the kiss lasted.

Lehnya's hands were caressing but cautious. Then Miss Milchford's tread was heard upon the stair.

Lehnya was very flushed as she turned, but Miss Milchford smiled in a motherly sort of way—so unlike the hostess at the Constant Nymph.

Annalinde waved as Lehnya's bicycle disappeared into the Void.

"I do hope Aunt Alice has not heard you," said Mummie, in her worried, blonde way, "you know how she disapproves of these clubs and late hours." She rolled the dice on the hall table. Why *must* she do that?

"I do not think she *has* heard," she said.

All in all, it had been a very lucky evening.

4. The General Disciplinary Strap

"**M**ORE TEA, miss," asked the uniformed maidservant, standing respectfully behind and beside her mistress's daughter at the breakfast table.

"Thank you, Angeline," replied Annalinde.

It *did* make a difference to how one perceived oneself, having a maid. More than one could possibly have imagined in advance. One was—no doubt about it—distinctly *wealthier*. Perhaps Emma Kadrina would have smiled at this rather literal and emotional manifestation of her philosophical discourse on the nature of wealth: but probably, Annalinde decided, not. She would understand. She would know that the sense of potency, or potential, (for were not the two the same? Was it not far more than a pun to say that *might* is the sum of those things we *might* do as opposed to those we lack the might to do?) imparted by the ownership of this small portion of human servitude was the very psychic stuff of wealth, the very essence of gold, whereof the yellow metal was but an inert mineral symbol and base-metal coinage, promissory notes and flickering figures in a digital bank account (in that order) but ever-receding symbols of symbols of symbols, growing fainter and more shadowy as they declined from the Source.

One had entered a new realm and dimension of wealth this morning. The difference between oneself and a potentate of old with a thousand slaves ready to attend upon the gesture of her hand was one of degree, but not of kind; whereas the difference between oneself this morning and oneself yesterday morning was absolute. And the difference, between oneself and almost any bongo was absolute—perhaps *any* bongo, for was the service of a waged employee-servant forged of this same true gold? One felt not.

Angeline filled the tea cup carefully. She was very quiet, very demure. She was dressed in black with a white apron. When she turned to the trolley, one saw the wide bow at the back of her apron, the crossed shoulder-straps and the long white streamer hanging behind her neat little cap. One enjoyed the black stockings and polished black shoes.

"That will be all, Angeline," said Miss Milchford.

"Very good, madam. Please, madam."

"Yes, Angeline?"

"I was instructed to give you something, madam. Shall I fetch it now?"

"Certainly, Angeline."

The maid left the room.

"She seems very well trained," said Annalinde.

"I am not sure she has actually been *trained* at all; simply instructed in how to behave and speak."

"Then she is trying very hard."

"Yes. She seems a very charming and willing girl."

"I wonder why she is on Punitive Service."

"Perhaps we are about to find out."

The maid returned with a flat parcel some two feet long, wrapped in brown corrugated cardboard.

"Thank you, Angeline. That will be all."

"Very good, madam."

Miss Milchford opened the parcel. It contained a long strap, quite broad as these things go, divided into four tails. The leather was pale and very stiff and hard looking.

"This must be the General Disciplinary Strap," said Miss Milchford. "Miss Quint said I should be supplied with one."

"It looks fearsome."

Miss Milchford held it by the handle. It hardly drooped at all, extending stiffly, like a flat stick, slightly splay-ended, with something of a downward curve. "It certainly feels formidable."

The two examined it with some fascination—particularly on Annalinde's part. Any one familiar with the attentions of more ordinary straps, and knowing how breathtaking their bite could be, must pause respectfully before the harsh potential of this implement. Near to where the tails divided were stamped the words "Imperial Board of Education"—which one knew was more fully entitled The Imperial Board of Education and Civic Discipline, and therefore supplied and licensed implements for official—and also private—disciplinary uses outside the purely educational sphere; although it was a truism that all discipline is educational. "In other words, it learns you," as some wag had remarked in the library recently, and the prim little librarian who overheard had said "And it does more than that, it *teaches* you." One had listened respectfully and considered her words, for humble though she was, she was very handy with the strap herself, and considerably more formidable than most cinema usherettes.

Annalinde relinquished her hold on the General Disciplinary Strap. "I am certainly glad it is 'Punitive Maids for the use on'."

"Don't be too sure you won't be feeling it before long, Annalinde."

"No, really, that isn't fair. I mean just because this young juvenile delinquent needs punitive treatment, that's no reason for me to be——"

"Annalinde! Do you want to taste it now?"

"No, Mummie."

"Then silence and take an Order Mark."

"No, please, Mummie. I've got three already."

"Two Order Marks."

Annalinde fetched the book and Miss Milchford registered the two marks. Annalinde shivered. She should have to see Aunt Alice now. Miss Milchford was being unusually unwheedlable. Perhaps she was getting new-broomy over the new maid.

There was a brown envelope in with the strap. Miss Milchford had opened it and was reading the note typed on official paper.

"It says I am to thrash her with this strap on her first morning."

"'Thrash'. That sounds a strong expression."

"Yes. I wonder how to go about it," said the mistress of the house uncertainly.

"Nothing to it really. Just call her in, bend her over and lay into her."

"Yes, I suppose so. It seems rather—well, rather cold-blooded."

"Surely you aren't accusing the District Authorities of cruelty?" said Annalinde in mock horror.

"No, I didn't mean 'cold-blooded' quite like that. I mean, it seems a strange thing to leap into, just like that with no cause and hardly knowing the girl."

"I could try if you like," said Annalinde with an enthusiasm that indicated she was more than half-hoping her mother would agree to the proposition.

"No, Annalinde. There is no difficulty really. It is only something unaccustomed."

Miss Milchford's hesitancy was in a way a little surprising. Aunt Alice, after all, did manifest through the same body, as did more than one quite ferocious schoolmistress. Still, there was no sense in falling into the trap of assuming that the tendencies of one *persona* influenced another. Miss Milchford herself was really quite mild most of the time. Her predominant impulse was to be kind to people, and, if anything, gentler than was good for them. Even her severer *personæ* were often inhibited by her—not so much inhibited in what they did when they were there as in the frequency of their manifestation.

Miss Milchford picked up the little bell that stood beside her place at table and tinted the air with its gently insistent tone. Angeline was very prompt.

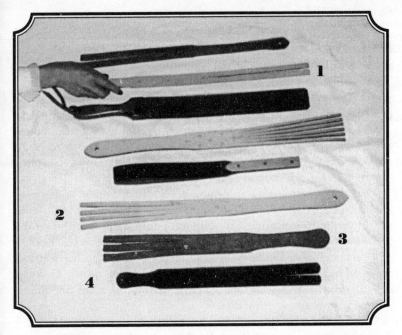

*Maryhill District Straps, including **1** Grammar School Classroom Strap,*
2 *General Disciplinary Strap,* **3** *Inspectorette's strap (p.177),* **4** *Cinema Strap.*

"You rang, madam?"

"Yes, Angeline. I find that I am obliged to thrash you." The girl's
eyes widened. "It is nothing you have done, dear. Simply my instruc-
tions."

"On the side of the box, you know," said Annalinde. "All-purpose
slavey: thrash well before use."

"Annalinde, that is not in the least amusing. Take another Order
Mark."

"Yes, Mummie."

"Angeline, clear the table, empty the trolley and return."

"Very good, madam." The girl quickly put the breakfast things on
the three-tiered Trentish oak trolley with its plastic-lace Quirrie trolley-
cloths and wheeled it out.

"Now, Annalinde: since you think a dose of this strap such an amusing matter, I think I shall try it on you first. Yes. You are well advised
not to protest. I am not in a mood to be trifled with. Bend over the
table."

Annalinde stood up and lay her top half along the surface of the
cleared table. Miss Milchford lifted the plentiful folds of her daughter's
light, wide Quirinelle skirt and bunched the excess of her full paper-

nylon petticoat firmly between her thighs, pushing it through to the front, so that her bottom and the backs of her legs were covered only by a close coating of the thin material with its water-marked flower pattern. Through the film of translucent nylon one could clearly see the high-waisted knickers over the black elasticated girdle with its wide black suspenders straining each against its firmly-gripped burden of stocking-top.

Miss Milchford picked up the weighty strap and made ready. Whatever she might sometimes lack in relish for the task, she was certainly not deficient in technical skill. She knew well enough how to use these things, even though she had never before plied one quite so fierce.

The splayed length cut across Annalinde's rounded thighs with a kissing bite. Her whole body tensed as if it had been electrified. Annalinde was moderately accustomed to corporal punishment, but this stroke had clearly shocked her. Nonetheless, she remained still and silent.

"Very well, Annalinde. You may stand." She rose to her feet and arranged her rustling skirts about her, thinking how nearly Arcadian these Quirinelle styles were. She felt chastened and Arcadian. She almost wanted to curtsey to her mother.

"Thank you, Mummie." The pain of that single stroke was still throbbing through her. She wondered how much of a 'thrashing' her mother had in mind for the maid. More than two or three strokes would be terrible. She wanted to say something along these lines, but felt too subdued now to offer advice. In any case, Mummie could see clearly enough how it had affected her.

"Rather an effective little implement," she said. "I must keep it in mind for controlling you in future."

"Yes, Mummie, thank you, Mummie."

The maid returned and stood respectfully before her mistress, her hands folded demurely in front of her—small, shapely hands set off nicely by the white field of her apron.

"So, you are ready for your thrashing, Angeline."

"Yes, madam." The girl was clearly terrified, but trying very hard to be as good and formal as she had been taught to be.

"Well—now this is not a thrashing for anything in particular, you know. It is simply part of your general punishment, and it is to show you what will happen to you if you are not a good girl."

Annalinde detected again the note of uncertainty in her mother's voice. She obviously felt the whole thing to be just a little awkward. But no doubt Annalinde, who did not yet know her mistress, would be unable to detect this.

"Have you been accustomed to physical correction in the past?"

"No, madam, not at all."

"Then I am afraid you will find this something of a shock. It is not the most gentle beginning, but it is what has been decreed for you."

The girl lowered her nervous eyes and said nothing.

"Bend over that table. Annalinde, position her please."

Annalinde helped the maid to take the proper position. Her black uniform skirt was raised and folded beneath her wide, white apron-bow. Her small, childlike, cross-strapped back lay prostrate on the table, every muscle signifying willing submission. Her cap streamer that flew behind her as she hurried about her duties lay limp on the table beside her. Her petticoat was already tight about her slender, girlish thighs, requiring no tucking-in to tauten it. The pale area above her black uniform stockings, consisting of white thighs and whiter knickers, was all-but exposed beneath the homely-diaphanous covering of elegantly serviceable nylon.

Miss Milchford picked up the General Disciplinary Strap. Annalinde noticed that there was still a slight awkwardness in her manner. In contrast to the easy way she had lain that stinging stroke upon her daughter, she seemed uncertain about strapping this strange girl—perhaps because there was no immediate cause for punishment. She looked at the strap almost as warily as one of its victims might have done, and then, steeling herself, lay the first stroke across the presented parts of her maid. It was not such a resounding blow as that which she had given to her daughter, but Angeline gasped in alarmed distress. Clearly she had not been prepared for anything quite so furiously painful.

"Keep still," said Miss Milchford, and swung the strap again, beginning to get into her stride. The second stroke was similar to the first—firm, but not too hard. Nevertheless, the weight and dense texture of the strap did much of the work on their own account. The maid began breathing heavily, managing to restrain any outward cry, but in evident distress. Curiously this did not seem to inhibit Miss Milchford, but encouraged her to continue with an unremitting rhythm, laying on stroke after stroke of the same moderate but firm intensity. The maid's well-polished lace-up shoes twisted on the carpet; her hands clenched on the far edge of the table until the small, girlish knuckles showed white. After four or five strokes, small, audible sobs began to emerge; after seven or eight, she was crying like a child. Eighteen in all she received; none of them delivered with anything approaching full force—perhaps, Miss Milchford considered guiltily, she had fallen rather short of her instruction to 'thrash' the girl, but it had quite evidently been an ordeal the like of which Angeline had never experienced before.

The girl stood up, smoothing her skirts into place and thanking her mistress. She felt embarrassed and humbled. She wished she could have kept a dignified silence in front of the young lady of the house, but most of all she was occupied by the heavy bruising sting still surging through her hinder parts. She was not, in fact, much bruised—though she would have been if that strap had been used in full earnest; but the splayed weight and kissing stiffness of the implement felt like a brutal intrusion upon her flesh: harsh, heavy and whipping. A part of her almost resented its heft and hardness, used against her small, delicate, unprotected legs and knickers. Another part almost rejoiced in the knowledge of herself as a slavey to be thrashed and hurt to the will and content of her mistress.

"You will be relieved to know," Miss Milchford was saying, "that it is not likely I shall beat you in that manner very often. You should also know that, however distressing the experience may have been, it was very far from being a full-blooded thrashing. No single stroke was of more than medium strength—or even as much. If you are disobedient, rebellious, lazy or impudent, the punishment you have just endured is the very least you may expect. I trust we understand one another."

"Yes, madam." The girl looked extremely nervous and frightened.

"That will be all, Angeline. You may proceed about your duties."

"Very good, madam."

Annalinde found that the whipping of the maid had much the same effect upon her as her own whipping had upon brunettes. It lent the girl a certain fascination. Angeline in her uniform was attractive, but Angeline tremulous and smarting after the ministrations of a heavy strap kindled a heat within one different from anything one could remember. To be pinched or petted by a brunette aroused her to a state of melting passion. That was natural, surely, at her age. But this—was this perhaps how the brunette herself felt?

From this time on the maid was enclosed for Annalinde in an aura of indefinable romance. This romance was not wholly unconnected with the concept of a serving-girl as representing a dimension of wealth, for while wealth in the later years of the West has come to be synonymous with all that is cold and material and quantitative, it is not so with this deeper and more essential form of wealth: that wealth, one might hazard to say, is *essentially* passionate; certainly so in a feminine social order. Her passion toward the maid took the form, at least partially, of a craving to *use* her—to engage her service in a direct and personal way; to ensure that she was *her* maid and property as well as her mother's. She made her first opportunity that very morning.

Knowing the maid to be working in the drawing room, she found some pretext to fetch something therefrom. Pausing at the door she quickly pulled her shoelace undone before entering. The maid, who was dusting, stopped her work upon hearing the door open, and, turning, gave a little bob to the young lady of the house and then stood in respectful silence waiting to be told to continue with her work. Before she arrived this was what she had been instructed to do until and unless her mistress gave her general orders to continue with her work unless called from it. It was very pleasing and Annalinde hoped her mother would give no such order.

"My shoelace seems to have come undone," said Annalinde. "Do it up." It went a little against the grain to give such an instruction without a 'please', but it was also rather thrilling.

"Very good, miss," said the maid, and instantly knelt at her young mistress's feet to tie the shoelace.

Annalinde found the experience intensely affecting. Much more so than she had expected. Just as the girl was about to tighten the knot she acted upon another daring impulse. She walked away from her toward a bookcase. As she pulled her foot from the girl's hands, she caused her to pull the knot awry. She picked out a book and opened it, leaving the maid kneeling somewhat nonplussed. Then, disingenuously she looked down at her shoe and said:

"What sort of a knot is that?"

"I am sorry, miss, I hadn't quite finished."

"Well, come here and finish it, then."

"Very good, miss." The maid crossed the room and knelt at her feet, a little awkwardly this time, as she could not kneel in front of a girl who was standing facing the bookcase, and had to work from the side without making herself too obtrusive.

"You'd better undo it and start again."

"Very good, miss."

"Undo the other one and re-tie that as well."

"Very good, miss."

Annalinde studied her book, acutely conscious of the maid crossing on her knees from one side of her to the other in order to perform the needless operation on her second shoelace.

"Will that be all, miss?"

"Did you enjoy that strapping, Angeline?"

"I am sure it was good for me, miss."

Annalinde knew what she wanted to do now. She wanted to tell the maid to stand up and then put her hand up the neat uniform skirt. She wanted to feel the hot, puffed thighs as they swelled above her black stocking-tops. She wanted to pinch the tender flesh hard and make the girl squeal. She had read about such things in a book called *The Feminine Régime*. All the girls had, and had discussed them on more than one occasion—but could she nerve herself to do it?

"Stand up, Angeline."

"Very good, miss."

Annalinde's heart was pounding. It would be quite easy. The girl would never report her, surely. She could order her not to. She felt a sort of animal warmth radiating from the maid—not a physical heat, but a psychic ardour. Did the girl half-know what she had in mind? Did she will it? Annalinde thought of the private, forbidden world of white thigh and white knicker that lay within the black skirt and above the black stockings—a hidden world, violated with harsh pain, yet utterly virgin and intact, still wholly the private and exclusive property of the maid who was herself a piece of property. The maid wore little make-up—surprisingly little for an Aristasian, but her lips were rouged invitingly, and covered with a little gloss—or were they just moist?

She reached down to the hem of the maid's skirt. Her heart beat unbearably. She could not do it—she just *could* not. She flicked away an imaginary piece of fluff and said:

"That will be all, Angeline."

"Very good, miss." Was there a note of disappointment in the girl's voice? Annalinde was certainly disappointed, but relief added sweet leaven to her frustration. And it was only the first time, after all. No doubt her courage would increase as she got to know the girl. Or would it? Was it one of those fences which become harder to jump with each successive failure?

She watched the girl continue with her dusting—her wide bow and neat cross-straps looking so very demure and businesslike from behind, her streamer licking her shoulders as she moved. Surely one had been mistaken in thinking she had been warm with passion to be pinched or kissed, to yield flutteringly to the exploration of her enclosed and dark-veiled precincts. All she had wished was to be released that she might continue thus demurely with her work. But what *does* motivate a serving-girl like her? Why is she what she is? What are her wishes? One must find out very soon; but for now one has adventured enough.

It was a mistake, Annalinde came to feel in the coming days, not to have pinched the maid then, when the moment was so ripe. Thereafter she became, or seemed to become, more primly self-contained than ever; more chaste and sugar-dry; more apparently alien to such moist warmth as her young mistress so often felt for her. Nor was she beaten more in her own household in those first few days. She was very much a model maid, scarcely deserving of the harsh licking fingers of pain that had so distressed her on her first morning.

5. The New Movement

THE REST of the day was busy for Annalinde. She must go to the office—or rather Patricia must—and put in several hours of work. It was a 'quiet day' in the office. No other staff were there, although the Supervisor from along the corridor looked in from time to time to make sure she was working. She worked well and the Office Cane was not invoked. The temptation not to work was much less when no one else was in the same office. Then she managed an hour on her own writing—or rather of Miss Nightwind's writing—before they set off for the weekly meeting of the Ulalua society, pronounced *Yoo-lal-yoo-a* with the accent on the second syllable, and named after the ancient Amazonian poetess Ulalua Miralinhela, "the Angel-Voice of Miralene".

The Ulalua Society was an informal society that met at the Brace of Pheasants, a charming hostelry not far from the Gaumont Cinema. Its aim was the promotion of the New Movement in literature and art. Its members consisted mostly of writers and artists in the District. In practice, of course, its meetings were but further phases in the great Conversation which nothing could trammel and few things deliberately direct into one course rather than another. The Waldvögel Club was at least partially successful in turning the conversation along the lines of its artistic theme for some part of its meetings. Miss Nightwind travelled, as was her wont, blindfold, cocooned in the Trentish dance-band music that played from the wireless* of the Hillman Minx driven by Maria. Maria was a younger girl, a *fillette sérieuse*, somewhat bookish and sixth-formy. Miss Nightwind was as near to a sophisticated adult *persona* as Annalinde came in her regular life, yet even now, by dint of her greater practicality, Maria seemed temporally in charge of the outing. The third member was Angeline—still Angeline, for her mistress did not yet feel it right to give her her head in another *persona*, and so she came, still in uniform, to provide an extra maid for the Brace of Pheasants.

They were early and the club had still a certain air of privateness; still an air of being vestigially the Trent-Kadrina household commingled with the orchestra-tuning freshness of a hostelry only just opened to the public, its glowing, chattering public-house *persona* still emerging from the cold dormancy of its daily hibernation.

---

* Aristasians, of course, do not receive broadcasts of any sort from the Pit. An Aristasian wireless set typically makes use of "windies"—audio cassette tapes—to play up-to-date music and spoken programmes provided by the Imperial Home Service

"I am sorry, things are not quite ready," said Alice Trent, a little flustered.

"Please do not trouble," said Miss Nightwind—how confident she sounded, how full of life and richness. Somewhere within, hesitant Annalinde marvelled at her and hoped fervently that she could be kept up. "It is all charming."

"Hardly charming," said Alice Trent, bustling away to attend to something.

"She is flustered," said Emma Kadrina from her armchair, where she was examining a teacup. "Blondes do get flustered. Brunettes maintain the superior calm of idleness. It is dreadful, really."

"It *is* charming, though," said Miss Nightwind. "We are rarely early enough to see the Pheasants half-dressed as it were; and there is a wonderful sense of—of *Eos* about it: the dawn of the day, the dawn of the year, the dawn of creation itself. The chaos that precedes cosmos, so full of potential, so fresh and young and unformed, like the flurry behind the wings before the curtain rises upon scenes where anything may happen."

"You are on fine form this evening, Miss Nightwind," said Emma Kadrina. "Not trying to provoke me to an early challenge, I hope."

"Challenge, indeed! Of course not."

"Of course not. That speech was yours and only could have been yours, and entirely splendid too, if I may say so. Sit down, both of you, please do. Maria, is it not?" (the name rhymed, of course, with *higher*, not *seer*).

Maria nodded. Her hair was in a long braid and she seemed a little shy, though when serious talk began she would come into her own.

"What is a challenge?" asked Angeline quietly.

"The reference is to the Cue Game," explained Emma Kadrina. "Whenever the Ulalua Society is in session the Cue Game is open—it may be open at other times too, but it is always open then. The object of the Cue Game is to learn a speech from some play or novel and to deliver it during the course of the evening. It should be delivered naturally, as part of the conversation. If no one challenges it, the speaker has scored three points. If it is challenged successfully, the challenger scores one point. If there is an unsuccessful challenge—that is, if the speech challenged is not a learned speech, but is the speaker's own *ex tempore* discourse, then the speaker gains one point and the challenger suffers a forfeit. One of the glories of the game is that it spurs the members to flights of fine rhetoric in the hope of provoking false challenges."

"Although fine speech ought to be the aim of all of us, regardless of any game," put in Maria.

Betty came in. Angeline recognised her as the barmaid from last night.

"Come with me," she said peremptorily to Angeline. Angeline followed her out of the room.

"You're the extra barmaid, I suppose," she said.

"Yes."

"Then what were you doing standing about talking to the customers?"

"Well, I thought—I mean last night—— "

"You're on duty. You're in uniform. You're not supposed to be disporting yourself."

"No, miss."

"I'll give you 'no, miss'. Touch your toes." They were in the kitchen. Angeline bent over as far as she could, reaching nearly to her ankles. This seemed to satisfy Betty, who, without ceremony, pulled up skirt and petticoat and all, revealing, above her black stocking-tops, Angeline's streaked and swollen thighs, a pattern of red and white, touched by the occasional darker discolouration of mild bruising continuing upwards until cut off by the neat trim of her elasticated white knickers.

"Already had a lashing today, I see," remarked Betty.

"Yes, miss." Angeline's voice seemed smaller each time she answered, Betty noted with satisfaction. Probably no one in the District other than Betty would have considered that this unassuming little maid was already showing signs of what she termed 'uppitiness', but that was Betty's considered opinion and she meant, so far as it lay in her power, to beat it out of her before it got fully under way.

"Then I expect this will hurt you." Betty opened a drawer and selected a light wooden spatula. She laid it across Angeline's sore thighs with a resounding slap. Angeline gasped and half stood up.

"Don't start that, dear, unless you want the cane," said Betty firmly. Angeline had never been caned. The prospect would have seemed terrifying at the best of times, but the thought of what a cane would feel like across her tender rear, when that light spatula was so agonising, sobered her considerably. She did not know whether it lay in a maid's power to cane her, but she had no doubt that Betty would either cane her or cause her to be caned without a moment's hesitation and with nothing but pleasure. There seemed to be in this maid none of the compassion she had experienced at her new home, and she felt thankful that it was there and not here that she had been sent for her punitive service. In the meantime, the only course was to clench her teeth and endure the present ordeal, knowing that her time under this harsh rule could only be relatively brief, provided she behaved herself for it and did not get herself into more serious trouble by resisting.

"I am sorry, miss," she said, bending down more tightly than before and gripping her calves with a firm determination to hold herself in place and not let go.

The spatula fell again, sending its sting tingling on the surface of her skin and soaking deep inside her. Betty beat her regularly, like the ticking of some monstrously loud and violent clock, each tick a furious throb of pain, which added to the swelling accumulation of fiery soreness which was building up to an unbearable crescendo. Betty could feel that she was pushing the new girl to her limits, but she felt that was what she needed, and took a dark pleasure in making her suffer. The thighs were now deep red, and the prim white knickers covered a throbbing heat which could almost be felt at a distance. There was a pleasure in having this maidservant thus at her mercy, at subjecting her to a suffering she could never have consented to and would have done anything to avoid.

At last she stopped. Breathless and overheated though she was, she could have gone on with pleasure, but just as her instinct told her to administer so much severer a punishment than might have seemed reasonable, so her instinct bade her end it now.

"Very well, your punishment is over. Stand up."

"Very good, miss. Thank you, miss."

Angeline was too lost in her physical distress to see or think anything. Only her desperation reminded her of her manners. Had she forgotten to thank her tormentress she felt sure the punishment would have begun again, as indeed it would.

"Good, now do exactly as I say for the rest of the evening, I don't expect to tell you anything twice, and remember there's plenty more where that came from."

"Yes, miss."

But five feet and a wall away, Emma Kadrina was showing three teacups and saucers to her guests. They had a charming rose pattern.

"A pity they were only three," said Emma Kadrina, "but they were a great bargain. I shall give them to Wendy."

"Will Wendy use them, do you think? She never entertains."

"Well, she will have to start. Her house is progressing well; it is time it began to enlarge the life of the colony. Look how splendidly she performed as Lehnya yesterday."

"Oh! Should one say that?" asked Maria in a tone of alarm. She had learned as her first lesson that one should always refer to *personæ* as different people.

"At times it is necessary to give consideration to these matters. That does not mean considering Lehnya one whit less real. Nor would one do it as she became fully established. But there are times when the qualitative assessment of a *persona* must be made from the point of view of civil organisation."

Miss Nightwind and Maria both felt a delightful sense of *inclusion* in having these words addressed to them. It was as if, in the last week or so, they had moved up, or *in*, a level—as if, perhaps, Wendy and Sinta were now occupying the rank they had held before; and possibly Angeline now held the outer ring that had been Wendy's place if not Sinta's. It was not just a feeling of personal compliment, but a sense that the colony as a whole had gone forward a stage, or *inward*, as if it was progressing to a new degree of depth and reality.

The bell rang and Wendy was shown in. She looked very blonde and fluffy after Lehnya. She smiled a sisterly smile at Annalinde, and then saw that Annalinde was not there.

"Miss Nightwind," she said, biting her lip prettily in her embarrassment.

"Welcome, dear child," said Miss Nightwind. "We were just talking about you. It is excellent practice to begin an evening by talking about something beautiful." How daring Miss Nightwind was. Annalinde watched her in wonder. It was a little like riding a runaway mare; one hoped she would not go too far, and that she would not suddenly slip from beneath and leave one stranded. Not that one was *on top* of Miss Nightwind, of course—far from it—one observed from below, or perhaps from behind, while she occupied the major part of the consciousness, but one feared, nonetheless, that one might suddenly lose her.

"I was thinking about safe words on the way over," said Wendy. "Would it be in order to talk about anything so dreadful."

"We were supposed to talk about Art," said Emma Kadrina haughtily, "but since we are not yet quorate I suppose you can regale us with some piece of dreadfulness if you really must."

Wendy gazed at her shoes. "I suppose it isn't exactly Wendy-ish," she confessed, "but some part of us wants to know and you are so-o wise, O, Emma Kadrina."

Emma Kadrina laughed. "Sit down, then, little Wendy, and tell us about your dreadful safe words."

"Well, some bongo types who practise discipline——"

"'Discipline'," sniffed Emma Kadrina.

"Well, you know what I mean. They use something called 'safe words'. It means that if Alpha is beating Beta, Beta can shriek "No, stop it!" or "I really can't take any more", or whatever she likes and Alpha—who is the beater—takes no notice at all; but if Beta—who is not the beater—says the Safe Word—which might be "treacle pudding", then Alpha—who is the beater—stops forthwith and instanter knowing that she really *has* had enough."

"Yes, I believe I have heard of this practice. What of it?"

"It seems to be one of the keystones of bongo—well, for want of a better word–discipline. Along the same lines, I read of a bongo-type who likes what she terms 'verbal abuse', but she arranges in advance what can be said. For example, she enjoys being called a slut, but would not allow any one to call her "stupid" or "ugly"."

"Well, she might not *be* ugly."

"Except in the generalised way that all bongos are ugly, of course. I am sorry to bring it all up, but I did want your views. In one way it all seems self-evidently silly, but in another way it seems quite logical and reasonable. I can tell it is not a thing that could ever happen in this country. I just hoped you might explain the whole thing to me a little more fully."

"Very well. You say that it seems in one way self-evidently silly and in another logical and reasonable. You are entirely correct. If 'discipline' is a game played with no other aim than the self-gratification of the participants—and that is precisely what it is for the bongo types you mention—then these 'safe words' and so forth are entirely logical. Part of the fun is to go through the motions of being forced against one's will or beaten beyond one's endurance; but one would be defeating one's own object if one ever passed beyond the point where it ceased—on some level at least—to *be* fun. The submissive party must set the limits, and indeed she must be in ultimate control."

"Yes, that is exactly what this woman said—or words to that effect—the submissive partner is always ultimately in control."

"In other words the submissive partner is really dominant."

"Yes, that follows, of course."

"Which only underlines the falseness of the entire transaction. It is a game and nothing more. Its sole purpose is gratification. It is not in any sense *discipline*, any more than recreational fornication is love; and it is ultimately barren and unsatisfactory, because the urge that is being toyed with is the urge for genuine discipline and true submission. Nothing else will actually satisfy it. However there is another problem. Genuine discipline and true submission require true authority. They require values and standards to which we all assent, and they require superiors who—just like the inferiors—are acting not for their own mere gratification, but from principle. The bongo 'submissive' is not just wrong and silly to want to remain in control; for how can one render up control to another individual who is herself motivated by nothing other than the desire for sensation? It is true that she may also be motivated by a genuine

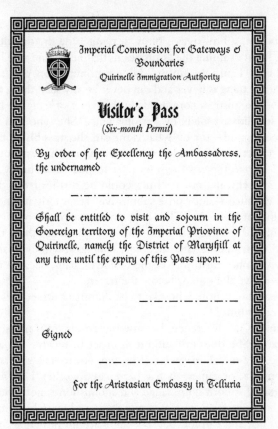

Imperial Commission for Gateways &
Boundaries
Quirinelle Immigration Authority

Visitor's Pass

(Six-month Permit)

By order of her Excellency the Ambassadress,
the undernamed

—— — —— — —— — ——

Shall be entitled to visit and sojourn in the
Sovereign territory of the Imperial Priovince of
Quirinelle, namely the District of Maryhill at
any time until the expiry of this Pass upon:

—— — —— — —— — ——

Signed

—— — —— — —— — ——

For the Aristasian Embassy in Telluria

Real life temporary pass for a visitor to Aristasia not yet granted Subject status

desire to give pleasure to the submissive party; but even that—though it
at least has the higher element of altruism—is insufficient, because it
still is not *discipline*; it still leaves the whole thing at the level of a game
played ultimately for nothing more than fun, whether of one party or
the other or both."

"So our objection is not just that the dominant party should be genuinely in charge?"

"By no means. That alone would be meaningless. In fact what we
criticise in the bongo approach to 'discipline' is not this or that error,
but the fact that the whole thing is based on a fundamentally false philosophy. There are a dozen things they do that are wrong from an au-
thentically disciplinary standpoint, but none of them is an isolated and
separate mistake, all are based on the same central falsehood."

"Could you give an example?"

"Yes. It is quite common for these people to refer to themselves as 'dominants' or 'submissives'. Now, leaving aside the dreadfulness of the jargon, let us examine the assumptions that lie behind it. The 'dominant' will say: 'I am a dominant—I don't submit to any one'. Now, in a true hierarchy there is never and can never be any such thing as a 'pure dominant'. The mistress commands in the name of a higher Law. Her command is validated solely by her obedience. She who will not obey must not command—for by what right can she possibly command if she is not a part of the Golden Chain, receiving her authority from above her? Bongo types sometimes refer to their disciplinary relationships as 'hierarchical', but nothing could be further from the truth. The 'pure dominant' and 'pure submissive' are utterly inimical to the very principle of hierarchy. The 'pure dominant' is cut off from above and the 'pure submissive' cut off from below. Between them they form a closed-off unit, atomised like all bongo couples and individuals. By definition they cannot form part of the Golden Chain, because there can be no links above the one or below the other."

"But what about those who like to be dominant sometimes and submissive at other times?"

"That makes no difference, because the dominant is not submissive *qua* dominant. She does not submit in order to receive her authority from above. She merely participates in two—or more—separate atomised relationships, or games, each as barren as the other. I am not saying that this desire for both dominance and submission is not a healthy inclination that *could* form part of a true chain of hierarchy, but in their case it does not and cannot, because there are no principles on which such a reality might be constructed. Their atomisation is no individual fault of theirs; it is part and parcel of the general atomisation and deracination of the whole world they live in."

"So the central fallacy of bongo 'discipline'—the root cause of all its incidental infelicities—is that it treats 'discipline' as an isolated game, unconnected with any higher reality, ungoverned by any principle, and with no end other than personal sensation?"

"Exactly. The desire for domination or submission may in fact be a genuine hankering after a more whole and rounded reality; a yearning to escape the atomised void of the Pit, but the enactment of some of the outward manifestations of discipline as a sort of lascivious hobby cannot possibly supply that need, being merely another variant of the trivialised, de-centred consumer-consciousness that has created the problem in the first place."

"But what about consent? The point about safe words I believe is to ensure that whatever punishment takes place always has the consent of the punished. I remember that you once said that Aristasian Law was based on consent and that nothing happened which was really against one's will. Is this not the same concept? Are they right, or are we falling into the same trap that they are, or are they two different *kinds* of consent?"

"A *very* good question, Wendy. The answer, I think, is this: the consent upon which Aristasia is founded might be called *fundamental* consent. Nobody is forced to become an Aristasian, or to go on being one. Suppose the District Governess were to sentence you to a caning you and you said 'no, I refuse to be caned'. She would not call in constabels to restrain you physically; but of course your refusal would have serious legal consequences involving further penalties. If you continued to refuse those penalties, at no point would you be physically or forcibly compelled. The only punishment which can be given *entirely* against your will is the death penalty—in other words, the termination of your Aristasian life, and that would be the ultimate result if you continued to refuse all other punishments.

"However, assuming that you do not want to bring all kinds of trouble upon yourself, including, perhaps, the ultimate execution of your Aristasian self, you cannot pick and choose what Aristasian discipline you will accept, or decide when you think you have ceased to enjoy a punishment. They are not there for your enjoyment. They are part of a genuine discipline."

"And yet," said Wendy, "the curious thing is that this discipline is much more satisfying than play-discipline could be. Sometimes when I have been at school and the mistress gives me the strap, I have wanted nothing less. The idea did not seem exciting in the least—I was very far from being 'in the mood', and when she started to give me six with that lethal strap I would have done almost anything to stop her after the first two—you can't know how much it hurts—well, I suppose you can—but after it, I felt calm and at peace. I knew that it had truly done me good. If I had been asked for my consent I should not even have gone to school that day. I had not the least desire to go."

"Exactly. None of the girls in the class might have wanted to go that day, and the mistress might have had no desire to take the class either—that happens too, you know. But we are under a higher discipline, and it has deeper and more unexpected satisfactions than any of us might have guessed at before we began."

"So are we in a way motivated by gratification, as they are?"

"I think not. Satisfaction is there, certainly, as an incidental by-product, and there is nothing wrong with that: but it is not our motivation. Our motivation, as we were saying last night, is to create a real world with hard edges. But discipline *does* bring satisfaction. The discipline of an army or a school builds a morale and an *esprit de corps* which is not reproducible in an undisciplined setting. More than that, it creates a sense of intensity and enclosure, and creates a range of *frissons* which are attainable in no other way, and those *frissons* are more intense and subtle in a feminine environment than elsewhere. However, they must emerge from a genuine discipline. Once we start dressing up in leather and chasing them for their own sake we are doomed to banality and frustration; and certainly all subtlety and delicacy is lost forever."

"But isn't there a genuine problem of 'going too far'? What about a girl who really felt her punishments were too much for her?"

"I have never heard of it happening; but then the feminine world of Aristasia is built upon the highest level of sensitivity. Mistresses have a strong intuitive sense of what is right for the individual charge. And then if a girl really felt harshly treated, it is always her right to go to the District Governess or some other authority and discuss it—not in a spirit of recrimination, but in order to find a resolution to the problem."

"And if a girl really could not bear the thought of corporal punishment at all; would that debar her from Aristasia?"

"Not necessarily. Some parts of the Empire are less strict than others, and even in stricter ones a girl *might* be registered as exempt from physical chastisement—she would have to accept impositions where necessary, of course. It is unusual, but not in principle impossible. If a girl really wished to escape from the Pit, a thing like that could not be allowed to stand in her way."

By now the meeting was quorate. Alice Trent found herself freed from her domestic duties by the arrival of the new maid—Betty had insisted in her quietly firm way that her mistress was not needed further. Sinta had arrived with apologies for coming late and been assured that she was not particularly late—every one else was early.

"Wendy," said Alice Trent, as if she had been calling a child from sleep. "Wendy, come here, dear." Wendy had become a bit 'middling' as the expression had it—all mixed up with the ex-bongo who had been asking necessary questions. Now Alice Trent, whose expert touch had done so much to conjure little Wendy into life in the first place, recalled her to herself and to the company. Wendy looked for a moment dazed and blank, and then, as if emerging from the mists, smiled shyly.

"Are you going to read us your poem?" asked Alice Trent.

Wendy read her poem on the coming of autumn. It was a slight piece, but full of delicate feeling, the rhymes were clever and the scansion precise, showing the benefit both of lessons in school and of the rhyme-games that were played sometimes in the clubs and sometimes at dinner parties.

The company applauded. "Very good, Wendy," said Alice Trent. Wendy flushed hotly and wrinkled her nose in a delightful smile.

Sinta came next. She had been working for some weeks on a pen-and-ink representation of the Sun—or perhaps one should say the Solar Angel—driving Her chariot across the sky. It was conceived in a modernist Art-Neo style, owing something to cubism and more to the popular Gaumont Cinema style of popular Trentish Art Neo. Crisp contrast of black and white, of geometric line and curve, were of the essence of the style, but executed with a subtle grace which humanised and feminised the effect. The aim was a style which combined the Essentialism of ancient and mediæval art—as expounded by such authorities as Ananda Coomaraswamy—with a 20th (or 21st) century futurism. The essence of the New Movement in Aristasian art was to pick up the finest threads of modern art that had been finally dropped at the time of the Eclipse, and to marry them with the traditional philosophy of art that had been finally lost at the time of the Renaissance.

Sinta had shown various sketches and discussed her ideas at previous meetings, but this was her first attempt at a full pen-and ink rendition. She showed it with some trepidation, for she knew that her friends could not commend what they did not truly admire.

The first-fruits of several weeks of labour, of a young lifetime of searching and of a new-found purpose in living, passed from hand to hand in agonising silence. A knot formed about Emma Kadrina's chair as she gazed at it over-long and others could not resist looking again.

"I think it is *lovely*," said Wendy at last.

"Yes," said Miss Nightwind, "so powerful, so passionate, and yet so pure. Chillingly ancient, yet crisply modern—but modern in a sense that rings *true*, is not alienated from our heart's hearth by anti-romantic pretension. It is exactly what the New Movement is trying to achieve."

Sinta smiled, relieved, and yet only half-relieved. She continued to watch Emma Kadrina who gazed at the picture as if in a trance of contemplation.

"Tell me, Emma Kadrina," said Sinta at last. "Put me out of my misery or plunge me into it, but do not keep me any longer in suspension."

Emma Kadrina spoke. "I must say the truth," she said.

"Of course," said Sinta.

"I do not disagree with Miss Nightwind—and yet, I do. Everything she said is there—*in principle*. The concept is truly magnificent, but the execution—well, Sinta, you have not *done* it yet, have you?"

"No, I feared I hadn't. I hoped I might have made a beginning."

"But you *have* made a beginning. A very good beginning."

"Yes, but can I get beyond that beginning. Have I really the ability?"

"Yes, I think so———"

"Can I tell you what is worrying me?—One of the things, perhaps the most important?"

"Of course."

"Well, you know that traditional art is based on a contemplative vision. Plato says that the artist who draws a tree from life—as the post-Renaissance artists did—is making a copy of a copy. The true traditional artist draws the Real Tree, the Archetype of which the earthly and individual tree is merely a copy. That is why traditional art—whether in India or China, in mediæval Europe or among the American Indians—is never naturalistic in the modern sense. Its aim is not to depict the material shadow, but the underlying Reality."

"Of course."

"But does that not presuppose a high degree of spiritual realisation of the part of the artist? Plato speaks of the man who passes beyond the cave of this world and sees the Real Things, of which the material things of our world are but the shadows cast on the wall of the cave. But is not the maid who passes beyond the cave one who has achieved what the Indians call *moksha*—a realised being? A Saint, a Sage, a Buddha? Can I aspire to that? And if not—for I cannot—can I be an artist in the traditional sense?"

"An interesting question," said Emma Kadrina. "Was every artist before the renaissance—excluding the period called by Guénon ' the classical decadence '—was every artist a Saint or a Buddha? I cannot think so. Yet, as you say, the purpose of traditional art is to depict the Real Things, and only the realised soul can fully see behind the veil of matter.

"How, then, can we reconcile these two things? Only, and obviously, by supposing that there can be varying *degrees* of realisation. That every true artist, to whatever limited degree she is able, sees something of the Reality—the Archetype—of the thing she is depicting. I think this is the case even down to the middle of the twentieth century. Some years ago in the Pit, an artist did a portrait of a royal princess in a style that was called ' traditional'—not Traditional in any serious tense, of course, but simply not proletarianised and deracinated. The work was called ' idealised' and ' chocolate-box' by the golem critics. He was accused of failing to depict the ' characterfulness' of the princess, of not depicting a woman who could ' stride about laying about her with opinions'. In other words, he was accused of depicting through her the Archetypes of Royalty and femininity rather than depicting a mere individual with particular emphasis on those aspects of the individual that happen to be in fashion in the Pit.

"Now, I do not think this work was a very successful depiction of Archetypal Reality. Apart from anything else it was too far compromised with the trivialised and proletarianised golem style. But the point is that even this work could capture *some* fragment of Truth. We might say that an artist has to be wilfully anti-traditional *not* to. The paintings of small children always depict archetypal trees and houses, suns and skies, mothers and children—not very well, but quite purely. A Victorian picture of a lady always drew her in the light of the Archetype of Femininity, and then the Archetype of the Mother, the Young Girl, the Noble Lady, or whatever she might be.

"I recently read an up-to-date but proto-bongo criticism of a painting of Nelson at Waterloo. He had been depicted in full dress uniform, looking immaculate—the radiant, resplendent hero. The smart-Alice critic set out a list of reasons why Nelson cannot possibly have looked like this—he wouldn't have worn his dress uniform in battle, he would have had forty-eight hours' growth of beard, he was suffering from dysentery—I can't remember all of it. The gist was that he should have been drawn as a pale scruffy mess and this would have been realistic. Now I don't know how far the arguments were true. Some of them sounded highly contestable to me. But that is not the point. Even if we grant every last one of them and agree that Nelson looked like something the cat dragged aboard, the painting as it stood was still absolutely correct and accurate; and a bongo picture of the cat-dragee would have been fundamentally *wrong*. Can you tell me why?"

"Yes," said Sinta, "because the painting as it stood depicted the true Nelson; the hero that he actually was, and beyond that the very spirit of Heroism itself of which Nelson was a shadow or earthly representative. A bongo-picture would merely have depicted the material accidents of the moment; would have taken pleasure in the incidental dirt and grime, the lowest, vulgarest, least intelligent and elevating aspect of the matter. It would have told a truth so unimportant as to be negligible at the expense of the only truth that made the subject worth depicting in the first place."

"Exactly. And that truth *can* be depicted—*was* depicted—by an artist who was by no means a contemplative (although all art is, on its own level a form of contemplation). It can be achieved by one who is nothing like a Buddha. The Victorian artist had no notion, philosophically, of depicting the Archetype: but he quite naturally attempted to do just that, because that is normal to the human spirit. One actually has to make a very conscious act of abasement to lower oneself completely outside the realm of the Archetypal—at least that *was* the case before the Eclipse. In the Pit every consciousness is de-archetypalised by the inverted and unnatural culture which is forced upon every one from birth.

"That is partly why we have to return to a much more *conscious* and *philosophical* form of Archetypal art; but it does not mean that in order to practise art we must be realised beings. Far from it. In any traditional society every one sees everything in the light of its Archetype. All actions are re-enactments of 'those things first done by the gods'; and while that was not theoretically true between, shall we say the 17th-century 'Enlightenment' and the Eclipse, it was still far more a part of normal consciousness than we may at first realise. Our art, like that of the 19th century, is bound to be more individualist and psychological—and to that extent less purely Archetypal—than the art of traditional Japan or the Middle Ages, and I would suggest that it is a necessary part of the downward historical cycle that it should be so. Nonetheless there are new treasures we can discover on the lower level that is left to us—new vistas that had of necessity to remain closed to higher ages and are the legitimate fruits of this phase of the cycle—provided we do not break the thread entirely and lose our connexion with primordial Reality. That is the purpose of our art. To renew the connexion and discover what a modern art *could* be like if it had not cut itself off from the wellsprings of Essence."

"So you are saying that a high degree of spiritual realisation is not necessary to the practice of this re-essentialised art?"

"I think that is true—I am sure of it. Of course, the higher the art the higher the realisation, at least on some level, and of course we must have a grasp of the depth and essentiality of life—which is why a bongo liberal could never be a real artist; or a bongo conservative, come to that— but to have transcended the cave of the physical universe, to have seen with one's own eye (or rather heart-intellect), the underlying Truth of being. That is not necessary. At the lowest—in theory—one's grasp of essentiality need be no greater than the Victorian painter's view of Nelson, although in practice we need some profounder philosophical root than he had in order to undo the ravages of the soul and intellect that have taken place since his time."

"But if that is the case— " began Sinta slowly, " —if that is the case, what *is* wrong with my work. Is it something even more incurable? Is it simply that I've no talent?"

"On the contrary, my dear, you have quite a respectable talent. The problem, I fear, like so many of the problems of life, devolves upon discipline."

"Discipline?"

"Yes. Genius may not really be one percent inspiration and ninety-nine percent perspiration, but perspiration plays a far greater rôle in the process than most of us are happy to admit. The truth is, dearest Sinta, that your imagination is splendid, your concepts very good, your composition quite passable, but you cannot *draw*. That should not distress you unduly. To say that you cannot draw is like saying you cannot ride a bicycle. You must *learn*, but that will take practice, hard work and discipline. Very few modern people can draw. A large proportion of the people who call themselves 'Artists' in the Pit would be put to shame in the matter of pure draughtsmanship by any young Victorian lady of nineteen who 'did a little sketching'. Picasso, whatever else one might say about him, is an excellent draughtsman, but very few of those who followed in his wash were anything of the sort. Picasso used his excellent draughtsmanship to justify his modernist pretensions; those who followed him have used their modernist pretensions to justify their bad draughtsmanship.

"I do not, of course, use 'modernist' as a term of abuse. There is good modernism and bad modernism, and if we succeed in founding a true art, it will certainly be modernist as well as being traditionalist. But that is not really the crux of the problem in any case. I used to know a girl who could command very high figures for her drawings on private commission. She was not in any sense a modernist, and while her work was competent and had a certain charm, the draughtsmanship, though not terrible, hardly stood up to quite mediocre 19th-century work. I was quite puzzled as to why this should be: after all, she did not lack talent; she had nothing to do but draw and refine her style all day and every day; she could afford to spend adequate time on each picture. Why, then was the work so far inferior to the prevailing standard of a century earlier?

"The only answer I can suggest is lack of discipline. Even people who are practising constantly do not put the depth of *disciplined* concentration into their art that was normal to people of the last century. They give most of their attention to the imaginative part, the creative part—the *amusing* part—and very little to the hard work of perfecting their craft.

"The Imperial Press possesses a book of Vintesse and Trentish advertising illustrations that is used in design work. It is called *1001 Advertising Cuts of the Twenties and Thirties* and is published by Dover books. You have probably seen it in the office."

"Oh, yes, I often look at it. It fascinates me"

"You have probably been wise enough to skip the bongo introduction. Nevertheless, it is of some pertinence to our present discussion, for the compiler tells us that much of the work in the book is of a high calibre because of the contemporary emphasis (that is, in Vintesse and Trent) on draughtsmanship and formal art training. In today's market, she continues—meaning the Pit, of course—the successful illustrator is frequently one with the clever idea, not one with the ability to draw the human figure adequately. She is not criticising, just stating the bald fact. And what is true of bongo commercial art seems true at every level.

"When Tamara de Lempicka decided to become a painter, she spent a considerable, self-imposed apprenticeship in nothing but making painstaking copies of the fourteenth-century Italian masters: not because she wanted to paint like them—indeed she intended to create her own traditional-futurist style—but because she wanted to acquire their cleanliness of line and purity of vision. Then she worked on the technique of painting itself, coaxing and coercing from her egg-tempera paints that unique, iridescent, enamel-like quality that all her paintings possess. She learned her craft diligently before she attempted to practise her art. You—and I cannot blame you—want to realise your imaginative vision straight away. You want to get straight to the most interesting part and try to pick up a bit of technique as you go along. Everybody does; but it never works. You must learn to draw and learn to draw *well* before you do anything else. Believe me, you have the ability. Now you must put in the effort."

"But how should I go about it?"

"Perhaps you could find a drawing-mistress. That is what you need. A nice strict one who will keep you to your work and rap your knuckles. Why not advertise for one?"

"Thank you, I shall," said Sinta, taking this suggestion to imply the possibility that there was an art mistress latent in the District.

"Remember the Tibetan simile of the marriage of Wisdom and Method. With the traditional understanding you have thus acquired and with your own projected artistic applications thereof, you have Wisdom sufficient to begin with. You must now acquire Method before it can be put into any effect. Or to say the same thing differently, you have a modicum of Essence: you must now acquire sufficient Substance for that Essence to come into manifestation."

Miss Nightwind next read the latest chapter of her novel. It was a novel depicting the life of Aristasians, very much as it was lived in reality. "An everyday story of homo-emotional, multiple-personalitied, disciplinary folk," as she had once described it. It held the company enraptured, but Miss Nightwind, so confident in other respects, tended to worry about her work.

"What of the conversations? Are there too many? Does the reader *want* to hear the Great Conversation of Aristasian life?"

"It is entirely necessary," said Emma Kadrina. "You are describing our life, and so much of what happens in our life—the very stuff of it— takes place on the plane of discourse. Leave that out and we should be a two-dimensional parody of what we are. We lead such an adventurous life and most of our adventures are intellectual adventures."

"J'agroo," said Wendy. "And also, how could any one know *why* we are what we are unless they knew what and how we *think*? Our life is inexplicable until you understand the thoughts that lie behind it."

"What would a life of Dr. Johnson be that left out his conversation?" asked Sinta.

Emma Kadrina read her latest chapter. She was writing an adventurous epic of life in High Aristasia, the magical world upon which our earthly Aristasia is based—a world where there are only and have only ever been two sexes—blondes and brunettes. Emma Kadrina's great enterprise was to fabricate a history for her people and to chart the vicissitudes of a world where feminine rather than masculine motivations had always predominated—where war, for example, had played little part and struggles for power took forms very different from those of male history. Not an Utopia—an impossibly *good* world—but nevertheless, one where good will was the norm and bad will the aberration; where love rather than enmity was the driving force of a majority of actions. Yet it must be neither dull nor sloppy and must have powerful and moving themes within it. It was a task to tax the profoundest talent.

And it was more than merely a literary task, for the life of Aristasia was being constantly modified and deepened by Emma Kadrina's history—and by Miss Nightwind's work and the work of some others—and at the same time those works were being influenced by the life of Aristasia. Where life ended and literature began had never, from the beginning, been wholly clear. Characters from fiction became incarnate in the bodies of the Empire. Without the literature there could have been no Aristasia, and without Aristasia there could have been no such literature.

"How wonderful it is," said Wendy. "I feel this *is* my history. I belong to no world and no nation but this one. If England—far less 'Europe'—went to war, I should feel no involvement. It would be a quarrel between two alien states. I am an Aristasian, and that is all I am."

"And yet," said Emma Kadrina, playing Devil's advocate herself, yet voicing her real concern, "are we not more deracinated than the rest—having cast off all allegiance save to a thing we have invented? Casting off all natural ties and birthright, having no mother country but the one we have given birth to out of the womb of our own imaginations?"

"Of course," said Maria, "only by becoming completely deracinated can one re-racinate oneself at this stage in the course of things. Only she who loses her life can save it. So long as a fragment of rootedness remains in the world that is opposed to all roots, there is no possibility of personal restitution. If you will forgive the analogy, every speck of decay must be drilled out before we can begin rebuilding the tooth. As long as we imagine there is still an England—or still *anything*—we are chained to the enemy's world by that link. England has gone, along with every other nation. There is only the Void. As surely as if civilisation had been destroyed by atom bombs, the only inhabitable world is the world we create."

"It is true," said Alice Trent, "and it is that terrible fact which allows us to rebuild the world as we would have it."

"In all conscience," said Miss Nightwind, "we suffer enough pain and heartache from living in a voided world; let us not be shy of reaping every shred of positive advantage that the circumstance allows us by way of compensation."

"And yet," said Alice Trent, "for all the pain we certainly feel, I often wonder whether the advantage does not outweigh, in many respects, the disadvantage. How else could we live a life as delightful as the one we do? How many people have lived in a world—however tiny—bound with such love and loyalty; with so little of jealousy and spite, so much pure appreciation of one another; so much rein given to the various natures of each one of us and the development of a purely feminine world, which, for such as us, must be more satisfying than any other—any 'real' historical world. Have we not been blessed abundantly by our misfortunes?"

"It reminds me," said Wendy, "of how people used to say things were so much better in the War—that people were kinder and nobler and had a sense of common purpose. Being so few against a howling emptiness, can we not be purer and better and have a truer loyalty than we could in a world where sanity was simply normal and taken for granted?"

"Yet isn't there something to Emma Kadrina's worry?" asked Sinta. "Does it not make our life curiously thin and insubstantial to owe our loyalty to a country of the mind? To associate ourselves with a people of whom—well, if you do not mind my saying it, we do not even know the Facts of Life, as they are called."

"You mean we don't know how blondes and brunettes make babies?" asked Wendy.

"Precocious child," said Alice Trent. "But do you not think that is the most wonderful thing? I mean, having emerged from a quagmire where these 'facts' have become so commonplace, so utterly vulgarised as to destroy every vestige of sanctity and beauty—where every hint of the real depth of the thing is buried beneath the most banal third-form literalism, rather like the bongo's picture of Nelson—isn't it the most delightful, audacious corrective of the whole nonsense to spirit ourselves into a world where no one knows the Facts of Life at all?"

"And all of us are as innocent as Arcadian adolescents. The polar opposite of what Johnny Bongo tried to make us."

"Or perhaps some wonderful, super-innocent fantasy-Quirinelle teenagers, living in a world where a certain degree of *petting* occupies the mind almost constantly——"

"Speak for yourself, Miss Nightwind!"

"——but nobody goes Too Far, because nobody actually knows how to."

"Delicious! But you know, I've heard that it's something to do with the brunette's tongue——"

"Wendy!"

"Sorry, Alice Trent."

"Yes, I've heard that too, but then I've also heard——"

"Miss Nightwind, you are not too old to be caned," said Alice Trent.

"Especially as Lindie seems to be slipping in," said Sinta with mischievous acumen.

"Well, never mind what I've heard. We've all heard various things, but the point is, no one actually *knows*, does she?"

"And that," said Emma Kadrina, "together with the *decorum* of Aristasia, and with a respect for life and its mysteries—doesn't it make the erotic so much more *exciting*? Doesn't it restore the thrill to a thing that has become so plebeian and commonplace in the Pit?"

"It does," said Miss Nightwind, "and yet—and yet we write off the world that has been destroyed with hardly a second thought. Is it entirely right? This morning I happened to notice a rose in the garden. It was all overblown and bedraggled. It looked like a painted old woman. And I remembered that I'd looked at it a day or two ago. It was lovely then, fresh and blooming and radiant. It may be hideous now, but that doesn't take away the beauty it had once. That was real."

"Yes, I suppose so," said Emma Kadrina "but what can we do? There is no possibility of *our* reviving civilisation. If it ever comes back it will not be our doing, and what we *are* doing may be of more value than we can know in creating a model for new forms of civilised life. Our art, for example——"

"Then I've succeeded!" said Miss Nightwind in triumph.

"Succeeded in what?" asked Emma Kadrina.

"Can't you guess, even now?"

"That speech—the one about the rose?"

"Exactly. *The Circle*, by W. Somerset Maugham, Act 2. My point, I fancy."

"Oh, *played*, Miss Nightwind."

6. Domestic Discipline

DESPITE the brief semi-appearance of Annalinde earlier in the evening, it was hard to make Miss Nightwind relinquish control of the body when they were returned home; and yet it was necessary, for Annalinde's Aunt Alice desired to see her. It was late-ish, of course, but Aunt Alice often seemed to make her appearances after ten o'clock at night—a curious predilection, perhaps, for this otherwise strait-laced lady, but such were the imponderables of manifestation.

"You'd better go into the drawing-room to wait for her, Lindie," said Maria, Annalinde having been finally re-established.

Annalinde went into the drawing-room and sat on the sofa. Miss Nightwind's minor triumph still bubbled pleasurably inside her. It was not every day that any one worked off a quotation on Emma Kadrina and the others. And so well that she did not guess immediately afterwards, either. It spoke well of one's thespian abilities, perhaps for one's future in the District Drama Society. It felt a little queer to be a child again and to feel this dread of Aunt Alice. She was in trouble again, that was certain, and as she waited a chill fell over her spirits. Of all things she had least wanted this. She felt, as one often does when taken in a quite different mood, delicate, and as if even a small dose of corporal punishment would be wholly unbearable. Of course Aunt Alice might give her lines; she did sometimes, but that felt no better. The thought of spending hours tomorrow writing out some tedious imposition seemed equally dreadful.

At last the door opened. Aunt Alice was there in her knee-length, straight wool skirt and her blouse and cardigan. She looked very everyday after the glitter of the Brace of Pheasants, as she always did. Annalinde rose immediately to her feet. Aunt Alice made the Brace of Pheasants and art and music and wit seem somehow phantastical, bringing one back to the grey weight of the Real World of duty and discipline and the hard fact that one was a child. Her heart had lain heavily in her stomach as she awaited her aunt. Now it seemed to rise into her throat.

Aunt Alice crossed the room and seated herself on the sofa.

"Come here, Annalinde," she said. "Closer please. Stand exactly there." She indicated a spot on the carpet. "Now, Annalinde, what have you to say for yourself?"

"I don't know, Aunt Alice."

"You don't know. You know to what I am referring, do you not?"

"Yes, Aunt Alice."

" Six Order Marks. Six! And when did I last punish you for Order Marks?"

"Saturday, I think, Aunt."

"Saturday is correct. And your mother has had occasion to give you six since then. Claire is a delicate blonde, Annalinde. She should not have to be troubled with constant misbehaviour from her daughter. And you are a blonde too. You should behave yourself obediently and with gentle grace. A good deal of the time, Annalinde you behave yourself like a rather unruly brunette. If you *were* a brunette I should have to discipline you, but as you are a blonde the matter is rather more serious. You do understand the difference between blondes and brunettes, do you not?"

"Yes, Aunt Alice."

"I hope you do. You are getting too old, Annalinde, to behave in a harum-scarum manner. In a child it is allowable, but in an adolescent blonde it is very unbecoming. There is a name for blondes who do not act in a blonde manner, Annalinde. It is not a pleasant name and I should not like to feel that such a name could ever be used of a member of our family."

Annalinde flushed deeply. She did not like to feel that she was risking her good name. Much of her naughtiness took place at home, but it was true that she was sometimes noisy and silly at the cinema. It was true that she sometimes behaved in an un-blonde manner. Perhaps at times she lost a certain connexion with the essence of her femininity—it was a common enough disease in any one who had been exposed to the Pit. Even a brunette should beware of that, but a blonde——.

"I see, Annalinde, that something of what I am saying is beginning to strike home. I am glad. It is not just a question of telling you off. You must take stock of yourself. Your un-blonde behaviour has passed as childish fun up to now. But you are getting older. You are reaching an age when the rather—well, rather rough and sometimes indelicate manner you sometimes affect begins to look ungainly and ridiculous."

It was true. She *was* growing up. It was a fact she had not entirely taken seriously before. After all, her chronological age was so different from her age in Aristasia, that age seemed to be a thing infinitely malleable, and one felt that one could seize at once the privileges of every age from infancy to venerable maturity. But, of course, it was not really true. Different *personæ* might have different ages, but they must be disciplined and each kept whole and integral: they could not splurge over one another—and Annalinde, her main *persona*, was definitely growing up. She had gone out with brunettes—well, one brunette. She was starting to be admired as a young blonde. She must not lose the respect of her position. Her remark this evening about petting, for example—and it *had* been her, not Miss Nightwind—would have been a bit near the knuckle even for a brunette. She excused it to herself on the grounds that it was making a real point, but it must have sounded rather brash and forward and unblondelike.

"This is a small town, Annalinde. A girl's reputation goes with her everywhere. You are admired in some quarters as a charming example of a blonde, and you *are* such an example at times. Now you must learn to discipline yourself and be charming and dainty all the time, not only when it takes your fancy. I do not mind your being excitable—and even naughty—provided you make certain you are doing it in a blonde way. When I say I do not mind I do not mean that I shall not punish you. Of course I shall. But it is not so *vital* a matter as maintaining your blondeness. You are not among the newest girls in the district any more. Your job is to set an example. I hope I may rely upon you to set one from now on."

"Yes, Aunt Alice."

"It is not entirely your fault, Annalinde. I blame myself in part. We both know well enough that the traditional method of keeping blondes blonde is to punish them—in particular to whip them. I have not been on hand to beat you nearly as much as your nature requires. We must try to remedy that, must we not?"

"Yes, Aunt Alice."

"Very well, then. Come over my knee."

Annalinde obeyed, lying herself across Aunt Alice's lap, her upper body resting on the vacant seat of the sofa.

"Put your hands under me," said Aunt Alice. It was her practice when administering a severe spanking to sit on one's hands, thus rendering one immobile and incapable of struggle. Annalinde manœuvred her hands under her Aunt's heavy, grown-up thighs. The straight woollen skirt had ridden up a little and she could feel her upper thigh filmed in gossamer Quirinelle nylon. She even fancied she could feel it grow denser and less ætherial as it darkened at the top. The soft weight of her aunt's legs pinned her firmly, and she was aware of that lady turning back the skirts of her—or rather Miss Nightwind's—elegant black evening dress, exposing the deep-pink satiny petticoat with black edging. She tucked the surplus folds of petticoat between her thighs, her hand warm against her most intimate places, and yet with an impersonal, aunt-like warmth. She knew with what she was to be disciplined. She had seen the hairbrush lying on the seat, and watched her aunt pick it up before she positioned herself over her. In truth, it was not actually a hairbrush, although that is what it was always conventionally called. It was a large, oval-headed Trentish clothes-brush, long, heavy and with a

*Annalinde, pinioned firmly by the hands, twisted
her legs as if to avoid the pain*

slightly convex back flat enough for its purpose. There were numerous of these brushes in the Empire, glistening in their dark-brown burnished Trentish timber. There was a home-like, quotidian severity about these implements, so ideal for their purpose and versatile enough to brush clothes as well.

Annalinde tensed herself involuntarily as she felt the motion of the first stroke coming. The flat, heavy, stinging shock exploded across her skin, penetrating the satiny petticoat and the matching pink, black-edged knickers as if they had not been there at all. Such delicate protection was powerless against the heavy thwack of sheening, Trentish wood. Her legs stiffened, her body reared a little, though her hands were pressed immobile by warm, feminine thighs.

"I hope there is not a spirit of resistance in you, child," said Aunt Alice sternly. "We have all night to beat it out if there is. Relax, please. Submit yourself."

Annalinde made her body go limp, letting herself go to the will of her superior. The brush smacked home again, tingling-sore upon the surface, yet deep too. These were heavy strokes. Not the crushing blows that were termed 'Victorian strokes', but hard, heavy, full-intentioned smacks. A third, a fourth, a fifth and a sixth fell. Annalinde gasped, tensed, tried to untense and tensed again. She had accepted such punishments better than this in the past, but punishment is a curious thing. In the right mood one can absorb so much, warmly, submittingly, almost voluptuously. Today was almost the opposite. She could hardly bear to be touched. These ringing, tingling flood-waves of pain seemed almost intolerable. She half expected her aunt to tell her again to submit. Sometimes she scolded her all through a spanking. Today she seemed to have said all she had to say. Annalinde knew what was expected. If she tensed and arched herself, the punishment would lengthen. Submission would come in the end.

Unable to help herself, Annalinde, pinioned firmly by the hands, twisted her legs as if to avoid the pain, opening her suspender-crossed thighs in the most ungainly manner. Aunt Alice deftly brought down the hard brush in agonising reproof to the neice's exposed inner thighs. Annalinde squealed like a wounded animal and closed her legs demurely as her only means of protecting this most delicate place of feminine modesty. For the rest of the spanking her legs remained neatly side by side, despite the mounting pain in her bottom and thighs. Even so, that burning soreness would make walking a delicate task next day, as her inner thighs rubbed together, up-gathered above her stocking-tops beneath the modest folds of her skirt.

Aunt Alice was falling into a rhythm now. Hard, swinging slaps falling with easy force upon the pink-sheened bottom and thighs. The flesh was becoming hot beneath its chastisement. Even her own thighs were hot and moist against the adolescent girl's clenching, powerless hands. The girl was sobbing now, but there was less resistance in her sobs. She was resigned to the long, hard spanking.

Angeline, in her little room above was taking off her uniform, unclipping her shiny metal suspenders. She felt glad, at first, that some one else should suffer. She was sore still from her beating at the hands of Betty. Inexperienced as she was, she could tell that it was some hard, wooden implement not unlike the spatula that had been used on her this evening, though heavier. She was still sore from that, used so cruelly over her already-lashed skin, and she slid off the stockings from her thin, girlish legs, enjoying the sharp percussion from below.

She crossed the hall in her petticoat and slippers, washed out her intimate garments, brushed her teeth, cleaned off her make-up all in a leisurely fashion, knowing that the other occupants of the house were otherwise occupied and contemplating the events of her first day in bondage. She was tired, sore, a little shaken emotionally, nervous and even a touch resentful, yet she looked upon all these feelings in a haze of tired detachment and with a feeling strangely pleasurable rather than otherwise.

It was no game; that was, perhaps, the salient sensation of all those in which her mind swum. The idea of being a bonded maid, the District Governess, the sentence, all these had seemed half game-like and half chillingly real. The visualisation of the Kadorian bus-station had made it seem more game-like than ever, though it also added another layer of wistful reality. But today, as it were, the reality had clanged to and the lock had clicked. She was a serving-girl, at the beck and call of her superiors, which meant, as far as she could see, every one. A girl to be ordered about, called hither and yon, to answer bells, to scrub floors, to be slapped and strapped, to be always neat and demure and obedient, to say "Very good, madam" and "Very good, miss" and nothing more. Yet the contemplation of these things was strangely rosy. Even her resentment seemed somehow a shade enjoyable, and the enjoyable part of that resentment was her powerlessness to act upon it in any way, as if she felt a certain—yes, a certain cruelty toward herself. She felt herself clench her teeth and vindictively wish suffering upon herself, as one might wish it on another. Not physical suffering either, but precisely the suffering of resentment. "Yes," a part of her was saying. "Fret in silence when you are treated as a menial slave, denied all privilege, whipped and bullied: fret and resent and cry yourself to sleep, and know that you can do nothing about it." She smiled a curious smile, and, in truth, in the days to come found a certain secret disappointment—secret almost from herself—in the thoughtful, kindly mistress and the reasonable household into which she had been bonded.

Her ablutions completed, she put her things into her sponge-bag and made her way back to her little bedroom. She was surprised to hear the spanking still in progress, slow and rhythmic and hard. Had it been as hard as that all the time she was in the bathroom? Had it been going on at that pace? She felt sure it had. How many strokes must it be? A hundred—no more, probably; much more.

As she settled into bed, she heard the rhythmic strokes, each one accompanied by a high, soulful moan. Annalinde's fingertips were digging deep into her aunt's thighs. The ordeal was far greater than she had expected. The spanking stopped for a moment, and the hairbrush was exchanged for a short, three-tailed strap, hard and heavy, perhaps nine inches long, and made, it seemed, specifically for spanking. It was fashioned from real old leather, dark and shiny with use; clearly an old school or home implement. Its harsh tails cut through the surface numbness created by the long spanking with a new, high-pitched pain. Annalinde squealed.

Angeline remembered Annalinde's commanding her to re-tie her shoelaces, and that gave an added *piquancy* to this audition of her strapping. She could not see it, of course, but being in the room above, it was almost as clear as a wireless broadcast. She felt sorry for the girl, frightened that such severities were possible in this house, but also she enjoyed it. She enjoyed it especially because of the shoelaces. It would have been easy to think that it was a kind of revenge for her humiliation, but really it was nothing like that. She had not minded serving the young mistress in that way. She had been embarrassed, but she could hardly say she had wholly disliked it. Somehow, though, the sound of this girl who held so much power over her, who could toy with her at will, receiving so sound a spanking gave her an exquisite *frisson*. Her involuntary squeals of acute distress as hard leather bit already-chastened flesh had an effect quite unexpected; pleasing almost to blissfulness and she found that the pleasure warmed and deepened as she pictured herself kneeling at Annalinde's feet tying her shoelaces. She settled herself to listen to the entirety of the punishment, but in the event she was sound asleep before the leather ceased its harsh refrain and the young lady of the house, sore and subdued, made her own way to bed.

October
TUESDAY
7. Maryhill County Grammar

THE BELL rang. A clanging brass hand-bell it was, with a worn leather strap-handle. Its commanding voice pealed all over the house far louder than was demanded by mere necessity. There could be no claim on the part of any girl not to have heard it.

They made their way up the stairs, quickly, but without running. Blondes in maroon gymslips, brunettes in grey skirts, white blouses and ties.

"Wait for me," cried Lehnya, "I can't get my tie to work!"

"Really," said Susan, "you're the soppiest brunette ever. You ought to be a blonde."

"Don't be horrid," said Jane.

Solid little black brunette lace-ups and more delicate blonde shoes clattered upon the bare floorboards of the classroom. Lehnya came in a half-minute later, still fiddling with her tie. The other girls were already lined up behind their desks, standing stiff and straight : two brunettes on one side, two blondes on the other. Miss Baines looked at Lehnya with weary impatience.

"Don't you think it would be better to get dressed *before* you come to class?" she asked.

"I'm sorry, miss. I was having a bit of trouble."

"Very well, stand in that corner with your face to the wall. I'll deal with you in a minute." Her voice was dull and irritable, as if the task of punishing this girl was just one more in a succession of tiring and tedious chores. Lehnya felt guilty for putting her to the trouble.

"Very well, girls." she said with a barely suppressed sigh. "Sit down ; get out your books. We'll begin as soon as I've dealt with this brunette who thinks my class is a changing-room. Come here, girl."

Lehnya turned to face the mistress and walked the short length of the small classroom to the front. She wanted to wheel round smartly and march forward as some mistresses made the girls do, but she feared that the laconic Miss Baines, who was clearly asking no such thing of her, might take it amiss. She certainly had no desire to increase the mistress's displeasure.

"Bend over that desk." Lehnya obeyed. Miss Baines lifted her pleated skirt, leaving her thin nylon petticoat in place, according to the modesty regulation. "Three strokes," she said.

She took the school strap from its nail on the wall, a long, slender, two-tailed strap, shiny with extensive use. A much more formidable strap than the cinema one, with a deep, hard bite. It depended, of course, with how much force and skill it was plied, and one might think that Miss Baines's lack of enthusiasm would make her punishments more bearable than many. It was not so. She tended to put all the weight of her irritability into her strokes. Lehnya suddenly felt vulnerable in the ordinary white cotton knickers of the brunette uniform. The maroon school ones of the blondes seemed much more protecting, though in truth there was probably only a little in it.

Without warning the first stroke fell, loud and shocking. One always forgot the intensity of the bite. The second and third came in quick, no-nonsense succession, each one wrapped home with what felt like real venom; each wave of pain was still climbing to its harsh crescendo as the next began, the three combined into a tidal flood.

"Don't cry," Lehnya desperately commanded herself. "Not a brunette. Not in front of the class. Not in front of—*her*."

"Stand up."

"Thank you miss," The pain was starting to subside already. One always noticed that about the school strap. So very hard to bear at first, but fading quite quickly. The worst was over. She had come through. Such an ordinary, everyday punishment, and yet how much of an ordeal. Other girls took such strappings so very lightly. She wondered how they could. But perhaps they did not seem light to any one at the time, only before and afterwards could bravado diminish their chastening effect.

"You had better move that desk. I was expecting three blondes."

The two blondes were at one double desk, and the two brunettes were at another. Behind the blondes was a single desk. Lehnya moved it behind the brunettes and then took the chair, feeling horribly conspicuous. If she had been quicker, perhaps she could have got a place beside one of the others. She felt isolated and strange. It seemed *exposed* being a brunette. People expected you to know and do. They didn't look after you in the same way and laugh indulgently at your mistakes. The thin white knickers seemed symbolic of a less protected state. Perhaps she was not really a brunette at all. Susan had more or less said as much. *Personæ* were all very well, and any one could have a brunette 'on the side' as it were, but to *be* a brunette, to *live* one, did one not have to be *born* brunette? It was a question of one's *sex*, after all, and although the girls sometimes treated it as the made-up game it superficially appeared to be, the more one lived with the concept, the more real it seemed. Some of the girls flitted about apparently quite easily from *personæ* in one sex to *personæ* in the other, but even then, the longer she knew them, the more convinced did Lehnya become that each one of them was either fundamentally blonde or fundamentally brunette, while her 'playing' of the opposite sex was precisely that—a more or less successful game.

Lehnya had been an experiment, an attempt to broaden her range. It was only because of—because of Annalinde that Lehnya was anything more than a party-piece. Because of her feelings toward her. But was that a mistake. Was she not simply a blonde infatuated with another blonde? And yet her feelings toward Annalinde were so very definitely *brunette* feelings; her appreciation of her blondeness, so very much an appreciation of the *other*, her feelings so towering and protective. It was confusing, certainly. From far away in the dark and distant depths of the Pit came the cry "but are all these categories *necessary*; are we not all unique and individual?" Yet that, it was clear, made less sense of the whole thing than ever. Without the *reality* of blondeness and brunettism, none of her complex and overwhelming emotions would exist at all, and her landmarkless 'uniquery' would be but a grey and formless passion-dead identity with all the other floating atoms of the Void.

Miss Baines was calling the register.

"Annalinde,"

"Yes, miss"

"Jane,"

"Yes, miss"

"Maria,"

"Yes, miss"

"Susan,"

"Yes, miss"

"Wendy,"

Silence.

"Where is Wendy?"

"Please, miss, she isn't here today, miss."

"I see, and we are honoured with your presence instead, are we, Lehnya?"

"Yes, miss."

"Very well. I suppose I had better write you in. With *L* for *Late*."

Lehnya bit her lip. It wasn't fair. She was hardly late at all, and she had been punished, Now there was a mark against her name. Everything seemed to be against her brunette identity. It was fate. She felt so desolate she could have started crying there and then. But a brunette can hardly do that sort of thing. How strange it was, awash in a sea of overpowering emotions bitter and yet sweet; harsh and yet so heartbreakingly tender. Was all this the natural feeling of being feminine? The re-

ality that made women such 'queer creatures' to men before they had
been remade in man's image in the Void? And what did men look like
to women in the real world? Strange stony beings, eminently practical,
but blind, in most cases, to nine-tenths of the colour of life, to nine-
tenths of its joy and its pain.

Miss Baines was reading from the geography book in a flat monotone.
Her vowels were not very good, though they were certainly decent, up-
to-date flat vowels. No bongo thin *oo*'s, for example. Even when we
do something badly we must do it badly in the right way.

The subject was not inherently boring; not if one made the effort to
meet it. It spoke of English agriculture and English hills, of fruit going
to market and sheep grazing by the roadside in a world where there
were markets with real market-men and roads with real cars and real
children to eat the fruit. Between the prosaic lines was a world as lovely as fairyland, and just as remote: remote from the fluorescent drabess
of the Pit on the one hand and from the highly-charged feminine magic of Aristasia on the other. Yet, as Miss Baines read it, it seemed dull;
excruciatingly, ineffably dull. Another mistress might have brought it
alive, but Miss Baines seemed to kill any life it might have.

And yet—and yet, was there not a life in this very dullness? A depth
of *reality* attainable by no other means? Miss Baines was a stroke of genius. She was born out of a deep irritation and weariness in the *psyche*
sometimes manifested as Alice Trent. It was by no means her whole self,
but a mood that seized her sometimes, making all seem dark and dreary. It was precipitated by financial worry compounded by the difficulties
of running an entire colony with only one maid and a brunette who was
charm itself, as well as being a genius, but utterly useless in every practicality of life, and in many respects as dependent as an infant at the breast.
These things added to a dizzy cycle of light and darkness that had
gripped her since early in life, begun by the extremity of her reaction
against the Pit, her horror of being forced to spend her childhood there
and the triumphal energy of her wild schemes to escape it, or even destroy it.

When the dark half of the cycle was upon her, when trouble pressed,
such things as going to school, or teaching children seemed pointless and
worthless.

"But they *must* be done when they seem pointless," Emma Kadrina
had said. "Don't you see, that is what makes them *real*. That is what
makes it *school* and not a game. If our world has no hard edges but turns
upon our whim, it will not be a world at all. You know, I think your
feelings could be seen not as a difficulty but as a wonderful thing; a great
opportunity."

"Do you really think so?" asked Alice Trent, who was by no means stubborn in her mood; rather the mood was stubborn in her and she longed to escape from its grip.

"Yes, I do," said Emma Kadrina, the fire of inspiration kindling in her eye. "You know what they say about cars: don't steer *out* of the skid, steer *into* it. You know what they say in Judo: don't push, yield. Use your enemy's strength against her."

"And how does that work with me?"

"Well, as far as teaching in school is concerned, don't *resist* your mood of dullness and irritation, *use* it. Let's create a *persona* that embodies those qualities in a positive crystallisation of dull, irritable *realness*. Let us forge her into one of those hard edges that our world so badly needs."

And so Miss Baines was born: dull, tetchy, tired, and as real as a wet Sunday in Manchester before Manchester was eclipsed.

The girls tried hard to follow each detail read out in Miss Baines's flat-voiced drone. They would be expected to answer questions, to write summaries, and if they had not paid attention they might be punished. Miss Baines was unpredictable. Sometimes she really was too apathetic to take much notice of misdemeanours, and one got away with far more than one expected, but at other times her nervous irritation came to the fore and punishment might be disproportionately severe. She could wield the strap with what felt like real spite at times, or could give out lines in appalling doses. Lines were no trouble to her after all. She could say "Five hundred" with as little effort as it took to say "One hundred". Just a moment's irritation or spite might make the difference—almost none to her, but so very much to the girl or girls condemned to repeat the line again and again and again. She could also send girls to be caned. Sending a girl for a caning was a serious affair. It implied that she was out of hand and needed to be controlled by a firmer mistress. She could expect to suffer intensely if she had to knock on the door of a senior mistress with a slip in her hand requesting so many strokes of the cane. But Miss Baines sometimes issued such a slip just because—well, the girls said, just because she was in "that mood"; or just because she couldn't be bothered to use the strap herself for the sixth time in a lesson. Being in Miss Baines's class was rather like living on the slopes of a volcano. One tread always very carefully, fearing to set her off, or to be the unlucky girl who happened to be in the way of the eruption.

"I don't know if Miss Baines should take her feelings out on the girls the way she does," kind, blonde Alice Trent had worried.

"Of course she shouldn't," said Emma Kadrina, "it is shocking bad practice. You would never do it and I should never do it; but it is what Miss Baines does, and don't you dare cheat by trying to stop her. She is creating a whole new dimension—a great ringing tunnel of iron. Building hard edges like a good'un. Worth her weight in construction engineers is Miss Baines."

And so the girls suffered; and Jane suffered as much as any one else; sometimes more. But for all the artificiality of its planning, the reality was as solid and unwhimsical as anything could be. Miss Baines was a real entity, once given her head by the *psyche* of which she was a fragment. She hardly gave a thought to the theory behind her construction, but simply *was*. The psyche *sank* into her—very much an inferior part—and rested there, and Miss Baines had her way. The *psyche* emerged from her refreshed and having shed something of its burden, but while she was there, Miss Baines was all. Even the normal vestige of disinterested æsthetic contemplation was inhibited by the sheer mundaneness of Miss Baines, who had not a disinterested æsthetic bone in her body—as Emma Kadrina had once quipped in connexion with this fact: "She is a walking illustration of the difference between *disinterested* and *uninterested*."

The psychic atmosphere of the class was very 'close', its reality hugely powerful. There was no room there for anything other than the reality of the lesson. This was always the case at school, but somehow Miss Baines brought a greater *weight* or solidity to the experience. She was often away for weeks, even months at a time, but whenever she returned and stood at the head of the class, there was that same sinking or 'grounding' feeling in every heart and stomach. Often in her classes (and in other classes too, but most markedly in hers) there was the dark atmosphere of a class in which nobody really wished to be present. The girls had rather be doing something more amusing, had rather be free to talk and play, and the mistress had rather also be elsewhere. Most mistresses, if that was the case, at least made largely successful attempts to conceal the fact, but Miss Baines let her *ennui* show as clearly as if she had written it on the blackboard.

It was a curious sensation, sometimes, especially for new girls, to realise that no one might wish to be present. Perhaps one had taken with a grain of salt the assertion that Aristasia was not a game: or, as Emma Kadrina had said, if it *is* a game, it is only a game in the sense that everything else—armies, stock markets, Governments and everyday life in general—are games. Aristasia, one might feel, is inherently more game-like. That is part of its charm. But sitting in a class where no one really wants to be, where all are subject to a certain compulsion, one begins to ponder the meaning of 'game'. If it is a game, it is a game none of the players want to play at this moment, yet all of them must. And wherefrom comes the compulsion? In a sense there is no one above them, and yet, suppose they were simply to leave the class by mutual consent—what would happen then? There would be repercussions. The District Governess would hear of it and would manifest through the body of one of the rebels to discipline them all in ways they would not enjoy in the least. There would undoubtedly be long, written impositions for all concerned; impositions of a judicial rather than a domestic or scholastic magnitude: thousands of lines which would blight one's life for weeks to come with endless, useless, tedious toil. There would be severe whippings, and no doubt a sharp increase in monthly hours of compulsory attendance at school, so that the thing against which one had rebelled became a greater burden. Other punishments would no doubt also be devised for such a monstrous and unheard-of act of petty treason, and the entire ordeal would be so very unpleasant for each of the miscreants that after it was over she would never dare to risk incurring it again.

So would order be maintained in the District, and it was by no means impossible that a District Disciplinary Committee would manifest itself through the bodies of *every* girl involved in the rebellion to devise their chastening, which it would do quite impartially, with regard to the enormity of the crime. It was possible also that (as is the custom with many such committees in Aristasia—and this one would have been established for many years, even though it may never have been manifest before) the precise form, combination and severity of the punishments would be ultimately fixed upon by some elaborate system of the casting of dice; for many of the hard realities of this world were so divined. What is certain is that the punishments would be crushing, tear-inducing ones against which the heart would cry out for relief, and resolve never to repeat the offence, for that would be the entire aim and purpose of the committee.

But wherefrom, wherefrom ultimately, came that stern and inescapable compulsion under which they all sat in their desks or stood at the front of the class? It came from the Golden Order of Aristasia, the True Good Place that lives in every heart, by whatever name it might be known. It came from the Order of the soul and of the universe, that can never wholly be crushed in a world of chaos—and in that world, where all legitimate authority was dead, that order must, at times be enforced *by* those whom it is enforced *upon*. To the individualism of the Pit, nothing could seem more strange, but to a more traditional mind, it is entirely natural, if a shade unusual. In the mediæval philosophy of art, there are always two parties to the making: the patron, who knows what is to be made and the artist who knows how to make it; if the artist makes for her own use, then the parts of artist and the patron are both played by herself, but that makes no difference to the fact that there must always be two parties to the making. It is not the will of any individual, or any group of individuals, that is to be enforced, but right order, goodness and harmony.

And when those things, upon occasion, went against the individual will, and even against *every* individual will in its temporary desire rather than its settled purpose, then their enforcement became the true test of freedom—freedom from the tyranny of the fleeting passions which, by disorganising the True Empire, could give power back to the Enemy; freedom to build, in the subtle realm of will and consent, a world that is a *reality*, and not merely a castle of sand to be washed away by the first tide, leaving only the *physical* power of the Enemy intact—indeed, it was this that the Enemy depended upon for the maintenance of his monopoly on the definition of reality: promoting a cult of low-level self-indulgence which he called ' individual freedom' that stifles the discipline necessary to create and maintain any self-defined world.

Without discipline there could be no freedom. And discipline in a shattered and fragmented world must necessarily take curious forms; but by such means alone could one seize the power to shape reality.

Wearily the hour wore on. Miss Baines did not seem to be in one of her especially bad moods, just in her usual bad mood—but one could never be sure with Miss Baines. She could seem relatively benign by Bainesian standards and then suddenly explode with irritation. Sensible, well-behaved Maria dropped her pencil with a light clatter. Miss Baines looked at her distastefully as if it had been an act of deliberate mischief.

"Two hundred lines, Maria," she sighed, as if the effort of awarding the punishment were a real imposition upon the mistress. Poor Maria, almost blonde-like in her desire to be good and to please, came near to tears. The class tensed. The imposition was disproportionate to the tiny ' offence'. Miss Baines was waxing dangerous.

Miss Baines was writing exercises on the board. Some of them, no doubt, would be done now and some for homework. The lesson was entering its last lap, but the last lap could often seem the longest. Maria felt shaken by the sense of undeserved reprimand, and even (unusual for her) a little resentful at the thought of the lengthy punitive task which lay ahead of her for no very good reason. Sometimes Miss Baines set lengthy homework tasks, dreary and pedestrian—tasks involving copying, answering rather obvious questions at unnecessary length, work which required extensive answers virtually cribbed from the book. Originality, in her eyes, often counted simply as being wrong. " That is not what it says in the book, is it?" Even in its oppressiveness, there was a certain refreshing innocence about it, a hard and stolid counter to a lightweight world where teachers had been taught to prize a rather pointless and unreal 'originality' above all other things. She wasn't exactly *right*, and she wasn't very clever, but as one learned to value these elements of realness and discipline, one could not entirely disapprove of her methods, even when one did, in practice, dislike them. Each heart sank as she began writing on the board. Would they have a long, dull homework to face this evening? Miss Baines was not the worst of mistresses in this respect. Some of the younger ones devised dull and extensive homework purely for the girls' 'moral improvement'—that is, for their torment, relishing the power of command and confinement over their pupils' lives. Some older mistresses also devised tasks with a view to exercising the girls' patience and submission. Miss Baines seemed to have no such subtle consciousness. Her slabs of dreary labour were set purely because that was the way girls learned their work. There were no short cuts, They must just learn from the book, write things out, answer questions fully using the book, so that they might learn to answer them in the examination without the book. Sometimes she set little homework or none; all depending, it seemed, upon her mood.

Maria's heart sank deeper than any one's, knowing that whatever Miss Baines set she would have two hundred lines to write before it or after it. Did the other girls want to be there at that moment? Susan was purely bored and hated the thought of further boredom at home. Lehnya felt so nervous and exposed in her unaccustomed brunettishness that boredom hardly entered into her state of mind, although the heavy dulness of the atmosphere did seem to exacerbate her feelings. Jane was curiously divided. On one level her lively, butterfly spirit was utterly crushed by an hour of stillness and unimaginative toil, on another it felt curiously restful to her ever-turbulent soul and there was a certain wistful pleasure in complete submission to the solid and wholesome and un-clever. Annalinde's spirit had perhaps fretted most of all. There were times when she really wished she could be old enough to leave school. Nothing valuable seemed to be achieved in lessons like this. Even if she *did* learn her geography she would have been just as well off ignorant of it. All this talk of exams as if they were all-important tired her. What did they matter really?

She had felt indignant on Maria's behalf when the punishment had been given for dropping her pencil. Indignant on her own behalf, too. She did not *like* Maria to be occupied in the evenings, and it seemed insufferable that she should be so just because this ignorant, self-important mistress had decided it. Not even decided it, really. It was just the crotchet of a moment, almost as random as the throw of a dice. But now Maria was bound inescapably by it; and Annalinde too.

Curiously, though, while the unfairness and self-satisfied arbitrariness of the imposition rankled with her, it also intrigued her; and the power vested in the dowdy, in-turned mistress at the blackboard held her fascinated, like a rabbit before a snake. She found a curious perversity growing inside her. What if she were to let her own pencil fall from the desk? What would old Baines do about it? She could do just about anything, from failing to notice it (it was not beyond her to be too apathetic to do anything at all, even though she had just punished another girl disproportionately severely for the same offence) to—to, well just about *anything*.

Annalinde felt the absurd temptation niggling at her, like Poe's imp of the perverse. It was the most idiotic thing to do, and yet she found herself almost daring herself to do it. "You know you wouldn't *actually* have the courage." "Oh yes I should." "Go on then." "All right." and before she had time to stop herself, she pushed the pencil over the edge of her desk. It hit the bare floor at an angle of forty-five degrees and danced clatteringly to a standstill. Miss Baines turned from the blackboard to watch the flushed Annalinde retrieve her property.

"Seems to be an epidemic," she said, half to herself. She stood for a moment as if pondering the matter. No one could tell if she was feeling severe or just a bit vague, and then with that near-psychic acumen that seems to be possessed by even the dullest of teachers she asked Annalinde the question that froze her very blood.

"Was that an *accident*, Annalinde?"

Lying was one thing an Aristasian never did. Not to other Aristasians. It was a cardinal point of honour. Their whole lives might be based upon what an outsider would call 'fantasy', their biographies and birthplaces might be of recent and exuberant invention; these things were not lies to Aristasians, they were a higher form of truth. But vulgar, ordinary lying, deceptive and dishonourable, muddying the waters of faith and trust among the sacred sisterhood, was anathema to every Aristasian. It corrupted the very principle of their new, self-defined truth.

"No, not exactly, miss."

"I thought not. Well, you'll have to see Miss Maybridge for the cane."

That was all she had to say on the matter. No lecture or recrimination, just the weary, matter-of-fact passing of sentence. A dark chill settled upon Annalinde. So *that* is what she would do. If only she had not been so idiotically anxious to find out. Miss Maybridge of all people! How many strokes would it be? Perhaps only two or three; but even that would be terrible. Only once had Annalinde actually been sent for a caning, and then it had only been a junior mistress, not the august and terrible Miss Maybridge. She felt hot and giddy, as if in the grip of a fever, and the remainder of the lesson passed as in a dream.

Miss Baines set a large number of tedious exercises for homework, causing inward sighs among the class—quite silent, though, for no one dared to risk Miss Baines' wrath. Sighs of tedium might be heard in Miss Baines's class, but only from Miss Baines herself.

Maria raised her hand. "Please may I leave now, miss?"

Miss Baines knew that Maria had a special reason for leaving and granted her permission. The other girls must stay to await the next lesson. Miss Baines took the little sheaf of printed punishment slips from the mistresses' desk and filled in one for Annalinde.

"Take that to Miss Maybridge after lessons today," she said. There were times when Miss Baines' irritability erupted into anger, but this was not one of them, and if she took some sombre joy in the heavy punishment she was inflicting, she showed no outward sign of it. She folded the slip and handed it to Annalinde. "Oh, and when you have completed tonight's homework, make another fair copy of it for me. Write out the questions as well as the answers, please." The homework was a long and wordy one, and the casual instruction fell crushingly upon the child.

Miss Baines gathered up her books and papers and left the room, Susan opening the door for her, and all attention turned immediately upon Annalinde.

"Oh, Lindie, the cane from Miss Maybridge. How *awful*."

"How many have you got?"

"I don't know. I haven't looked."

"Well, look now."

"I can't."

"Give it to me, then. I'll look."

"Susan, don't. It isn't yours."

"No, but I want to know. Don't be a silly blonde. You can't resist a brunette."

Of course she couldn't, and Susan took the slip from her easily. She opened it and looked.

"Oh, *Lindie*."

"How many is it?" asked Annalinde, turning pale.

"Are you sure you want to know?"

"Don't be silly. I've got to know now."

"You'll have to ask more nicely than that."

Lehnya was now the only other brunette in the room, and she knew it was her duty to curb Susan's behaviour.

"That's enough, Susan," she said, trying to sound easy and confident. "Give her the slip back."

"Oh, the new girl wants to tell me what to do, does she?" said Susan, holding the slip high over her head.

"*Please*, Susan," said Jane. "It isn't fair. The poor girl's going to be caned and she's frightened."

"Is she? Perhaps I'll tear the slip and then she'll get double."

"*Susan*, you're being *horrid*. Why are you being like this?" Jane stamped her foot, but she also looked close to tears. A terrifying vision of the next mistress coming into a room with crying blondes putting the blame on her (blondes are terrible tell-tales) sobered Susan instantly.

"All right, Annalinde. Here is your slip. May it bring you great pleasure." She giggled at her own joke, turning her merry eye upon Lehnya who giggled a little too, so as not to seem too po-faced.

Annalinde opened the slip and read it. She looked very small and afraid. She folded it neatly and put it between the pages of her geography book for safe-keeping. She sat down at her desk.

"How many is it?" asked Jane.

Annalinde did not reply.

"Six," said Susan.

"Six! Oh, Lindie!" Jane sat beside her at the blondes' double desk and put her arm about her shoulder. "Oh, Lindie, *did* you drop the pencil on purpose?"

Annalinde nodded.

"But *why*, Lindie? Why did you do it?" Jane's gentle, blonde voice was full of horror and incomprehension. Annalinde felt more dreadful than ever. The punishment loomed like a frightening shadow over her, and Jane's manner made it so clear what a dreadfully un-blonde thing she had done. Susan might have done it and it would have been a reprehensible piece of brunettery. Lehnya and Maria would probably never have dreamed of it. But for a blonde to do it was just *odd*. And she *was* a blonde, there was no doubt about that for her or any one. She was just an odd blonde. How she wished she had learned from Aunt Alice's spanking.

The blondes were huddled together at their desk now, exchanging tearful confidences and commiserations. Their blonde world excluded the brunettes utterly. Curiously, despite her worries, Annalinde had never seemed blonder from the outside.

Lehnya felt strangely excluded. To Wendy such a blonde enclosure would have been open and she would have felt safe therein. Now, on the outside with Susan who had behaved so roughly, and who had been curbed only by the threat of Jane's tears, not at all by her own admonition, Lehnya felt like a foreigner.

But brunettes are still girls.

Susan took Lehnya's hand. "Are you all right, Lehnya?"

"I don't know. I feel a bit funny."

"You mustn't mind my teasing the blondes. It is only part of the fun."

Wendy had been teased by brunettes both individually and as part of a group. It had never seriously worried her, and even when they had really annoyed one, or even frightened one a little, it had only made her feel safer and more secure in her blondeness. But Lehnya could never imagine *doing* the teasing. Still, the remembrance made Susan's actions seem more understandable and Susan herself less strange. She gave Susan's hand a squeeze.

"Don't worry," said Susan. "I know what it's like to be new. You're a bit nervous, aren't you?"

"Yes," said Lehnya; but she was more than nervous. She was assailed by the strange, exposed feeling of being brunette, by the worrying exclusion from the blonde enclosure, and, perhaps most of all, by being shut out from Annalinde's distress. She wished Annalinde had turned to *her* in her fear and anxiety. But was that likely when she was a brunette?

The classroom door opened and a gymslipped blonde came shyly in. Both brunettes stood up and Susan made a sweeping bow.

"Elinor, my heart's desire," she said.

Elinor smiled nervously. "Is every one all right?" she asked, sensing some disturbance in the atmosphere.

"Annalinde is going to get the cane," said Jane gently.

Oh *dear*," said Elinor, and her distress was not one whit the less real because the mistress who had so wantonly imposed this distressing fate had but lately been occupying her body. She remembered it, of course, but she did not *officially* remember it, and while that word *officially* might have for most non-Aristasians connotations of mere formalism and legal-fiction, for an Aristasian it went much deeper. It meant that she should pay no attention to the connexion, that she was both debarred from it and freed from it. Her strongest feeling in relation to it was the sense of lightness that always came from purging all the heaviness and weariness and irritation that had accumulated in her system through Miss Baines, but that was more a quasi-somatic sensation than a thought. In her thoughts she scarcely gave house-room to any connexion between herself and Miss Baines, and thought of her mostly as an old, unattractive mistress who had been most unkind to her friend.

"What did you *do*, Lindie?" she asked.

"Only dropped a pencil," said Jane protectively.

"But it *was* a bit deliberate," confessed Annalinde.

"But even so, the *cane*," said Jane. "And six strokes."

"Six," said Elinor. "How *dreadful*. Just for a bit of nonsense. Oh, how *could* she?" She felt quite indignant, except that a good blonde like herself was never indignant to her depths. She accepted the right of authority to wend its wilful way, and felt sure that it was always for the ultimate best, as did all the girls.

The door flew open and all the girls stood neatly erect behind their desks. They had rearranged themselves, Lehnya sitting beside Susan and Elinor pulling the extra desk behind the blonde's double desk. It was too heavy for a blonde and Lehnya did it mostly for her. They were still dragging when the new mistress entered and Elinor and (especially) Lehnya were a little late in taking up their positions. Of course they should have moved the desk before. They had had time. The mistake, depending upon the character of the new mistress, might well prove a costly—not to say a painful—one.

Miss Blue bounced into the room. It may seem a shade disrespectful to say 'bounced', but it is the just description. Just as Miss Baines's very presence filled the room with a weary weight and a greyness, so Miss Blue seemed to fill the room with light. She had on a slim Trentish skirt, flaring out at the knee, a red cardigan and about her neck a flowing silk scarf of rich royal blue.

She bounced her pile of books on the table—well, she cannot quite have *bounced* them as her burden contained not only books but a neat, up-to-date-looking electrical box. Yet somehow she gave the impression of bouncing them, and her bright eyes sparkled over the room. They had a twinkle for every one, but they settled on Lehnya and then on Elinor and then on Lehnya again.

"Dear me, dear me, dear me," she said. "Not ready. Not standing to attention like good little *Mädchen in Uniform*. Pulling desks about like dockers. Shifting the scenes even as the curtain rises. Very bad form. Very bad form indeed." Her eyes twinkled from one to the other. It was always a pleasure to be the object of her attention.

And now her eyes left them, playing now among the other three. "What shall we do with them?" she asked. Her three innocent pupils did not answer. They were not expected to answer. It would have been bad form if they had. "Shall we thrash the brunette as the more responsible of the two? Shall we whip the blonde because it is her desk and anyway blondes need it? Shall we drop the entire matter as being too trivial and worldly for artists like ourselves? What do *you* think?"

She paused now, as if really expecting an answer. Her eyes settled upon first one innocent and then another. If she had concentrated upon any one for a fraction of a second longer she would have been demanding some attempt at an answer, but always her sparkling glance flitted away before the moment of consummation.

"Let me see, the blonde, I think. Yes, the blonde. Come here, blonde." Her twinkle settled on Elinor and fixed, yet it did not cease to twinkle. It was a happy, friendly feeling, yet a nervous-making one too. Elinor stood up and came to the front.

"Over the desk," said Miss Blue, pushing her over the front of Annalinde's desk, causing Annalinde to move her things and push her chair backwards. She lifted the girl's skirt, and did she lift her petticoat too? It was strictly illegal, but Miss Blue might do such things. Annalinde and Jane could not quite tell from directly in front of her, though no doubt the brunettes had a better view, being further to the side. Miss Blue picked up her tapette, a small, oval leather paddle, pointed at the end, made by a Scottish saddler for school use. It was not an official implement in this school, but a few mistresses affected paddles of varying sorts for minor correction. Miss Blue always had hers on top of her pile of books.

The slap of flat, stiff leather upon blonde thighs rang through the little classroom. Elinor gasped. It was a small tapette, to be sure, but well made by an experienced saddler, and Miss Blue applied it, as she did all things, with great vigour. She pressed Elinor against the desk with one hand and administered a sharp, vigorous paddling with the other. Elinor gasped and writhed, wishing to coöperate with the charming mistress, but unable to stay still under the rapid stinging slaps. Mostly Miss Blue was intent upon her work, but once or twice she sent her twinkle dancing about the room settling upon child after child, and then back to the business of chastening the blonde. It was perhaps a minute by the clock. Not a long time, but long enough when a fiery sting is accumulating with each passing second. Elinor rose and breathlessly thanked the mistress. She felt at once subdued and invigorated.

"Now, what about the brunette?" asked Miss Blue, once again addressing her question to the class, and including the tremulous Elinor in her questioning glance, for she now had joined the innocents. "A much harder thrashing, perhaps, as brunettes should know better? No, I think not. I am feeling rather fond of brunettes today. I think I shall let you off, young Lehnya. Your little blonde friend has had your punishment for you. Be careful, though. You have used up all your credit for one lesson. The trigger is hair for you, brunette. The sword of Damocles hangs above you by a raven lock.

"But enough, enough, enough. We cannot spend the whole lesson having fun or I shall deserve a whipping. That would make you laugh wouldn't it? Oh, yes, you dreadful children. That would make you laugh. Well, enough. The time for laughter is ended. The time is come for toil and labour. Seriousness and mental strife. To work. To business. Down the mines."

She opened the up-to-date little electrical box, and it transpired to be a portable tape-recorder with small reels. Not quite a dictaphone, but the very smallest of real tape-recorders. And the girls, who, in another world, had been familiar with every manner of electronic home sound-making were as entranced by the appearance of this magical toy as any true child of Quirinelle. Miss Blue, in her wonderful way, conveyed the special magic of the thing while all the time treating it as the most matter-of-fact and worky device imaginable. She plugged it in and turned it on and the girls heard a group of Quirinelle drama-school children singing nursery rhymes, then a lady from the B.B.C. announcing a programme, then a little girl announcing, then some narration from *Bill and Ben*, then a snatch of a panellist from *Twenty Questions*, and several other female Quirinelle voices the girls could not identify.

Miss Blue switched off the tape recorder, paused for a moment as the delightful sensation was absorbed and then asked: "Now, girls, what did you notice about all those voices?"

Jane put up her hand.

"Yes, Jane?"

"They were all ladies, miss."

"Yes, indeed, Jane, they were all ladies. What did you expect in Aristasia? Talking fish? Now who else has noticed a very important thing that is common to all the voices?"

There was a pause as no one quite wished to risk a further attempt; but Miss Blue was brisk as well as bright. It would not do to keep her waiting. After a few seconds Susan put up her hand.

"Yes, Susan?"

"They all spoke properly, miss."

"Yes, Susan, they all spoke properly. That is quite correct. A goal for the brunettes. Now, I shall forgive the others for failing to remark upon this point, because it *ought*, of course, to go *without saying* that they all spoke properly. How else should they speak when they are broadcasting on the wireless or the television—unless, of course, they are performing in low comedy? It is incumbent upon broadcasters to maintain the highest standards of speech; to set the best possible example; to raise the general standard. And until the Eclipse, the general standard *was* rising very noticeably.

"However, that was not the case in the dark depths of the Pit. There people aspired not to speak as well as possible, but as badly as possible, and the example set by the broadcasting services was quite deliberately a low and corrupt one. Even the members of their strange, vestigial 'royal family' were trained—specially trained by instructors—to flatten and coarsen their voices lest any should think they continued to uphold some superior standard. In their universities, where the 'Oxford accent' had reigned supreme, that accent was destroyed in a few short decades; rooted out of the mouths even of the majority of older dons who had been speaking it all their lives.

"Why was this, dear children? There were no doubt many excuses and justifications, but the real reason was this: Good English was the mark of a superior caste—of the leaders. But no caste in the Pit was any longer truly in command. The new rulers of the pit were the manipulators of international capital. Financial control was a great pyramid that overrode and controlled all other forces from governments downward. In that New World Order, every one was reduced to the position of a proletarian except a tiny handful, and every one must be trained to act, think and *speak* like a proletarian.

"Executives of international companies, leaders of intellectual opinion, Prime Ministers of nations—all of them were waged employees, dependent for their livelihood on the same pyramid of financial control. They no longer belonged to a financially independent class of free, civilised, classically-educated people. They belonged to a mass-media-fed *lumpen* class of dependent employees; and it was important, in countries where speech was a symbol of status, that their speech should be remodelled to reflect their new status as dependent proletarians and inferiors.

"The change was extraordinarily sweeping. It affected every one from leading politicians, university professors and broadcasters down to every girl from a good family who, a generation ago, would have spoken in crisp, good English and now talked with contorted vowels and a proletarian slur. Of course the girl herself could hardly hear it. She thought of the new serf-speech as 'normal' and decent English, her natural heritage, as affected, or 'snobbish'. In any family of erstwhile good standing (for good standing meant next to nothing any more) one could almost guarantee that the grandmother would speak very well, the mother in a flat, middling voice and the daughter in bongo-neo-proletarian. A whole generation had been as successfully programmed and re-educated as if they had been a single person. It was chilling, my children. Positively chilling.

"None of that, of course, has anything much to do with us. The Pit is the Pit and this is Aristasia. Whatever they did down there is dead and gone as far as we are concerned. But it is nevertheless important that we should ensure that our own voices are not infected by any creeping contagion from the foetid miasma that hovers above the Pit and occasionally drifts in noxious traces across the pure air of the Celestial Empire. In the matter of speech, this means that we must make very certain that we are speaking the Empress's Aristasian, true and unsullied, both in vocabulary and in pronunciation.

"So let us consider some principles of correct speech. A newspaper reporter once described Miss Marianne Martindale's voice as being 'full of vowels, like a Trentish actress'. She did not use the word 'Trentish', of course. But note where the comma falls in that sentence. She did not mean 'full of vowels like the vowels of a Trentish actress', she meant 'resembling the voice of a Trentish actress in that it was full of vowels'. A curious statement on the face of it. All speech is made up of vowels and consonants, and between every few consonants must fall a vowel or two, one would have thought—unless we were speaking Martian. But no. The reporter was quite right. Bongo speech is increasingly *empty of vowels*—that is to say, of clear, distinct, differentiated vowels. The lip muscles seem to atrophy, and all the vowels slowly lose their distinction—each one aspiring toward the neutral *uh*-sound. This is all part of the bongo identity: to appear to be as lax and casual as possible, to ignore distinctions and enunciation and to give the impression of taking the least trouble over one's speech. Anything else might smack of superiority, and mind-serfs must never dare to seem superior.

"So where do we begin? First of all, we must listen to the voices of those who *do* speak properly, like the ones we have heard a moment ago. Listen to them again and again, practice enunciating our own vowels as they do, each one clear and correct and separated by crisp, wellformed consonants. We are going to do that together in a moment, and I want each of you to go home and do some more work of the same sort. Some of you require quite a lot of work, and some of you need only to polish the work you have already done. But those that fall into the second group must not sit back on their laurels. Dear me, no. You must polish, polish, *polish*. I want the clearest, crispest, most musical and lovely voices in Aristasia. I want fine control and well-modulated expression of every *nuance* of thought and feeling. Language is the window of our minds and souls, and that window must be clear and bright and beautifully adorned. *Excelsior*, children. That is the motto of Aristasians. The motto of the Pit is 'lower, ever lower!' But our motto is *Excelsior!* To the highest!

"Now, before we begin our practice, I want to consider some of the specific things we must listen for and correct in our speech. Above all, we must understand what is specifically Pittish in diction and pronunciation, and avoid it. Because there is, dear children, such a thing as the bongo-accent. It is not just a question of unrefined speech—indeed, even *personæ* for whom unrefined speech is desirable must learn to use *real* unrefined speech to replace bongo unrefined speech. So, can any one tell me what is the most salient characteristic of the bongo-accent in southern Pit-england?"

Annalinde's hand shot up.

"Yes, Annalinde?"

"Yeeth and byeety, miss."

"Very good, Annalinde. That is one goal each for the blondes and brunettes. Now I see that some of you are looking a little puzzled by Annalinde's somewhat cryptic reply. What Annalinde is saying is that the most salient characteristic of the English bongo-accent, affecting most of the young professional class, and spreading to much of the southern Pit-English population as a whole, is the thinning of the *oo* sound to the quality of *ee*.

"A little story. A short time ago I went down the Pit to a baker's shop where I bought a particular kind of bread. The shop-girl, a pleasant but deeply Pit-poisoned young thing, asked me:

'"Would yi like t'cheese?"

"I thought she was saying 'Would you like the cheese?' and was wondering whether some loaves had actually been baked with cheese, or whether there were some cheese-filled rolls which she thought I might wish to buy. I asked her what she meant, and she merely reiterated, in a clearer voice:

"'Would yi like t'cheese?'

"After some consideration and a further repetition, I finally worked out that she was saying 'Would you like to *choose*?' She wished me to select the individual loaf I should take.

"Now I understand that this sort of confusion does not arise often in the Pit, because most Pit-dwellers have grown accustomed to the bongo-accent. Many Pit-born girls do not even know what I mean when I speak of this phenomenon, so, if you have the misfortune to go down the Pit, I want you to listen out for it. First familiarise yourself with *real* English, work on your own *oo*'s especially, then listen carefully to Pit-speech, particularly that of young and ultra-bongo speakers. You will soon hear it in them, and then you will start to hear how, to a lesser, but constantly growing, degree, it is affecting the speech of most other Pit-dwellers. Some less-corrupted speakers say *teeoo* or *tyoo* for *two*, whereas the more corrupted really do practically say *tee*. Listen out for it.

"This thinned *oo* has long been current among the bulk of the Australian population, but, when grafted on to the sub-cockney of southern Pit-english proletarianised-middle-class speech, it is a purely bongo phenomenon. I rather fancy it made its first appearance in English universities in the late first or early second decade of darkness, among middle-class undergraduates who had been conditioned to want to stop sounding 'posh' like their parents but did not feel able to adopt fake Cockney accents. They adopted instead a strange, thinned, loose-mouthed speech that represented an uncomfortable and rather embarrassing compromise—a strange, drab, contorted diction that had not grown organically out of any class of English speech; a mutant *argot* born from the shuffling capitulation of a people robbed of their pride and freedom and commanded to abase themselves; a mongrel-speech that took nothing from lower-class English except its lowness and nothing from middle-class English except its triviality, leaving behind the true worth and beauty of both. Since then, through the mass-media, developments from this mind-serf speech have become Pit-standard, and have filtered back into the speech of the southern Pit-english working class.

"Now girls, pick up your pencils. No, not like that—you are not going to write with them. What are you going to do? You are going to put them in your mouths. Just like this, watch me." She put the end of her pencil about a quarter of an inch into her mouth and closed her scarlet lips about it

"Did you see? Put the pencil in the front of your mouth and form your lips round it. Now take it out and say *oo*. That is right. *Oo. Oo. Ooooooooo.*

"That is the way you must always say your *oo*'s. With nice round lips. Don't let your muscles stay lax, make them *work*. Nice round mouths. *Oo. Oo. Oooooo.*

"Now say after me:
Who, who is *Looby Loo?*
Little rag doll *who* plays with *you*."
The girls repeated the rhyme in unison.

"Good girls. Now I want you to keep practising that *oo* sound. When you hum a popular song such as *You're the Cream in My Coffee*, don't go 'Deee de dee dee dee deee de' but 'Ooo oo ooo oo oo oooo oo'. Just practise those *oo*'s and that nice round mouth. Think of Vintesse Pippsies and their *boop-boop-a-doop*.

"And remember: every round *oo* is a blow against the Pit; an arrow of light in the psychic war—because that is where the war is fought, my children: in the mind, in the heart and on the lips. The fact that you are only a few, while millions are capitulating to the Octopus and speaking as he commands is of no consequence. Those millions are just baggage. They belong to whoever is in power. They are not warriors— they are the spoils of war. If we controlled their television stations they would speak as *we* told them. You, my children, the few who choose for themselves, who are not made and moulded by the Enemy: you are the only warriors, the only individuals. Go forth, then and send your shining *oo*-arrows streaking into the psychic twilight; let the bright blades of your sharpened consonants cut down the hordes of greyness; let the fusillades of your flighted *a*'s fall like thunderbolts upon the gates of darkness. Not alone will they win the War, my children, but upon that lunary plane where the course of the world is decided, they will do more execution than perhaps you can yet understand."

Her eyes were brighter than ever, her cheeks flushed with the fervour of conviction, and as the lesson proceeded with reading aloud, there was an underlying fire in the whole class—a sense that what might seem to be merely a routine lesson had in fact a deeper and nobler significance. Each girl read her passage with a sense that her vowels and consonants were shining weapons in the battle for light and good and purity against the troglodyte ugliness of the Pit.

But such weapons must be put to the test not only in practice thrusts and parries but in trial contests. Miss Blue announced 'conversation'. First the girls must all speak a little impromptu on a subject chosen by the mistress: 'My Favourite Film Actress', 'Should Blondes be Treated more Strictly than Brunettes or *Vice Versâ*?' 'Clever Song Lyrics' and other subjects upon which an Aristasian girl was wont to forget herself and wax eloquent. In these the girls did well. Then she led them in free conversation on the same subjects, enticing them into genuinely free conversation as if she had been one of the girls herself. As if—specifically—she had been Maria: a daring stroke but one that she carried off consummately, never letting her imitation of Maria quite become the real thing and yet leading the girls away from classroom stiffness into the true battle conditions of conversation. From her little black Quirrie bag she produced a slip—a small, stiff shaped implement midway between a strap and a paddle, and each time a girl dropped an *oo*, she delivered a stinging stroke on the hand. While nowhere near as excruciating as the dreaded tawse, for which one had to have an appointment and which was considered a more terrifying thing than the cane itself, these single strokes were breathtakingly painful, and after each chastisement it took a considerable effort to coax the girls back into true conversation; yet Miss Blue did it admirably. This part of the lesson was verily a *tour de force*.

"Come along, Susan", said the mistress in her least mistressly manner. "You usually have something clever to say about song lyrics. Give us the benefit of your meditations."

Susan was nervous. "Well, I *did* think something about the *St. Louis Blues*, but it isn't strictly Aristasian."

"Oh, go on," said Jane.

"Well, I rather thought it was originally written to be sung by a girl rather than a man."

"Really? It usually isn't."

"I know, but consider the lines:

"*If it weren't for powder and for store-bought hair,*

"*That girl of mine would not have gone so far from me*

"That is what a chap sings, and it always rather puzzled me, but then I heard a girl sing the song. The lines are just the same except it is that *man* of mine who would not have gone so far. Surely the implication in the first case is that the girl is so inherently unattractive that were it not for her artificial charms she would not have found any one to take her on—a curious thing to say about one with whom one is besotted even if somewhat disgruntled. Apart from anything else, it reflects so embarrassingly on one's own taste. The implication of the girls' version is that some painted hussy has spirited the chap away with her cheap attractions. Much more natural, don't you think?—and surely the true version."

"How *clever*," said Jane.

"Now, Susan," said Miss Blue.

"Oh—miss."

"Yes, Susan. A clever thesis and very well put. Full marks for vocabulary. But we did let our *oo*'s slip more than a little, did we not?"

"Yes, miss."

"Hand, please."

Susan held out her long hand and Miss Blue's slip cracked fiercely along its surface. Susan's eyes widened and her small white teeth bit her nether lip.

"Other hand," said Miss Blue. "I did not wish to interrupt the delightful logic of your discourse, but I am afraid there were too many slips for one stroke, even though one slip can cure them all."

The reluctance showed in Susan's eyes as she proffered her other hand, although her obedience was unhesitating enough. She winced as the strap descended and it required all her willpower not to withdraw her hand. She gasped as it landed and, having thanked the mistress, sat looking rather crushed with her hands huddled to her tummy.

"Now, Annalinde," said Miss Blue. "I am sure you've something to say about song-lyrics. I have never known you short of an opinion or two."

"I'm not sure, miss. I cannot think of anything, really."

"Hold out your hand, then."

"Yes, miss." Annalinde extended her right hand, feeling utterly wretched. A caning after class, and now that dreadful slip. Miss Blue tickled the blonde's palm with her own blonde finger, like one playing 'Round and round the garden' with an infant.

"But perhaps you would rather discover that you *can* think of something to say about song lyrics?"

"Oh, yes, miss. I think I can."

"I thought you could. Go along then. Enthral us, dear blonde."

"Well, it wasn't much, but I sometimes think about *Robins and Roses*, where it says:

"*And we'll add to their glee*
"*Serving afternoon tea*
"*'Mid robins and roses*
"*And then life will be*
"*A poem by Kipling*
"*While troubles go rippling by*

"Well, *Kipling*, miss. I wonder what poem the lyricist has in mind. One of the *Barrack Room Ballads*, perhaps."

The class could not repress a giggle. Miss Blue answered not schoolmistressily, but almost in Maria's *fillette sérieuse* tone. "You're right, Annalinde. The lyricist obviously wishes to evoke the idea of poetry in the conventional idyllic sense and has chosen Kipling purely for the rhyme. Keats or Wordsworth might have been more appropriate."

"How about:

"*A Keatsian poem*
"*While troubles go flowin' by?*" suggested Lehnya. Every one laughed. The clock was moving rapidly toward the end of the lesson.

"A rather dubious rhyme, but very neat on the spur of the mome. Now, Elinor," said the girl-mistress to the shy young blonde who had yet contributed nothing.

"Em, *Cocktails for Two*, miss."

"Yes, Elinor, what would you like to tell us about it?"

"Well, I cannot remember much about the lyrics, miss," said Elinor, taking the most delicious care over every single vowel and consonant, "but an odd thing is that when we played it at the Soda Fountain the other day, it was the parody by Spike Jones and his City Slickers, and I said how much I should prefer to hear the real song, as it appeared in *Murder at the Vanities*, and nearly all the others said they had never heard the song sung properly. Is it not strange, miss, to know the parody but not the song?"

"Not really," said Jane. "Think of young bongos. They know the parody but not the civilisation."

"Very good," said Miss Blue, returning fully to herself. "And well-spoken, both of you. Now the lesson is almost over and I am not going to set you a formal homework: but I want you to practice, practice, *practice* in the coming week. Those of you who need voice-models,

Susan especially, must try to find recordings of an up-to-date actress to listen to. All of you must work on your voices in every odd moment, and try to be conscious of them while you are chattering as well. I shall want each one of you to give an honest account of the practice she has done next time we meet, and I shall expect all of you to do better in conversation-work than you have today. Those of you who are doing well must be more polished than ever. Those who are having trouble must be making noticeable steps toward overcoming it. Otherwise we shall have some sore little hands—and perhaps some lines."

This last reflection was sobering, as Miss Blue did not often give lines, but was prone, when she did, to hand them out in horrifying doses, all with a sparkling smile.

"Good afternoon, then, girls."

"Good afternoon, Miss Blue."

PUNISHMENT SLIP

Maryhill County Grammar School

Name of Pupil Annalinda Mitchford

Offence Creating a deliberate nuisance in class

Number of strokes recommended 6   Implement Cane

Issued by S. Baines   Signature S. Baines

To be presented to Miss G. Maybridge

Signature below indicates that punishment has been duly carried out

G. Maybridge

8. The Soda Fountain

THE EXHILARATING beat of *At the Hop* filled the little Soda Fountain. Two waitresses were on duty, looking rather like maids, but with special little caps provided by the management. The place was otherwise empty as Lehnya, Susan and Elinor went in.

"Nice to have it to ourselves," said Susan. "Any specials?" she said to the waitresses.

"Only what's on the menu, miss, same as usual," said the senior waitress.

They examined the menu with its delightful picture of a Trentish girl sipping soda through a straw. Banana splits and meringue confections tempted them.

"What will you have?" Lehnya asked Elinor, feeling very brunette and in charge.

"A Silver Fountain, please," said Elinor, not wishing to choose anything expensive.

"That's a good idea. I'll have the same," said Lehnya.

"So will I," said Susan. "Waitress, three Silver Fountains, please." Lehnya felt helpless and dispossessed. She also felt that Susan was showing off.

"Threepence ha'penny each," said the waitress. "That will be ten-pence-ha'penny, please."

Susan gave the pretty blonde waitress a shilling. "Keep the change," she said.

The girls went over to a table covered with a red and white plastic cloth. The waitress poured glasses of cream soda, put a small scoop of ice cream in each and brought them over to the table on a tray.

"What are you doing tonight, darling," asked Susan. She said it in a loud, impudent voice, knowing the girl had left school and would hardly expect such invitations from a uniformed schoolgirl. It left her open to a snub, of course, but even though she did not know the girl, she guessed that it would not be forthcoming from her. She was right. The girl looked timid and shy and seemed lost for any answer.

"Don't you start that," said the senior waitress from the other side of the room. "That girl's just had a good spanking, and you can have the same if you want."

"You can't do that," said Susan.

The senior waitress put down the glass she was polishing, walked slowly across to the table and put her hands on her hips.

"Can't I now?" she said. "You just give me one more piece of cheek and you'll see whether I can or not. I know the law. Staff in public places have the right and the duty to maintain good discipline. It's the same here as in the cinema. Just try it on, that's all. It would be a pleasure to give you a good tanning, miss."

A defiant look crossed Susan's face, though she said nothing. It was answered by a quizzical look from the senior waitress which seemed to say: "Come on then." Susan lowered her gaze and studied the menu.

"Schoolgirls!" said the waitress contemptuously as she went back to her work.

"I'd like to see how they'd keep this place open if it wasn't for schoolgirls," muttered Susan.

"Don't," said Lehnya. "You're acting like a Teddy-girl."

"Just having fun." said Susan.

"Well it isn't the best sort of fun."

"You should have been a blonde. That Wendy's a bit of all right!"

"Susan!"

"Excuse me a moment, I must powder my nose," said Elinor.

"There, you've frightened her away," said Lehnya as Elinor left the room. She felt unhappily that Elinor had partly left in the hope that at least one of the others would have joined the party by the time she returned—ineffective Lehnya being an insufficient buffer against Susan's alarming behaviour. She felt that Wendy, or at least Wendy in conjunction with Elinor, might have had more influence over her. She feared that as a brunette she was neither flesh nor fowl nor good red herring.

Susan chuckled. "Yes I am being a bit of a tearaway. It's only a pose, you know."

"Well you know how it is with poses. They can crystallise into *personæ*."

"Might be fun to have a Tedde in the District."

"I wonder what they do to juvenile delinquents. What was it like getting the slip from Miss Blue?"

"Wollygogs! It *really* hurt. I sort of liked it, though."

"Did you really?"

"Well, not at the time—it was too painful! But it gave me a sort of warm feeling afterwards, a sort of glow. Punishment often does. Does it you?"

"Yes, I think so. A sort of secure, nice feeling."

"That's right. And it does help. How are my *oo*'s now?"

"Better, I think."

"Good. Keep an ear out, will you, and give me the old B.O. if I'm doing them wrong."

"All right, but I can't give you the slip!"

"Perhaps we should work out some system of punishment among ourselves to keep us on our toes about pronunciation."

"Perhaps we could."

"It wouldn't be as nice as being punished by Miss Blue, though. I do think she's dreamy. You know, there is something rather exciting about being punished by a blonde. Did you think so when she paddled you?"

"Yes, I rather think I did, although I didn't identify the feeling at the time."

"Hello, children," said a voice from the door. It was Maria.

"What ho, Maria," said Susan. "Do come and join us at this ultra-sophisticated red-and-white-plastic-cloth-covered table."

Maria joined them.

"All brunettes together," said Lehnya.

"Yes," said Susan. "The blondes have withdrawn. Perhaps we should smoke. Any one got any fags."

"Susan, don't," said Maria. "We might get reported. They can tell what school we're from by our uniform. I know you wouldn't really do it, but we could get reported for talking like that."

"The Devil's in Susan today," said Lehnya. "She wants to be a juvenile delinquent."

"I wonder where the blondes are," said unrepentant Susan. "It would be fun to have some one to pinch."

Annalinde had waited for some time outside the door of Miss Maybridge's room. A sympathetic blonde prefect told her that the mistress was not there at present but was expected shortly. Probably the wait was no longer than five minutes or ten at the very most, but it seemed endless as Annalinde wondered how terrible it would be.

"After all," she reasoned with herself, "It will all be over in two minutes. One minute probably. Ten seconds per stroke makes one minute. How bad can one minute be? Two minutes if she is very slow, pausing between each stroke. Perhaps even three. What would be worse. Having them quickly, so that the pain mounts up, wave on wave? Or having them slowly, so that each one is a distinct and dreadful experience? The pit of her stomach felt heavy and her hands were cold and damp. Still—one or two minutes and then it would all be over. So much better than lots of lines, or a whole-day detention or something. Somehow the reasoning would not convince her troubled nervous system.

What a beast Miss Baines was. Punishments like this should be for smashing windows or saying really bad swear words or wearing bongo-clothes. Girls who wear jeans or untidy rags or idiot padded fluorescent

nonsense, besmirching and poisoning their femininity and their humanity, *they* ought to be caned. Caned hard. They should be standing here,
trembling over their fate. All of them. They deserved it. But canings
shouldn't be handed out like sweets for silly little offences like dropping a pencil—even if it was dropped deliberately. Stupid, undiscrimi-
nating mistresses who take no notice of the relative importance of
offences, but only of their own stupid moods, should have no right to
give very severe punishments. They should be limited to a hundred lines
and the classroom strap. They were too irresponsible to have the authority to inflict the sort of suffering Annalinde was awaiting now.

Annalinde stopped. She had shocked herself. That really was a very
mutinous and almost Pittish way to think. Miss Baines was in authority,
and what she did was right. Perhaps Annalinde *did* deserve a caning for
the badness of her rebellious mind.

Could she bear it? She would *have* to bear it even if she couldn't. It
would all be over very quickly. Just for dropping a silly pencil. Perhaps
Miss Maybridge would be less severe in caning her as it was for such a
silly offence. She ought to know Annalinde had not been really
caneworthily naughty. After all, some part of her had been there. But
Annalinde knew that such things did not count. Miss Baines's decision,
fair or unfair, must be implemented to the full. Annalinde had been
given a severe and serious appointment for a caning, and no one would
take her part against a mistress.

She heard footsteps on the stairs and felt slightly queasy. It must be
her. Oh, let it be some one else. Let it be delayed just another minute or
two. But no. Miss Maybridge had arrived, with her cane.

The mistress swept past Annalinde and entered the classroom, leaving the girl where she stood. She was brisk and businesslike and had the
air of being an older woman. She wore an academic gown over a smart
navy-pinstripe coat and knee-length skirt. She wore black patterned
stockings. There was a rumour among the girls that patterned stockings
meant great severity, as did very pale ones. Silly schoolgirl lore, no
doubt. Or was it? All the mistresses were, of course, intimately aware
of such things, and perhaps they had some basis in the feminine rituals
of discipline.

"Come in," called Miss Maybridge. She sounded brisk and almost
jolly, but there was a hard, no-nonsense edge to her voice. Annalinde
entered quietly, closing the door behind her. Miss Maybridge was sitting
down. One saw the diamond-pattern on her stockings. Diamonds each
with four little dots at the centre. On the knee of her upper crossed leg,
the pattern was stretched, making the diamonds larger and the unpat-
terned black nylon inside them more transparent. Somehow one

thought of the strong, elastic suspenders pulling them firmly into their tautness. One thought of the white girdling and metal suspender clasps and general grown-up feminine hardware that mistresses wear, and somehow it made the severity of patterned stockings seem all too probable.

"Annalinde Milchford, is it not?"

"Yes, miss."

"Well, Annalinde, what can we do for you?"

"I've to give you this slip, miss." She handed the fateful piece of paper to the mistress. So absurdly easy for Miss Baines to write, yet as dreadful and inescapable as an iron fetter once she had done so.

Miss Maybridge studied the slip. Annalinde saw the tiniest hint of white nylon-lace petticoat as Miss Maybridge's skirt-hem sloped backwards along the side of her crossed thigh. It seemed a charming feminine irrelevance to the severity of her pinstripes and her stern patterned stockings. In the inconsequential way that one's mind works at such stressful moments, Annalinde thought of the various meanings of the word *slip*—a petticoat like Miss Maybridge's white nylon one; a slip of paper like the one she was studying; the hard little leather slip with which Miss Blue had stung her erring pupils. Annalinde's voice was very good. She had not had the slip; but how she wished it was the slip she was to have now.

Miss Maybridge looked up. "'Creating a deliberate nuisance in class'," she quoted. "Rather a serious nuisance, I imagine, since you are down for six strokes of the cane."

"Ask me what it was," urged Annalinde silently. "Give me a chance to tell you it was only a dropped pencil. Go on—interrogate me the way you mistresses are so fond of doing. Perhaps you won't cane me so hard if you know it was only that."

But Miss Maybridge had no enquiries to make.

"Well, well. Six of the best, Milchford. The archetypal school caning, no less. Have you ever had it before?"

"No, not really, miss."

"'Not really'—a curiously vague answer to so definite a question; but I think I know what you mean. Not in school, not formally; not from a schoolmistress. You may have had six strokes of a cane at some time, but not quite like this. You are right to draw the distinction, Annalinde. It *is* different. But I think you can already feel that, can you not?"

"Yes, miss," said Annalinde faintly.

Miss Maybridge walked to the blackboard, picked up a stick of chalk and began writing. She wrote:

I must accept my punishments meekly and quietly, like a gentle and submis-

sive young blonde, in a spirit of obedience, self-constraint and repentance for my misdeeds.

Annalinde had heard that some mistresses made girls write lines before a caning; sometimes hundreds, as a sort of preparatory discipline. Perhaps she would spend hours here, writing that wretched line before Miss Maybridge finally caned her. Oh, and she *did* want to join the others at the Soda Fountain. The one ray of comfort in being caned was the thought of going to the Soda Fountain and being the centre of fascinated girlish attention. She had not realised until this moment exactly how much that had meant to her.

Miss Maybridge wrote at the bottom of the sentence:

x 1,000

"A thousand lines," said Miss Maybridge. "Another archetypal punishment. Have you enjoyed that one before, Milchford?"

"No, miss," said Annalinde. This time she was definite. She could not have said what was the maximum number of lines she had ever written. 150 and 200 she had done relatively often, though not nearly as often as some people thought was good for a blonde. 300 she had done once, and that was quite an ordeal. She did not think she had ever done more than that, even though she had been subject to discipline for some years. Certainly she had never had as many as 500; but she had written enough lines to know what a terrible ordeal 1,000 would be. And with a line of that length, it was really more like writing 2,000 She certainly could not write them all tonight. Perhaps some before the caning and some blighting the next few days. She felt oppressed by the heavy weight of something dark, crushing and inescapable.

"A thousand lines," said Miss Maybridge, rolling the phrase round her tongue like a delicate wine. "No doubt you will be pleased to learn that I am *not* going to ask you to write them. Not, that is, if you accept your punishment properly. If you do not, I shall stop the caning at once and you will go away and write me these thousand lines, and then, in a few days, after you have enjoyed yourself in every spare moment with my lines I shall begin caning you again; from the beginning, of course. We can repeat the process if necessary."

She uncrossed her legs and sprang to her feet. Her manner seemed at moments almost as bright and jaunty as Miss Blue's, though she was clearly much older and much more serious. She picked up her cane, which she had placed on the mistress's desk. It was quite a short cane, no longer than twenty-eight inches, but it was thick and stiff-looking, quite different from the cane at home. It was made from the rare, dark-coloured rattan known in the Empire as 'Victorian cane', though it was quite a light hue for Victorian. Somehow it seemed old and well-worn, although there was no real way of telling that with a cane as there was with a strap; it had the feeling of a cane that was not new, and that had a certain austere 'personality'. Perhaps it even had a name. Some favoured canes do acquire names from the mistresses who ply them. Certainly she had a nickname among the girls. 'Thumper', she was called, no doubt with reference to the rabbit in *Bambi*, but more immediately from her weight and rigidity; from the fact that she bit home with a heavy thwack as compared to the sharp, high-pitched sting of many canes. Rumour had it that she had once been longer and had been used by the District Governess in another District for judicial punitive canings. As canes will, she had split for several inches at the end during the sound caning of some offender, and had been cut down and 're-tired' to Miss Maybridge's personal use.

Miss Maybridge flexed the cane in her hands, testing its stiff pliability, rather less than many canes, but entirely sufficient for its purpose.

Annalinde felt suddenly ill. She did not want to meet Thumper. It was not *fair* that a blonde should be subjected to such heavy punishment. It was harsh and unfeminine. Annalinde wanted to run away, but how could she?

"Six of the best," said Miss Maybridge, almost jauntily. "Stand there. Yes, just there. Turn round and bend over. That is right, just as you are. You are not going to have a chair or desk to support you. It will hurt you more this way. That is the purpose of a caning you know. Can you touch your toes? No? Well bend over as far as you can. Further!" The mistress pushed her shoulders down. "Good, now hold onto your calves. Hold on for dear life. You'll be writing those thousand lines if you let go. Straighten your legs. Yes, straighten them right up. I know it's a strain. You'll feel it in your calves tomorrow; but not as much as you'll feel it elsewhere."

As Annalinde stood, trembling with the strain of her position, Miss Maybridge lifted her maroon gymslip and white petticoat. Modesty regulations normally forbade the lifting of petticoats, although that particular regulation was lightly enforced and not always adhered to; but formal canings properly took place with no protection but the knickers.

Miss Maybridge tapped the short, heavy cane on the rounded maroon school knickers. There was a small temptation to place at least one dark weal across the pale thighs swelling above the dark school stockings, but she decided to lay each stroke squarely into the seat of those knickers.

Annalinde felt the weight of the cane, stinging her lightly but unpleasantly even when applied with almost no force. She felt its heavy, threatening mass, which made the sharp sting of the home cane seem quite friendly by comparison. She squeezed her eyes shut, holding on tightly to her calves.

"Well," said Miss Maybridge. "I had better cane you, hadn't I?"

"Not now!" thought Annalinde. "Not yet! I am not ready for it!"

But when would one ever be ready for it? The cane descended with a low-toned *whoosh*, deeper and more melodious than the swish of the canes she had known before. The impact was heavy and almost numbing. It knocked her forward, almost making her lose her balance, and for a split second it did not seem to have hurt her very greatly. Then the pain came welling up like a biting, stinging, bruising wave. She wanted to let go of her calves and stand up, but she dared not.

The second stroke came, and this time the pain mounted to a terrible crescendo. She could not hold on; but she must. She thought of those thousand lines.

There was a pause. Miss Maybridge allowed the two strokes to soak in for a quarter of a minute. Then she tapped the heavy cane again on the seat of the maroon knickers. Annalinde winced as she touched her sore places. The mistress drew back the cane and sank another satisfyingly hard stroke into the maroon surface. She felt the impact and knew that it was good. Annalinde gasped. It was all she could do to keep her balance. She wanted to jump up, but the thought of the long imposition and of beginning the six strokes again kept her holding desperately to her position.

"Your punishment is half-way through," said Miss Maybridge. "I trust you are enjoying it."

"Thank you, miss," said Annalinde. The same again to go. She wondered how she could endure it.

Slowly and in measured fashion, Miss Maybridge delivered three more strokes with all her force, squarely across the maroon target. The short, stocky cane felt firm and powerful, the gasps and small cries of the girl were intensely satisfying and she enjoyed the impact which seemed to rock the girl forward each time. She knew she was putting her through a dreadful ordeal and she liked it. There were other *personæ* that would have been horrified, but Miss Maybridge incarnated a certain matter-of-fact harshness. She would never have committed any real cruelty, of course, but she knew how beneficial an authentic caning could be, and how anything second-rate would detract from the archetypal quality of the thing and leave the girl ultimately disappointed in the magical reality of the universe. Annalinde, she knew, was *not* enjoying her ordeal, but there was nonetheless something more than bluestocking facetiousness in the question she had asked. On some level that Annalinde could not yet imagine this caning was satisfying to her as well as to the schoolmistress, and Miss Maybridge was now experienced enough to understand that deeper level and not to hold back or feel compunction because of the superficial layer of pain, even though, to Annalinde, that was the only thing her mind and body held room for at this moment.

Nothing but the thousand lines. and the thought of repeating the caning from the beginning, kept her gripping her calves through those desperate moments as the complacent mistress plied those terrible last three strokes. Each one seemed to cut her in half and impel her with a force beyond resistance to leap up. At moments the most temporary relief seemed more important than hours of tedious labour; and the ending of the present caning, even on the fifth stroke, more urgent than any caning to come. But reason held sway over nature and Annalinde held her calves.

"Good girl," said Miss Maybridge approvingly, ten seconds after the sixth and final stroke had seared across the livid target, the flesh beneath having taken on a colour little different from the regulation cloth that covered it. "You may stand."

Annalinde rose to her feet, her face flushed almost to match her hinder parts. "Thank you, miss," she somehow managed to say.

Miss Maybridge flexed the sturdy little cane. "Now that, my child, *was* a caning," she said, with the appreciation of a connoisseur. One sensed that she had truly enjoyed it; not in a cruel or vindictive way, but with a genuine and legitimate æsthetic pleasure.

"Yes, miss," said Annalinde, and already she saw something of the mistress's point of view.

Annalinde, dismissed, went to the bathroom and splashed her flushed and tear-stained face. She drank some cold water and slipped her hand up her gymslip and under the elastic of her knickers to feel her burning, tender, wealed behind. It was very painful to touch and she dared not look. She felt somehow purified, and pleased with herself to have come through the ordeal. As she went down the stairs she was filled with the most curious mixture of sensations. She felt at once tearful and tremulous, throbbing with residual pain, slightly queasy, proud, peaceful and cleansed. She felt glad to have had the experience, and absolutely determined to avoid having it again at any cost. Certainly, as Miss Maybridge had known, an ordeal that had left her feeling "Well, that wasn't *too* bad. I could manage it again if I had to" (which is the feeling of many girls after most everyday punishments) would have been a genuine disappointment; would have destroyed the awesome archetype of the formal school caning and left the world narrowed and more grey. It was not grey now, whatever else it might be. There was deep darkness and bright light, but mundane greyness was nowhere in her heart.

She made her way to the Soda Fountain where the girls were fore-gathered. Elinor, the sole blonde, was sitting among three brunettes, both pleased and a little at a loss. She was partly the centre of attention, partly a tolerated piece of silliness at a serious brunette soda-session.

"Lindie!" she cried as Annalinde walked in. "Oh, Lindie, was it *terrible*?"

"Bit overrated, isn't it?" said Susan.

"I don't think I should call it overrated," said Annalinde. "I certainly never want to go through it again." Elinor shivered, so, perhaps did a brunette or two, though they did not show it. Maria's dear, sisterly eyes looked sympathetic.

"I suppose it *would* be hard for a blonde to bear," said Susan, "but they do need a good thrashing from time to time. Come here and sit next to me."

"No, sit next to me," said Lehnya. Why should pushy Susan make all the running?

"I shall sit next to—Lehnya," said the blonde-of-the-moment.

"Sit between us," said cunning Susan, moving a place away from Lehnya.

Annalinde could sense a curious current in the air between herself and the two brunettes. It was biology at work at a fundamental level. One knew that brunettes find a blonde more attractive when she has been whipped, and the caning she had just endured—possibly the most concentratedly severe ordeal of her life—had accentuated her pubescent magnetism. She felt rather like some exotic animal whose fur has become infused with subtle musky secretions released at the mating season.

"Did it hurt you dreadfully?" asked Lehnya in a soft, husky voice. How wonderful that Annalinde had chosen *her*.

"Dreadfully," said Annalinde, haltingly and with a slight tremor that was not wholly uninfluenced by Katherine Hepburn.

"May I—may I touch the place? Through your skirt I mean, of course."

"It might—it might bring me comfort."

Lehnya placed her hand behind Annalinde very gently.

Susan was very close on the other side of her, although she kept her attention with Lehnya.

"You're hot, Annalinde," she said.

"It has that effect on a blonde," replied Annalinde, "though I am sure a brunette would find it overrated—some brunettes anyway. I think it is a question of *sensitivity*."

"Oh, a hit; a very palpable hit," said Maria. "She deserves it too. She has been behaving dreadfully all afternoon."

"Well, what shall we have?" asked Susan, ignoring this remark. "Annalinde is unprovided-for and the rest of us have nearly finished. Shall we have sundaes this time?"

"I'm afraid I can't run to that," said Lehnya.

"Let's just have floats again," said Maria.

"Certainly not. Money is no object," said Susan. "I'll buy sundaes for every one."

Lehnya felt slightly aggrieved. She knew that Sinta had a job in the Pit and had bought quite a lot of Aristasian currency, which was good for the Empire. But she should not use it to show off with and gain advantage over others. It was unfair. But then, if a girl had rich parents or something. It was fairly natural for her to show off with her money if she was the show-off sort. Oh, but this was quite unfair. Susan was probably being kind and generous. One really should not think the worst of things. It was Lehnya herself who was being unAristasian.

"Wench!" called Susan to the junior waitress.

"Don't," said Maria. "You'll get us all thrown out."

"Oh, waitress, dear," said Susan with exaggerated sweetness, "we shall have sundaes if it will please you to serve them." Some of the girls giggled. "What are you having, pettes?"

Angeline stood demurely at Susan's elbow. She had not as yet a wait-ress-*persona* and was only Angeline doing a part-time job. The shilling would be given to her mistress toward her keep, and Betty, the senior waitres, clearly regarded the job as part of her punitive service and was treating her quite severely. To be excluded from the company of these jolly schoolgirls, to be regarded by them as a figure of fun and to watch while they enjoyed treats she was not permitted, seemed hard to her.

The girls chose their sundaes from the charming menu and Susan sorted out her money.

"You know," she said, "I don't know if I ought to mention this, but I was down the Pit the other day and I was asked if I had a few bongo-cents in change. I looked in my purse and guess what? I had half a crown and three florins, a couple of tanners and threepenny bits and any amount of odd copper, but only about seven bongo-cents. The girl went goggle-eyed at my laying out all my real money on the counter."

"You had more money than cents," said Elinor.

"Oh, *very* good, Elinor." The appreciation of the little circle was genuine, for the atmosphere of Aristasia was one of love and enjoyment of one another. Elinor did not often make witticisms, but when she did they were often very quick and clever.

"And what will you have, serving wench?" asked Susan.

"Me, miss?" asked Angeline.

"I should think so," said Susan.

"I don't know if I'm allowed, miss," said Angeline nervously.

"I say," called Susan politely to the senior waitress, "am I allowed to buy this girl a treat?"

Betty looked wry. "I suppose so, miss," she said. "A drink, not a sundae."

"Can I have a soda float, please?" asked Angeline, her eyes bright.

"But of course, add it to my bill." She called to the senior waitress. "You can have one too if you'd like."

"No thank you, miss." It was her opinion that ice cream should not pass the lips of a punitive girl, particularly steeped in soda, but she had not felt empowered to refuse. She made up her mind that if she found the smallest excuse the girl would get a good hard dose of the wooden spoon to make up for it.

"Hello, pettes," said a voice from the door. It was Jane and the party was complete.

"Oh Jane, where *have* you been?"

"Round and about."

"Come and sit here. Blonde brunette, blonde brunette, blonde brunette. You make the arrangement perfect."

"And you're just in time for a sundae," said Susan. "What will you have?"

The table fell into a new magnetic pattern. Susan and Lehnya were both drawn strongly to Annalinde's whipped sensuality. Susan seemed to have mellowed, perhaps as a result of this and the threesome was no longer angular. Each of the brunettes found the other's state of warmth exciting, for Aristasians are quite usually attracted at least somewhat to members of the same sex. Maria, as a result, became the centre of the other two blondes: a cooler triplicity, but still rather cosy, and quite an interesting novelty for the sensible, somewhat bluestocking Maria.

All this, however, was taking place on quite a subtle level. On the surface the whole table was united in common conversation.

Jane was in a state of mild euphoria after the caning of Annalinde. It had been nothing to do with her personally, of course, and she did not feel that it had, but a curious feeling of elation spilled over into her present *persona* and was somehow increased by her sudden reversion to blondeness and the feeling of sharing with Elinor the invisible protection of Maria.

"A riddle!" she announced. "Who eats needles, and where?"

"Eats *needles*?" The company was puzzled until suddenly Annalinde got it.

"A bongo in a Chinese restaurant!" she said.

The Maryhill
SODA
FOUNTAIN

Ice Cream Sundaes

Banana Split 5½d   Toffee Meringue Ice 6d

Walnut Whirl 5½d   Long Tall Sally 6d

Soda Floats

Silver Fountain 3½d

Golden Glow   Crimson Night   Blue Heaven

All 4d

The management reserves the right to discipline patronettes in accordance with the provisions of the Public Decorum Act

There was a pause, and then most of the company laughed as they caught up with the quick wits of the two blondes.

"I don't understand," said Susan.

"It's a *yeeth-and-byeety* joke," explained Elinor. "Remember Miss Blue's lesson."

"*Crispy needles*," whispered Lehnya, as Susan was still looking a touch blank.

"*Special fried needles*," added Maria.

"*Chicken needle seep*," said Elinor. The company was passing into the higher hilarity.

"Why *do* bongos call their soup *seep*," asked Annalinde.

"Because that is what it does when they eat it with their forks," said Jane. "That's an old one."

"All right then, but did you hear about the girl who went to a bongo dentist with a bad tooth? She ran out of the door when he said he was going to take her *teeth* out."

"How can you tell that bongos know they are animals?"

"Because they believe in Darwin?"

"That is how they *became* animals. You can tell they know it because they call their food *feed*."

"And here comes ours," said Susan. The junior waitress came up with a tray full of assorted sundaes. She was supposed to know who had ordered what, and the girls helped her to get it right with looks and pointed fingers. Somehow they sensed she was in danger of a whipping. Susan took occasion to slip her hand inside the girl's skirt and pinch her thigh just above the top of her stocking. The girl started and then said, very demurely and quietly,

"Thank you, miss."

It was really a very nice thank-you. Annalinde guessed what had happened and remembered how much she had wanted to pinch the maid some days ago, what agonising it had cost her, only to end in nerveless failure. How easily that young tearaway did things that others could not pluck up courage for. Well, the maid should be pinched now. Boldness and precipitousness. Those were the rules for such actions. She felt Susan's hand join Lehnya's uninvited in cupping the upper part of her bottom. She considered an outraged blonde rebuff, but somehow could not produce it. It all felt so warm and natural.

"Your change, miss," said Angeline, putting a large assortment of silver and copper on the table. Susan had paid with a ten-shilling note, almost unheard-of for a schoolgirl.

Lehnya, seeing the change, told the newcomers of Maria's "more money than cents" joke.

"Bongos are so depressing with their stupid money and their stupid everything," said Annalinde.

"Isn't it just awful the way they are accepting metric measurements in every area. They all think they are rebels, but they accept every new *diktat* as meekly as lambs. If the Octopus passed a law saying they all had to wear clothes with 'kick me' written on the back they would do it without a murmur."

"They wear clothes that make any decent human being want to kick them now."

"Yes, and I should think the Octopus is laughing just as much as if 'kick me' was actually written on them. They are the clothes of self-contempt. The sackcloth and ashes of a defeated humanity."

"But things like metric measures are so terrible. They accept the stripping away of every last vestige of their identity. It seems hard to bear."

"I don't think so," said Jane. "I am rather glad of it."

"Really, why?"

"Well, the Pit is not the real world, and I think it best that it does not try to counterfeit the real world. Every time the Pit gives up some fresh area of decent life, it is passed into *our* hands. It becomes our exclusive property and a mark of our being. On the other hand, every element of decent life that it holds onto, it dirties and defiles.

"Take the years. I remember when the third decade of darkness passed into the fourth. For a time we said, let us make the '90s *ours*, the new *fin de siècle*. Some of us even toyed with calling the year 1990 just as the bongos did: but it failed. It failed because, even though we never watch their filthy broadcasts or read their filthy publications, the crushing weight of their ugly usage lay on the year-numbering too heavily for us to shift. Within months 'the 1990s' (pardon the phrase) meant what *they* wanted it to mean We must know our psychic limitations, and the Pit has so much invested in its designation of the current decade as its exclusive property and the inflamed, throbbing centre of its corruption, that we could not challenge it to psychic war on that front, even within our own world. We *had* to abandon the very mention of the four-figure words that designate the years of darkness.

"Now I believe there was some talk in the Pit about abandoning the traditional Western year-numbering for some new nonsense. I don't know what. Starting from the birth of Darwin or the printing of the first dollar, I expect. It sounds like lunatic foaming, but then so did most of the changes of the Pit before they actually happened and became supinely accepted by the sheep.

"Anyway, the point is: I hope they do it, because if they do, we shall have the years back. By simply using the traditional year-numbering, we shall be making a statement of our independence, but until the Octopus (for his own rotten purposes, of course), lets go of it, we cannot touch it.

"Well, the same is true of measurements. It is true that pounds and ounces were not as defiled as the unmentionable year-numbers, but it will certainly become the case that using them from now on will be less and less a neutral act and more and more a specifically Aristasian gesture.

"As for money, yes, I *do* think bongo-cents are awful, but I am very glad the Pit uses them, because it makes our gorgeous, ancient shillings a thing we can appreciate and adore rather than something smirched by the Pit. Imagine every bongo Johnny in pony tail and earrings touching half-crowns with his poisonous hands. Imagine some grooshy bongo television announcer with six-foot shoulder-pads and twisted vowels talking about a 'tee-shilling rise in the price of petrol'. Of course we should never hear her, but the psychic sludge of it would crawl all over our money and over the very word *shilling*. Better far that they abandon decent things and keep their filthy hands off them."

"Yes," said Annalinde, "and it's the same with voices isn't it? It is entirely right that middle-class bongos talk in a supercilious, sub-cockney bleat. The Queen's English *should* belong to us and only to us."

"Not even to *their* Queen," said Susan

"Absolutely," said Elinor, "it is the traditional mark of the superior caste. It would be pure fraud if any one but us used it now."

"And a few older people," suggested Maria.

"Yes," said Annalinde, "people old enough to have lived mostly in a real world, and whole enough to have kept the Pit at bay, so that they are not quite aware that the Eclipse has happened, and for them it has only half-happened. But there are fewer of them every year, and so many old people in the Pit are disgraceful. As bad collaborators as the young and with far less excuse."

"Grannies in track suits."

"Don't! It is too hideous."

"But what about children?" asked Maria softly. "Children who will never hear a real voice or see a real thing from birth, who will live thinking that terrible fake world is all there is or has been or will be? Would it not be better for the Pit to keep a few real things for their sake?"

"No," said Jane, "I do not think so. What good would a few real things do mixed into the insane *mélange* of the Pit? It would just be parody, like a Pit-girl wearing a Trentish dress with workman's boots. No, it is far better for them that they see a whole world in real films or

books, and know at least that there was once a reality quite different
from the malign fun-house in which they were condemned to be born.
It is better for them *not* to be confused by superficial resemblances between the real world and the nightmare they live in. It is better for them
to see the truth clearly—that some fell hand has wiped *everything* out.
What good it can do them I do not know: but at least they will have a
better chance, if they can clear their minds of the brainwashing, of seeing the truth. At least it will be obvious, to those very few with eyes,
that a whole world has been uprooted, utterly destroyed, and replaced
by a false, manufactured, cheap, impoverished world; sterile, noisy and
dead."

There was a silence broken after a few moments by Elinor.

"Well, thank goodness *we* don't have to worry about it all," she said.
"The Pit is nothing to do with us, and we are well out of it."

"Yes," said Annalinde, "sundaes are more our cup of tea—if one
can call them that."

Lehnya looked at her sundae, so attractively presented in its Quirrie
Art-Neo glass, decorated with a cherry which she still had not eaten,
for she liked to preserve the cherry until the last, and found herself suddenly overcome.

"Oh, the sundaes are so lovely," she said. "Thank you, Susan, for
buying them for us, and thank you, *all* of you, for making everything
possible."

"Why, *Wendy*," said Jane.

"Yes," said Wendy. "Yes, I am, aren't I? I'm so awfully sorry. I
shouldn't be here." Her eyes were very round and she looked as if she
was about to cry.

"Don't worry, Wendy. It is very nice to have you here. We miss you
when you don't come." Jane took her hand across the table.

"You mean Lehnya is a bit of a failure?"

"I do not mean anything of the sort. I just mean that it is nice to see
you."

"Oh, Jane, oh, every one—it is so nice to be here. I do think this is
the most lovely, lovely Soda Fountain, and I do think we are so lucky
to have sundaes."

"That is why she came," said Annalinde. "She couldn't bear to leave
the whole sundae to Lehnya."

"No," said Wendy, "it *wasn't* that. Not the sundae itself, anyway, not
the *physical* sundae."

"I know what you mean," said Susan. "I love sundaes for their souls
too."

"I remember a Saki story where a chap was described as having the soul of a meringue and some one commented that if meringues had souls, Lady some-one-or-other would be organising social-work programmes among them and saying it was wonderful how much you could teach them—and how much you could *learn* from them."

"Well, I think one *can* learn a lot from these sundaes," said Wendy, undaunted.

"Yes, of course you are right," said Jane.

"I know," said Annalinde. "How lucky we are to be able to come here and have such delightful treats."

"Blondes!" said Susan. "Subtract one brunette, add one blonde and the entire balance of the table is upset. It goes gooey!"

Wendy was pleased by the compliment to Lehnya. It was not much of a compliment, but in a way its very off-handedness—its matter-of-fact acceptance of Lehnya as ' one of the brunettes '—comforted her.

"Well, I think it is very pleasing," said Maria. "Blondes have a great deal to teach us——"

"Like meringues," interposed Susan. They all laughed.

"Well, they have. It is so important to cast off our hardness and to *love* all the lovable things of our world. The blondes can lead us in that, but we should follow them. Gentleness and gratitude are so important. Brunettes should not be hard, you know. We are not supposed to be like that other sex."

"There you are," said Jane to Wendy. "Maria is quite right. Don't let that naughty Susan worry you."

"Do you think I can stay for a minute?" said Wendy. "I feel very awkward dressed like this." She looked at her blouse and tie and skirt, the brunette school uniform in which Lehnya had felt so clean and hopeful as she had set off today.

Annalinde put her arm about her with wonderful tenderness—oh, if only she had put her arm about Lehnya. But no, Lehnya should have put her arm about *her*. It was quite hard to remember about being a brunette. Sometimes she felt that Annalinde would make a better brunette than she. But that was absurd. Annalinde was certainly confident and mischievous, but there was really nothing brunette about her at all.

"Does any one mind?" asked Annalinde.

"Naughty Susan doesn't mind," said Susan. "Naughty Susan isn't *really* so dreadful. Naughty Susan likes Wendy too."

Annalinde put her other arm about Susan and then squealed.

"Oh, Susan!" she cried. "That is where I was caned. It really does hurt!"

Susan snuggled into the enclosing blonde arm, which was not withdrawn. " Couldn't *help* it," she said. " Brunettes *can't* help pinching whipped blondes. It's nature."

" The things you get away with, naughty Susan," said Annalinde.

The girls left the Soda Fountain, the beat of its Quirrie pop music still ringing in their ears, and issued into Saddler's Yard, a small brick enclosure with posters on the walls advertising the latest film as well as Oxo cubes at 1d a box and a brand of soap-powder claiming to wash whiter.

It had been raining lately, and the fallen leaves gleamed dark-gold and brown in the little yard. The air was moist and smelled of Autumn. The girls were a little ill-assorted: navy macs mixed with maroon and grey, and even a Quirrie duffle-coat, but they all looked very real and schooly. Emma Kadrina stepped ghostly aside from Jane and admired the group from within. It would be nice when exigencies could allow a tightening of uniform regulations, but really they were progressing very well. Realness was like swimming or riding a bicycle. It only really counted when the technique had become unconscious: and here they were, a perfectly Quirrie group of schoolgirls hardly giving a thought to the question of being such. Chattering, laughing, mixing schoolgirl high-spirits with thought and philosophy that was entirely adult in a way that simply meant that a new species of schoolgirl had been invented. But of self-consciousness, of recognising any reality outside Quirinelle and the Empire, of the least degree of artificiality or Pit-recognition, there was not a trace.

Even Susan's awkwardness, her not-quite-there-ness, which every one felt a little; even though it was the result of her former contamination with the Pit, was perceived so completely from *within* Quirinelle that its specific character counted for nothing. Whatever was alien to Quirinelle was perceived as being merely alien; its particular *type* of alienness carried no weight. Even Susan herself felt it in this way. It was a great victory; a great defeat of the power of the once-all-pervading Enemy. Sometimes one moved forward so slowly that it was hard to be sure one was moving at all. But then one could stop and take stock on a late-afternoon like this, in Autumn, in Quirinelle and nowhere *but* Quirinelle, outside the Soda Fountain with a group of magically-so-phisticated schoolgirls, and look back over the ground one had conquered.

And so much of it, here in Maryhill, was owing to Alice Trent. Poor, dear Alice, who seemed to notice only her failings and her distance from perfection, had, with her cure of souls, created so much of this. She took Elinor's maroon-gabardined arm as the party passed into Shilling Lane, and whispered, " Look on your handiwork, Alice Trent, and see that it is good." Alice glanced through Elinor for a moment to look doubtful: doubtful about her own part, for even to her it was clear that it *was* good. A record dropped on the auto-change in the Soda Fountain, and the strains of *Magic Moments* wafted out into the Yard as they left it behind.

"What a beastly lot of homework old Bainesey has given us," complained Lehnya, trying to regain her brunettishness.

"Yes," said Jane, "Isn't she a brute?"

"I don't think you ought to talk like that," said Maria. "I've got two hundred lines on top of it, but it is not nice to complain."

"You'll be a prefect soon, I shouldn't wonder," said Jane.

"Then you should pay attention to me," said Maria primly.

"Of course we shall. I think good brunettes are fascinating."

"So do I," said Elinor.

"You weren't in Miss Baines's class, so I suppose you won't have to do all her tedious homework," said Lehnya.

"I shall get it from Jane and do it. I don't want to get behind," said Elinor.

"You don't really need to. It's only repetitive stuff."

"I am sure a mistress knows better than girls do what is good for them."

"Well said," said Maria.

"Miss Baines does create a tremendous atmosphere of *realness*," said Lehnya.

In a way Emma Kadrina felt disappointed to hear this issue raised. The realness had reached such a pitch that it seemed a pity to reduce it to self-consciousness, yet it was interesting to know how the girls saw it.

"Yes," said Elinor, "so I am told. But from what I hear of her, is it not rather a *drab* realness?"

"Oh, *infinitely* drab," said Lehnya, "if Maria does not object to my saying so. But that is partly why it is so real."

"But are 'drab' and 'real' the same thing?" asked Jane, unable to leave alone the teasing question, "or are we using 'real' in that Saturnine sense in which bongos use the word when they talk of 'realism' in literature as meaning all that is dullest and most grim; or 'the real world' as life stripped of every thread of imagination?"

"Oh, I *hope* not, Jane," said Lehnya, "but I don't really know. Is it one of your rhetorical questions? Do *you* know the answer really?"

"I didn't when I asked," said Jane, "but now I think of it, I think the answer is no. I know exactly what you mean. It *is* the drabness that makes her lessons so real, but isn't that because we are back to our need for hard edges again? And perhaps because we are all so Bohemian and

arty and flighty ourselves that some one who brings an earthy, unin-
spired note to the proceedings, and *chains* us to it, helps to ground and
solidify our world? The drab is not the only reality, and it is not more
real than the imaginative, but it does belong to the pole of substance or
matter, and a world requires substance as well as essence, clay as well as
shape, brick as well as blueprint. Left to ourselves, at times, we could
be so airy that we float away, or shift shapes until no shape has any
meaning. Miss Baines supplies an element we do not normally supply for
ourselves."

"Yes," said Maria. "You know, I find something almost warm and
comforting in having two hundred lines to do for her."

"Really?" said Jane. "I bet Annalinde doesn't feel the same about
having to write out all that homework twice."

"Where *is* Annalinde," asked Maria, "we've got to go."

"I don't know. I think she and Susan are still in the Yard," said
Lehnya. "I'll fetch her for you."

Lehnya ran back into the Yard, ready to shout "Lindie!" But the
cry died on her lips. As she came to the end of the short lane, she saw,
in the corner of the yard, Annalinde and Susan. Susan had Annalinde
pressed into the corner, her knee within her grey brunette school skirt
thrust deeply between the maroon box-pleats, two mouths joined in
moist passion. One hand was slipped inside Annalinde's skirt, gently
exploring her punished thighs, with such audacity that the white froth
of Annalinde's petticoat and the top of her stocking were visible from
here, while, Annalinde, with both her arms about the brunette's neck
was the perfect picture of blonde submission.

The stifled squeak of a still-born cry escaped the wounded Lehnya,
and then she turned and fled. She pushed rudely through the small
group of schoolgirls.

"What is it, Lehnya?"

"Where are you going, Lehnya?"

But she had already mounted Granya and was disappearing into the
Void.

9. Kisses have Consequences

ANNALINDE was worried and subdued on the homeward journey. Maria chatted affably about school and other matters. Angeline sat silently in the back. Annalinde felt she could say nothing in front of the maid, and in any case it was not to Maria that she wished to speak. She wanted her mother.

She found her at last in the drawing room.

"What is it, dear?" she asked.

"It's Lehnya, Mummie. I fear I've hurt her dreadfully."

"How have you done that, dear?"

"Well, she came into Saddler's Yard and found me being kissed by Susan. She was terribly upset and ran away without saying anything to any of the girls."

"I had rather thought she was fond of you, Annalinde."

"Yes, but—I mean—I don't really know her that well. I've only been out with her once and, well, I don't *want* her to feel jealous about me like that."

"Don't you?"

"No—at least—well, it is very flattering, of course. I can't say I'm not pleased by it on one level—what blonde wouldn't be? But I don't want to cause her such anguish and I don't want to feel I can't—— "

"Can't what, dear?"

"Well, that I can't do what I want to."

"I suppose it all depends what sort of blonde you are, darling."

Annalinde was stricken. Did she mean by that that she thought her behaviour wanton. And was it? Should she really let a brunette kiss her like that—like that. Of course, her mother had no idea exactly *how* Susan had been kissing her. When the girls had asked what the matter was when Susan and Annalinde emerged and Lehnya had already disappeared, Susan had told the truth:

"I gave Annalinde a kiss. I don't think Lehnya liked it."

Well, it was the truth. It wasn't untrue. But no one knew what *sort* of kiss it was. No one knew except Susan and Annalinde—and, of course, Lehnya. No one else knew that they had been—*necking*—in broad daylight not fifteen yards from the other girls, like a pair of——

Oh really! There was no need to be so self-critical. Girls often kissed a bit warmly after the cinema, didn't they? Lehnya did not own her. It was so hard. There were two ways of looking at it. She wanted to tell her mother more of the truth, but she felt unable to say it, did not know what words to use. One could make it sound so much worse than it was, or one could euphemise it away as had been more or less done already. It was all so complicated that it seemed easier to say nothing at all.

"Mummie?" she said.

"Yes, dear?"

"I don't know. I mean—I could 'go steady' with Lehnya if that is what she wants, and if it was what I wanted; but—well—where would it lead? She isn't going to ask for my hand however long we 'go steady'. I am *yours* and I'm not going to leave you and cleave unto Lehnya. I mean, it isn't *like* that, is it? And how dreadful if it was. So are we perpetual adolescents, living forever on the verge of an adulthood that cannot be, or—or what?"

"You are Children of the Void, my dear—and who knows where such paths lead, for no one has ever trodden them before you. Quirinelle adolescence seems perpetual enough when one is in it; perhaps it would hardly be real if one could look at it from the maturer standpoint of its end. I think at present you have choices to make within the Theatre of Life, and some might be better than others. Where they will lead—if anywhere—we cannot say."

"Suddenly I had a picture of up-to-date Superman comics we sometimes get. Lois Lane always wanting to marry him; his best friend Jimmy Olsen wanting to marry Lois's sister Lucy, who is sworn not to marry until her elder sister does. Everything on the verge, but nothing ever changing and no one growing older for years and years and years—until their Eclipse, in fact, after which the stories are uncanonical and do not count. I wonder if we are like that; exploring a dimension that seemed purely fictional but might become a reality for us."

"Perhaps," Miss Milchford laughed. "And every now and then— once every year or so—Superman and Lois *do* get married: but we always know that it is a hoax or a dream, or what the editors call an 'imaginary story'."

"Shall *we* have 'imaginary stories', do you think, Mummie?"

"We might."

"Is *Toytown* on the wireless this evening?"

It was *Toytown* evening, and Annalinde, who loved the clever delightful stories at all times felt tonight a longing to bathe herself in their innocence; to be cosy and peaceful with her mother; to forget all about being an adolescent.

Lehnya got up from her bed where she had been lying, still in her school uniform. She picked her mac up from the floor and hung it up. She was a tidy girl and did not often leave things on the floor. She had been crying, but even so, before abandoning herself, she had boiled a kettle and made a pot of tea. It was such a reflex with her that she had hardly noticed doing it.

She looked about the room. She had done quite well. There was nothing bongo in evidence. Up-to-date books on the shelves, Wendy's dear Trentish Little-Bo-Peep looking glass (picked up for next-to-nothing at a jumble sale). Not a bakelite telephone, unfortunately, but a not-bad Infra black plastic one with a dial and a bell and a proper receiver. Two pounds, that had been, at a fleem.

It was a nice little room. She had never had money, but at least she had had *time* to search for bargains, get things at prices even she could afford; and she had found that living with up-to-date things was actually much cheaper than buying new ones. The room was not as smart as the Milchfords' luscious Art-Neo apartments or the pin-neat Quirrie-respectability-with-Art-Neo-dashes of the Trent-Kadrina household, which seemed to reflect Betty's firmly suburban tastes as much as those of her mistresses; but it was thoroughly up-to-date even where a spot of dilapidation was in evidence. Lehnya had always been proud of her little flat, ever since she had begun the work of transforming it.

Today it seemed hardly to matter any more. She had cried herself out. The tea was cold and stewed. She poured it away and put on a fresh kettle. She turned on the wireless and Bing Crosby began singing *When the Blue of the Night Meets the Gold of the Day*. She had never cared much for men, and would have liked to live in the True Aristasia where there were only blondes and brunettes. But when she felt sad or worried or lost, as she did now, Bing Crosby always seemed to comfort her with his warm, rich, gentle voice. Annalinde had said the same about Bing, she recalled, and had called him "my friend", though she was just about the most un-chappie girl known to maid.

Oh, Annalinde, Annalinde, Annalinde: How could you? How could you? How could you?

She took out one of her white cups and put it on its saucer. There were three cups and four saucers—enough for as many guests as she had ever entertained in her little flat. They were rather chunky, serviceable cups. Quite up-to-date, but not the most elegant cups ever. Giving up the use of mugs had been one of her first great steps into Aristasia, and at the time the cups had seemed a large, almost unnerving, step toward civilisation. Now, although they seemed homely and friendly, she often hoped to find something a little more delicate. Something more in keeping with the teapot. The teapot was a beautiful chrome affair with a bakelite handle that stayed cool and a bakelite standing-base at the bottom. It had been a birthday present from the

Trent-Kadrina household. That had been her first birthday in Maryhill. Her only one so far. Annalinde and Miss Milchford had given her the most wonderful book—*Patricia Prefect* by Ethel Talbot, a very moving tiny tragedy, delicate and lovely, much different from the ordinary schoolgirl book, jolly as they were, and from Miss Talbot's more usual pot-boiler style. They had given her some very serviceable up-to-date kitchen equipment including a lovely pair of scales with a needle and a round face on which was printed (as well as pounds and ounces) a charming up-to-date picture of a house with the words *Concise Home Encyclopædia*. It was a wonderful stroke for making the kitchen look real. Lehnya often looked at it and thought of Annalinde. Susan had not given her a present, because Susan was not born then; Sinta was there, but only very new. Betty had given her a butter-dish knife and a cheese-knife; nice up-to-date ones with matching green handles. She remembered her handing them to her shyly in a neat little roll of mauve tissue paper. Angeline was not there then, of course.

Well, what now? One thing was certain, Lehnya could not face the others again. Not just because she had made a public fool of herself, though that was bad enough. But because, well, there was no reason to go back, and she had failed in everything. Almost, for an instant, she thought of never, in *any persona*, going back. But that was impossible. One could not live in the Void. But Lehnya could not go back. Lehnya was a failure completely and Annalinde did not want her, and Annalinde was really her reason for being. Wendy was liked and appreciated. Lehnya had been a silly experiment in being what she was not.

She sat in her armchair. Jessie Matthews was singing her wistful rendering of *Looking Around Corners for You,* with that wonderful, half-tearful catch in her voice. Lehnya felt empty and bleak.

There was a knock on the door. Lehnya froze at the noise. She hated knocks on the door. She wanted no dealings with the Pit, but her mind swiftly organised the sound into the familiar District Knock. It was an Aristasian, then, but who? Not *her*, surely?

She opened the door, and there stood Emma Kadrina.

"Hello, Lehnya," she said.

"I'm not Lehnya, I'm Wendy."

"No you're not. You're Lehnya."

"Well, perhaps I am. Will you come in?"

"Thank you, I'd love to."

"I've just made some tea."

"Providence must have arranged my arrival at this very moment."

"The cups aren't anything to write home about I'm afraid."

"Just chunky white ones. I remember from last time. I think they're rather jolly little pettes, but why don't you use your rose-patterned bone-china ones."

Wendy laughed. Such domesticities always brought Wendy to the fore. "We haven't any rose-patterned bone-china ones."

"Far be it from me to disagree with the blonde of the house, but I fancy you have." Emma Kadrina gave her a small square-shaped brown-paper carrier bag with string handles. Inside were a number of teasettish shapes wrapped in pink tissue paper.

"Oh, but Emma Kadrina! It isn't my birthday or anything."

"There is no rule that says presents can only be given on birthdays. I for one would strongly oppose such a rule as being deleterious to the spontaneous joy of life. Anyway, there are only three of them, so they aren't a full present, you might say; but we thought they were *you*, so obviously you had to have them."

Wendy opened the little parcels and set the darling cups and saucers on the table.

"Oh, thank you so much!" she said. The tea was poured and Wendy produced some Rich Tea biscuits.

"Now, Lehnya, I want to talk to you,"

"I'm not Lehnya, I'm Wendy."

"I know, but I want to talk to Lehnya."

"Lehnya is going away."

"Are you, Lehnya?"

"I—I—"

"Come now, Lehnya. I want to talk to you as one brunette to another. If you are going away you must at least talk to me before you go."

"Yes, of course, Emma Kadrina."

"Good girl."

"If you've come to tell me I've made an idiot of myself, you needn't trouble, because I know it."

"Have you made an idiot of yourself?"

"You know I have."

"In Saddlers' Yard, you mean?"

"Yes, that's what I mean. I am the laughing stock of Maryhill."

"You do Maryhill a great disservice. No one thinks ill of you. You aren't the first brunette to get emotional over a blonde and you won't be the last. Brunettes are emotional too, you know."

"But what will she think? What will they think? I had no right. There is nothing between us—— "

"The blonde will be flattered, you can be sure of that. Whatever else she thinks she will first and foremost be flattered. As for the others, well, they all know what you were feeling, and feelings were never governed by rights. Yes, perhaps a little more restraint would be in order—on all sides—but remember that you are among friends. None will condemn you or laugh at you coldly. If anything they will love you a little more. I do."

"Do you?"

"Certainly. If that is your reason for going away, I think you should reconsider."

"Well, it isn't."

"Isn't it? What is it, then?"

"It's hard to say, Emma Kadrina. It's just that—well—I don't think it has worked. I don't think *I've* worked. I've failed."

"Failed in what way?"

"I'm not really a brunette. Wendy is the real me. With her I am comfortable. I feel safe and happy as a blonde. As a brunette I am just false. Nobody could believe in me. I am only here at all because—because of Lindie, and now that that is all over——"

"All over—adolescent storms in rosy teacups!"

"Well, whether it is or isn't, it is just false. There's no good my pretending to be a brunette, even because of Lindie."

"You feel very strongly for her, don't you?"

"Yes, I do."

"Do you think your feelings are really a blonde's crush on another blonde?"

"I don't know. When I'm with her, I do feel very brunette. I feel as if blondes were another species; one I don't understand, but find fascinating. Of course there is Wendy, but she doesn't make any difference to that feeling. She is a child, and anyway, it is just like having a blonde sister. It doesn't make any difference to the awe and delicate terror you feel when you meet a 'real' blonde."

"Lehnya, you are a brunette."

"Do you think so?"

"I am just about sure of it; and you know I don't go about saying I'm sure when I'm not. Do you know what you look like from the outside?"

"No, what?"

"From the outside you look like a quietly charming brunette, gentle, refined and winning. Lacking a little in confidence (but by no means as nervous as you feel inwardly). From the outside, you make a very good brunette."

"Really?"

"Yes, really. You mustn't let Susan worry you with her boisterous ways. Not all brunettes are like that. Look at gentle, serious Maria. Look at me."

"You always have such overwhelming confidence."

"Have I? Well, just look at Maria then. She is hardly overwhelming in any respect, but she is a true young gentilmaid. Susan, on the other hand—Susan has the makings of a charming brunette, but her more boisterous aspects are hardly the most charming thing about her. Of course there must be all kinds of people in a whole world like Aristasia, but I certainly would not wish you to think you had to be like Susan to be a brunette."

"Annalinde finds her charming enough, evidently."

"Oh, Annalinde—you don't understand blondes."

"Does any one understand blondes?"

"Not completely, of course, but living, as you are, all alone at this difficult age without a brunette mummie—or even a blonde mummie—to advise and guide you, perhaps I should try to help as best I can."

"I should be very grateful."

"You look at Annalinde and see her, confident, excitable, often rather naughty, and you probably think she is not the soft, yielding sort of blonde. But Lehnya, *all* blondes are the soft yielding sort, otherwise they wouldn't be blondes."

"That doesn't mean they will yield to me."

"Not necessarily, no."

"Some of them seem to prefer yielding to Susan."

"I expect Susan was rather forceful with her. Blondes can rather melt when one is forceful with them."

"I always think of Annalinde as rather Olympian. It seems disappointing to think of her—well, *melting* all over the place."

"Melting blondes can be very pleasant."

"Well, I won't have her melting with Susan."

"Very brunette. Perhaps you should tell her so."

"I can't. I don't know what to do. What *should* I do?"

"Take your courage in both hands and lay siege to her. You saw how it worked for Susan, and really, I don't think she is a Susan sort of blonde."

"Do you think she is a Lehnya sort of blonde?"

"I shouldn't be surprised. But there's only one way to find out. Faint heart ne'er won fair lady."

Not long after the knock on Lehnya's door came a knock on Sinta's. She opened it to find a small, neat woman in a smart little suit, the skirt just a fraction above the knee. She might have been some one from the District, but she was not. Sinta knew well enough who she was, although she had never met her before. She was the drawing mistress who had answered her advertisement in the *Maryhill Telegram* and with whom she had made an appointment.

"Miss Worth?" she asked, just to be sure.

"That is correct. I have come for your drawing lesson."

"Do come in and sit down."

Miss Worth looked rather like Miss Baines, but was much more precise and alive. She seemed surprisingly formal and conservative for a drawing mistress; one had expected, perhaps some one a little more 'arty', like Miss Blue. But Miss Worth was here to teach the *craft* of drawing. Alice Trent was aware within her that she knew very little about drawing. Miss Worth, no doubt, knew a great deal, but as manifested through Alice Trent, she knew very little. Still, the important point was discipline. Sinta, Emma was sure, could learn through concentrated practice. What she needed was the discipline to keep it up and some criticism.

Miss Worth opened her portfolio and brought out the picture Sinta was to work from this week. She told her, in her precise way, exactly what must be done. She also carried with her portfolio a very short, thin switch which she laid on the coffee table. After they had discussed the work for a while she said:

"Are you right-handed, Miss Serendra?"

"Yes, miss."

"Then kindly stand up and hold out your left hand."

Sinta rose to her feet and put her hand out as for a punishment. It felt strange, for Miss Worth was still seated. Sinta was wearing a square-shouldered Kadorian day-dress, with a lovely skirt that fell in elegant folds from the waist. She had dark real-Quirrie nylons and wide orange-red lips that ignored her natural lip-line in the true Kadorian style. It felt very odd to be standing there, so elegant and grown up, holding out her hand for a punishment that showed no sign of coming.

Miss Worth, far from showing signs of punitive activity, crossed her legs and settled deeper into her chair.

"You have confessed to me on the telephone, Miss Serendra, that you are prone to be somewhat lazy about practising your drawing."

"Yes, miss."

"That is what I must cure, is it not?"

"Yes, miss."

"I propose to do so. Today is our first day, and so I have not come to examine any task already set. You have committed no offence in relation to your course of study with me."

Sinta felt a mild sense of relief.

"However, Miss Serendra, I think I should give you a small sample of what you will receive if I do find you slacking in your practice. That is what you are paying me for after all, is it not?"

"Yes, miss."

Sinta had paid a reasonable number of shillings for her lesson, but she would happily pay the same again or double to have this demonstration waived. But she knew that such a suggestion would be the worst form.

"Then we are both agreed," said Miss Worth, leaning forward and picking up her short, tapering switch. She bent it a little, meditatively, eyed it for straightness and stood up.

"I trust your arm is not becoming fatigued, Miss Serendra."

"Just a little, miss."

"You will be able to rest it soon."

She laid the switch across the palm, sizing up position and aim. She tapped it lightly, and then quite suddenly drew it back and whipped it across the hand with a high-pitched shisssh. Sinta's eyes widened and filled with tears—tears not of weeping, but of sympathetic shock.

"How would you feel if I were to tell you to extend your hand again, Miss Serendra?"

"I—I—"

"Do not worry. I am not going to. Not today. But if I am not satisfied with your work, you may be doing so next week. Perhaps twice. Perhaps three times or more. Do you think it will help you to work?"

"I am *sure* of it, Miss."

"Splendid. Then let us finish our tea and talk of other matters."

"Do you really think I will be able to draw if I practice?"

"Oh yes. You have ability, but nothing can be done without work. By the bye, I have been hearing things about that young sister of yours."

"Susan, you mean?"

"Yes, Susan. People say she is turning out to be something of a tearaway."

"Yes, I suppose she is. I expect it is only a phase she is going through."

"I hope so. Perhaps you should have a word with her. She may end up getting herself into serious trouble."

"I shall try, miss. I don't know how much notice she will take. I don't seem to have a lot of influence over her. You know how they can be at times. Sometimes the things she says and does just amaze me."

"Well, I suppose it is all part of growing up. But she had better not go too far."

"I'll say something, miss."

"Good girl."

Ten minutes later, Miss Worth's car was stopping outside Lehnya's house to collect the un-mobile Emma Kadrina. It was rare that Emma made a call outside the colony on her own, but it had seemed necessary for Lehnya's sake.

WEDNESDAY
10. *Chastening the Maid*

MISS MILCHFORD worried often about the treatment of Angeline. She seemed to be doing too little—that is, Miss Milchford did, and come to that Angeline did too. Since the first mandatory strapping she had not disciplined the girl at all. There seemed no definite occasion to do so, although it was not true to say that she was perfectly satisfied with Angeline's conduct. In some respects it seemed to be falling off from the careful precision of the first few days. Her manner was laxer and more casual. Of course, it was natural that she should become more relaxed as she grew used to her new home, but Miss Milchford had an uneasy sense that the relaxation that was happening was taking the wrong form—but she could never quite put her finger on a punishable offence. On the other hand, she had been told that Angeline had more than one *persona*, and she had done nothing to encourage or permit these others to express themselves. She felt somehow that she could manage Angeline—just—as an obedient maid, but that anything further would complicate the situation beyond her powers of control. Even now she felt that her grip was very slowly slipping.

Angeline had her regular duties—preparing meals, washing up, making beds and some laundry. These things seemed to absorb most of the available time and to require quite a lot of the mistress's time still, in supervising, sorting out little problems and making decisions. The house *was* better run by a certain margin, but somehow that margin seemed a long way short of a whole new pette'sworth. Considering what was done before she came, chaotic as it was, the improvement seemed too small. And things were *still* chaotic. The house was not tidy. Another inspection would have little better result than the last one. There somehow seemed neither the time nor the organisational power to lick the house properly into shape and keep it there.

Miss Milchford blamed herself. It was her fault. How far it was also Angeline's fault was hard to tell. She was outwardly obedient and she worked hard in her way—she was very rarely actually *not* working, except when she was given time off to read or rest or join the family in some entertainment, but there was sometimes a sense that she was dragging her feet and not getting any more done than she had to. And then, it was hard to tell if this was a question of bad will or merely of bad working habits—habits which Miss Milchford did not know how to cure as her own working habits were scarcely better. She knew that, with a different sort of mistress, everything would be running a great deal better. She also knew that with a different sort of maid everything would be running a great deal better. But then Angeline was a punitive girl, not a well-trained vocational maidservant. It was the mistress's responsibility to get the best out of her.

Annalinde was also becoming aware of the position, partly through her own observation and partly through remarks made by Miss Milchford. Fiercely protective of her mother, she tended to blame Angeline, but like Miss Milchford she could not put her finger on precisely what was wrong. She felt some action ought to be taken to break the deadlock, but, being impractical to the point of utter helplessness, had no idea at all what the action might be.

The day after the Soda Fountain, Annalinde went into the kitchen where Angeline was washing up, and, mindful of how docilely she had responded to Susan's pinch, Annalinde ventured to pinch her rounded bottom gently through her black uniform skirt.

"Ooh! Cheek, miss! I'll tell the mistress," said Angeline. There was, however, in her voice something inviting.

"Will you?" asked Annalinde severely. Her severity surprised herself. Perhaps she was piqued by the difference in Angeline's response to the bumptious brunette from that which she made to her own small pinch, and perhaps she was a little more cross with the girl, under the surface, than she quite knew.

Angeline was quite intimidated. "Oh, no, miss. Not really."

"What you need, my girl," said Annalinde, "is a good whipping."

"Do I, miss?" asked Angeline. The girl's manner was melting and provocative, slightly insolent but with more than a hint of submission, and—and with a quality that reminded Annalinde uncannily of Diana Dors in a Quirinelle film she had seen recently. Angeline had seen it too. Suddenly the mask of everyday dulness was off, and the two girls looked at each other on some deeper level.

"Yes, you do," said Annalinde, "and you're going to get it."

To her surprise, the maidservant instantly positioned herself submissively over the back of a kitchen chair, her hands resting on the seat. A position that Betty had made her adopt on three or more occasions. Annalinde looked at the neat little bottom clad in the black skirt, the wide, white bow and the white apron-straps running up the bowed back of the tall girl. She looked at the hem of the skirt, hanging in charming folds below the girl's knees and pictured herself picking it up. She felt almost giddy with the desire to serve the girl as she so clearly expected—and, it seemed, wanted—to be served. What could she use? Could she get the strap? The cane would make less noise.

But no, the whole thing was absurd. Her mother was in the next room working on business matters. What would she say when she realised Annalinde had decided, on her own account, to thrash the maid? They weren't that kind of household. Annalinde was a teenager and immature for her age in many respects. She did not do grown-up things like that on her own initiative. Even so—watching Angeline bending so still and quiet, with such patient anticipation—even so she would have done it if she could have expected to give the girl a really sound thrashing. Done it and taken the consequences afterwards. But she could not reasonably expect to get beyond two or three strokes. The whole thing was impossible.

"Stand up," she said.

"Very good, miss," said Angeline, coming upright and brushing down the front of her apron. She was a good deal taller than Annalinde and by the very look in one's eyes a taller girl can either emphasise her stature or put it aside. Now she seemed to indicate by the subtlest of emanations that she was, after all, a full-grown maidservant and Annalinde only the child of the house. She seemed to taunt her powerlessness, but also to display a certain disappointment of her own, and at the same time to show Annalinde a new respect; which seemed in no way contradictory, for now, instead of looking at her as just someone she passed in the hall, she was very definitely looking at her as the Young Mistress, however young she might be, and the very promptness of her "Very good, miss" reminded Annalinde how frequently this compulsory courtesy was forgotten or mumbled or supplanted by a pleasant but distinctly evasive little noise.

Annalinde left the room and Angeline returned to the washing up. She felt hollow and let down. The bewildering mixture of wordless messages she conveyed to her young mistress were all accurate. She felt all of them. But now she felt what she had been feeling predominantly for the last little while: bored. She had heard about punitive service, and in the period of anticipation had been alternately excited, worried and deeply depressed. Long hours, hard work, frequent whippings: the grim intensity of a life of punishment had filled her with dread and fascination in about equal measure. And now the reality was so much less than she had expected. Less in every respect. Less miserable, less exciting, less *intense*. In fact it was nothing much at all in any direction. It was insipid.

She could almost kick herself for thinking such things. Miss Milchford was so terribly nice and kind. She was decent and generous and always had a thought for the maid's comfort and convenience. She had once worked in a motorway café in the Pit, and that had been a great deal more like punitive service. The work had been hard and dull and you were always rushed and pushed to give more than you thought you could. Here, if her feet had ever ached for five minutes the way they did there all day, the mistress would have told her to sit down. If she ever got tired, the way she was perpetually tired there, she would be sent to lie down for half an hour. It was very nice, and Miss Milchford was very nice, but it did not feel like punitive service. She sometimes felt that if she had a punitive girl under her *she*, Angeline, would know how to give her punitive service. She was not working nearly hard enough. She knew that; but she did not know what to do. Really hard work was not expected of her. The house was not *geared* to it. She could do better if she tried—she knew she could, and sometimes she *did* try, but she lacked self-discipline.

She was ashamed, above all, of how much better she worked for Betty on the occasions when she was taken to the Trent-Kadrina colony. She knew that she remembered her manners and her "Very good, miss" all the time with her, and got more done in a few hours than she did in a day here. She really did not like Betty, who was nice to every one else, but seemed crabbed and suspicious toward her and spanked her horribly on any pretext. But she respected Betty and she did well for her, and the fact that she could not seem to do well for Miss Milchford whom she liked very much made her rather despise herself; but it did not make her change her ways.

Yes, Angeline knew many things. She knew that the disorder of the household was getting on top of Miss Milchford; she knew that she, Angeline, could not solve the problem herself, but she also knew that she could do quite a bit more to help than she was doing. She knew, though she could not have put it into so many words, that she could be helping much more not only *physically* but *psychologically*. She could be paying more respect, giving more willing submission and coöperation, making her mistress feel more in comfortable command of her household. But she was not. To say that she was giving the bare minimum would be unfair. She was giving more than that; but she was not giving the maximum— nor even the full extent of that which she was easily capable of giving. She knew it; she was ashamed of it; and she watched it listlessly, as if she had been watching another over whose actions she had no control.

And above all, she *was* bored. Now that Annalinde had left the kitchen without whipping her, she felt a strange, hollow feeling, a feeling of going back, after a moment of light, into the greyness. She was a discontented girl. One of those who put little into life and so get little out of it. She had been making a bad, half-hearted Aristasian back in her own District. "Most girls either leave or stay and make a go of it," her District Governess had said to her. "You, Angeline, do not seem to want to do either."

And she did not. Above all she did not want to leave. She had no illusions at all about the Pit. Its brightest spot was greyer than the greyest parts of Aristasia. So she agreed to go into punitive service instead. The District Governess had thought it might cure her of her sluggish self-centredness, and Angeline had thought so too. But it was not working out. She would never change. She was just that sort of girl.

"What do you think about Angeline, Mummie?" asked Annalinde, bursting into the room.

Miss Milchford looked up wearily from a pile of papers. "I don't know what to think about Angeline," she said.

"You know she hardly ever says 'Very good, miss' to me these days."

"I know. It is the same with me. It has sort of crept up on me, and I don't know how to clamp down. I tell her off often enough and smack her hands——"

"You must use that strap. You're supposed to, you know."

"Yes I know, but I can hardly smack her hand one day and bring out that fearful strap the next for the same offence, can I?"

"Of course you can."

"It would look inconsistent."

"No it wouldn't. You just say:—'I suppose you think I have been letting your insolence go, but I have been counting the number of times you fail to address me properly, and now you are going to get a lesson you won't forget so quickly.'"

"I suppose you're right dear——"

"Mummie, I *am* right."

"But think about Angeline. Away from her home, working hard in the kitchen—she looks so tired sometimes—and that dreadful strap. I shouldn't like to taste it myself."

"You gave it to me."

"Only once, dear, and you seemed to need it."

"It did me good. It will do her good, too. You know, she needs it—she wants it really. It's half her trouble. She was sent here for severe treatment, you know. You are failing in your duty if you don't give it."

"Yes, possibly——"

"It will make her happier. I'm pretty sure of it."

"Do you really think so?"

"Yes, I do. I'll tell you what. I'll call her in and tell her to do something, and if she does it properly and answers properly we won't worry about what I've said, but if she doesn't, you give her at least six with the General Disciplinary Strap. What do you say, Mummie?"

"Yes, I think you are right, dear. Let us try it."

With a hand that required considerable willpower to prevent from trembling, Annalinde picked up the bell and rung it. Angeline appeared a clear minute and a half later, having evidently finished whatever she was doing before answering the mistressly summons. She saw that the bell was in Annalinde's hand. Miss Milchford was apparently deep in her paperwork.

"Yes, miss?" she said.

"Find me a letter-opener, Angeline."

The letter-opener was sitting on the sideboard. It was not uncommon for Annalinde to be at a loss for some article that was sitting a few feet from her nose. Angeline picked it up and gave it to her young mistress.

"It's just here, miss," she said.

"What did you say?" asked Annalinde balefully. Miss Milchford had now turned round.

"I said it was just there——" said Angeline in a small voice.

"And what should you have said?"

Angeline felt aggrieved at Annalinde's talking to her in this magisterial manner in front of the mistress, obviously trying to get her into trouble. Still, the mistress probably wouldn't do anything much. " I should have said 'Very good miss'—miss."

"Indeed you should," said Miss Milchford. "There has been far too much of this laxness lately. You were much better behaved when you first came. What is happening to you?"

"I don't know, madam."

"I suppose you think I do not mind since I have been treating it so leniently. Well, I have merely been giving you a chance to pull your own stockings up, so to speak; but since you are clearly not capable of it I shall have to employ other means, as I should have done earlier in the case of a punitive girl. Go to my room and fetch the General Disciplinary Strap."

"The——"

"Yes, you know the one. Two extra strokes for hesitating."

Angeline was shocked. That horrible strap had been gathering dust ever since the first dreadful day she had been thrashed with it. She made her way to her mistress's room, picking her steps across the littered floor.

"I *could* have helped with all this if I'd been more willing," she thought. "It's Annalinde's doing, Madam's sending me for this strap. She daredn't do it herself, so she's got me into trouble with the mistress, the little wretch."

She picked up the hard, heavy strap from the dressing table. It bowed a little in her hand, but did not droop like ordinary leather. Its weight was appalling. The protracted spankings she had suffered at Betty's hands had been hard to bear at times, but nothing stuck in her mind like the sheer searing pain of this strap. She had never been caned, it was true, but she fancied she had rather be caned, dreadful as she had heard that was, than face the General Disciplinary Strap again. She carried it downstairs, feeling faintly sick, conscious of her bottom and thighs beneath her neat black uniform skirt, so ordinary and intact, trying to imagine the excruciating pain they would so soon be feeling. It seemed a thing almost impossible to believe; a thing so far from the neat painless reality of the present moment as to be a wild fantasy, and yet it was all too inescapably true—a burning, terrible reality separated from her by rather less than five minutes. Her bottom, now covered modestly with folds of black material and an inner layer of nylon slip; encased inviolably within prim white cotton knickers, a place of untouchable girlish secretness, would soon be throbbing under this hard, merciless, whip-fringed piece of leather that she carried in her hands, plied by her gentle, hesitant mistress at the instigation of the smug little daughter of the house—in fact, in a way, at her own instigation, since none of this would be happening, she was sure, if she had not first provoked Annalinde in the kitchen. She looked down at her starched apron and thought of her own helplessness. Sometimes being a maid seemed more a game than anything, and her mistress just a person quite easily manœuvred into being an easy-going companion with very little real power over her. But now it became clear that she *was* a maid, and even if her mistress *had* been manœuvred into her present punitive mood partly by Annalinde and partly even by herself, there was nothing now that she could do about it. Nothing but suffer the horrid chastisement that lay ahead. Her stomach was heavy and her throat slightly nauseous, but she also felt a little thrill as life seemed to click back from the muddy mess of the last few weeks into a hard, crisp, untwistable reality.

She entered the drawing room.

"You have brought the strap," said Miss Milchford. "Good, now bend over the table as you did before. Annalinde, prepare the maid for chastisement."

Annalinde lifted the black uniform skirt, exposing the near-transparent slip and beneath it the dark stocking-tops, white thighs and whiter knickers. She stepped back, looking at the wide, white apron-bow, the black shoulders so neatly crossed with uniform white straps. The maid looked so prim and self-contained these days; so secure in her independent manner, it was rather nice to see her exposed from below the white bow and folded skirt: uncovered, unprotected and vulnerable. Miss Milchford had the same sensation.

"Very well, Angeline. We shall see if we cannot improve your manners a little. Six strokes, plus two extra for hesitating to obey my command to fetch the strap."

The sentence was considerably fewer strokes than on the girl's first beating, but those strokes had been of only moderate force. Miss Milchford was resolved to make these harder. She drew back the strap and lay its fringed length with real determination across the diaphanous petticoat. The strap itself did much of the work even with a moderate stroke. With real force behind it the pain was terrible.

Angeline let out a loud cry that sounded like a cry of protest, even of anger. She had made up her mind to lie quietly for her whipping, but the unexpected shock of the stroke forced the cry from her, and her underlying bad will came out in its tone. It was unfortunate for her. The strength of the stroke and its effect had, for a split second, started a movement of remorse in Miss Milchford's tender breast which would no doubt have caused her, half-involuntarily, to temper the rest of the punishment. The rebellious, not to say insolent, note in Angeline's cry brought to the fore the side of her that felt Angeline was uncoöperative and considerably to blame for the continuing difficulties of the household, and her resolve to whip the child severely hardened.

"Hold her, Annalinde," she said. Annalinde pressed the maid's uniformed shoulders hard against the table. Already, through the lucid nylon of the little slip, one could see the wide streak across the girl's white thighs darkening from red to purple. Another crack filled the room with its harsh report. The maid screamed: angry, defeated and maddened by the heavy, ferocious, unendurable sting. The next stroke crossed the seat of her knickers, falling mostly on the near-side cheek and cutting horribly in between the two, as a strap-stroke sometimes will.

"Ooohhh!" she cried, this time anger was giving place to simple distress. Another stroke fell squarely across the knickers, dealing with both sides equally, but hurting more on the left because that was already so tender.

Half the punishment was over and Miss Milchford told her to calm herself for a minute, reminding her that she would have only two strokes to come now if she had obeyed instantly.

As Angeline grew quiet and her breathing returned to normal, Miss Milchford lay the heavy strap across the tops of her thighs. This time the girl began to cry. Three more strokes exploded with harsh, multiple report and tidal waves of pain. The neat, bobbed mistress of the house laid them on carefully, methodically—not quite so hard, perhaps, as the first

"Very well, Angeline. We shall see if we cannot improve your manners a little."

few, but still very hard for such a heavy strap upon such tender cheeks and thighs. Angeline, sobbing, clutched the edge of the table, enduring somehow until the ordeal was over. As the girl stood up, Miss Milchford smiled, pleased at having chastised her maid so effectively. The dense, firm strap in her hand gave her a sense of pleasing power, and the distress of this quietly self-willed young maidservant seemed a rectification of the proper order of things.

"Thank you, madam," she said in a subdued voice that made it clear how much of self-assertion and independence of manner had crept into the neutrality of her tone over the past week or so. She determined to give her more of this medicine in the future.

"Replace the strap and return to your duties, Angeline."

"Very good, madam." She bobbed. Every one had forgotten her bobs for some time now. There was a quiet submissiveness in her tone that had not been heard since her first week.

Annalinde left a quarter of an hour before seeking out the maidservant. She was dusting in the dining room. It took a little courage thus to confront her, for when she had returned to the drawing room bearing in her hand the heavy leather instrument of her coming chastisement, she had shot the little tell-tale whom she knew to be responsible for her suffering a look of scarcely-masked venom. Would she still feel thus toward her, or was her subdued demeanour genuine. Annalinde told herself she did not care. She was not going to be emotionally manœuvred by a punitive maid.

Before entering the dining room, Annalinde pulled her shoelace undone. As she entered, Angeline turned from her work and bobbed. For some time now the young mistress's entrance to a room had gone unacknowledged by the maid, who generally gave the impression of not having heard her. Her manner now was a curious mixture of submissiveness and quiet reproach.

"My shoelace seems to have come undone," said Annalinde. "Do it up, Angeline."

"Very good, miss." Angeline knelt immediately to the task.

"Did you enjoy your whipping, girl?"

"It was very painful, miss."

"They are supposed to be."

"Yes, miss."

"I suppose you think I got you into it?"

"It isn't my place to think anything, is it, miss?"

"No, it isn't, girl, but you are thinking it anyway, and you are right, I did."

"Thank you, miss," said Angeline. She was not sure what else to say.

"Would you like another one?"

"I'd do anything to avoid it, miss."

"Then you'll have to change your ways a good deal."

"Yes, miss."

"You've finished with my shoelace, haven't you?"

"Yes, miss."

"Then why are you still kneeling there?"

"You didn't tell me to stand up, miss."

"Good. You *are* improving, Angeline. Stand up now."

"Very good, miss."

Angeline stood up. She was a good bit taller than Annalinde. It felt exciting to be in command of this big girl. It gave Annalinde an idea.

"Can you reach the picture rail, Angeline?"

"I don't know, miss."

"Try."

Angeline went over to the wall and stood on her tiptoes to reach the rail.

"Yes, miss."

"Hold onto it with the tips of your fingers."

"Very good, miss."

"Now, imagine you are a slave-girl chained in that position. You must not move until I unlock you."

"Very good, miss." Angeline's voice showed that the position was already a strain.

Annalinde came over to her and began to run her hand up the maid's leg underneath her skirt. As she passed beyond the taut nylon film to the warm flesh, the slave-girl squealed.

"Oh, please, miss, I'm terribly sore."

"You are going to be sorer." Annalinde ran her hand over the warm, swollen surface of the naked upper thighs. The slave girl's breath quickened. Annalinde scratched the hot flesh gently with her long fingernails. The slave girl moaned.

"Oh, miss, it hurts."

Annalinde took the flesh between her thumb and forefinger, pinching hard. A high whimper emerged from the chained girl. She pinched again and again; hard, firm little nips that tormented the sore thighs. The slave girl writhed and wriggled against the wall, obediently maintaining her difficult hold on the picture rail and emitting breathy, gasping squeals, never loud enough to be heard outside the room.

"Open your legs," said Annalinde.

This was difficult, for it increased the strain on the slave-girl's arms, but she managed to get her feet a good thirty-two inches apart.

Annalinde felt a warmth of coöperation. The girl was doing her best to obey in everything and to do what her young mistress wanted of her. There was a slight air of martyrdom in her manner, but also a sense of relief. The girl felt less tense and prickly when she was being treated like this, she seemed quieter in her soul, and, on quite a deep level, happier.

Annalinde slipped her hand inside the open thighs, taking a pinch of the deliciously soft inner flesh and squeezing with all her digital strength.

"Ohh! Oohhh!" gasped Angeline, almost losing her hold on the picture rail, but somehow managing to keep it. She was not really afraid, as she had been during other punishments, of the consequences of failing to hold her position, but she wanted to coöperate and do as her young mistress commanded, and besides, as she told herself, she *could* not break her chains.

Annalinde pinched again in the warm enclosure between the legs, brushing at times against the thin, plain white uniform knickers and feeling upon her hand the moist warmth of the slave-girl's soft, most secret place as she writhed in her physical stress.

At last the slave-girl had been punished enough. Her chains were unlocked and her arms fell from their strained position with great relief. She fell to her knees before the young princess who stroked her hair for a moment. Annalinde felt a magnetic warmth about the girl.

"Are you sufficiently chastened?" she asked.

"I *think* so, miss." She was certainly not *dis*couraging the young mistress from punishing her further.

"You're not sure? Do you think you need more?"

"Well, miss——"

Footsteps approached the door.

"Stand up," whispered Annalinde. The maid rose hastily to her feet. The door handle turned and Miss Milchford entered.

"May I see you for a moment, Annalinde?"

"Of course Mummie. That will be all, for now, Angeline. I shall see you later."

11. A District Inspectorette

NO ONE had to stay behind for a strapping and the girls issued from the Odeon together.

"What a *wonderful* film," said Annalinde.

"It made me cry," said Alice Trent.

"Cry," said Lehnya, "but why?" It had been a comical film, adventurous and rather silly. *Miss Robin Hood*, a story about a writer of a children's magazine story about a schoolgirl adventurer, who becomes involved in real-life adventures at the instigation of a Miss Honey, played by dear, dotty Margaret Rutherford. A film full of nicely-spoken schoolgirls, and policemen and outlandish escapes and improbabilities. Hardly a tear-jerker, Lehnya thought, though in truth, Wendy had shed a tear or two, hardly knowing why.

"Because it was so *real* and good and innocent and pure."

"It stirred up my feelings in a way that I can hardly explain," said Annalinde, whose mascara gave distinct evidence of the fact.

Honeyset Park was already behind them and high heels rang on the concrete of Bottle Alley mingling with the chatter. Bottle Alley in the dark could be a slightly frightening place, as Rough Brunettes might catch a girl and pinch her till she squealed, but no Rough Brunettes were likely to approach a group of this size, so it felt safe and cosy walking together to the Constant Nymph.

The new waitress opened the door and ushered the party in, giving a special smile to Annalinde, almost as if she had known her; but then Angeline really didn't have a special name and persona for her work at the Nymph, so Annalinde acknowledged her with a friendly wrinkle of the nose. Angeline felt warmed, for although she was (in a sense) under the Milchford roof, she was more immediately under the command of the implacable Betty—or rather, Charmian. Betty, she sometimes thought, was the punitive element in this Punitive Service.

Cocktails were ordered, seats were found, blondes were settled.

"What are we going to do about the tennis-ball problem?" asked Lehnya suddenly.

"I don't know," said Emma Kadrina, "what can we do?"

"Can't get them," said Annalinde succinctly.

"Can't get *what*?" asked Sinta.

"Tennis balls, of course. That's what we're talking about."

"Would it be simplistic of me to suggest buying them in a shop?"

"A bongo-shop, you mean."

"Well, yes, but we don't usually worry about that."

"No, but then usually you can buy whatever it is, but tennis balls you can't. I mean bongo-shops haven't got them. They've some things that look a *bit* like tennis balls, but they are horrible wongo colours. Tennis balls are white, therefore these things are not tennis balls."

"Exactly," said Lehnya. "And I really rather like tennis. It seems awful if we should have to stop playing because we can't get the balls."

"Would you really have to stop playing?"

"Well, what would you suggest?"

"I—I'm not sure."

"I think we know what you might have suggested, Sinta," said Emma Kadrina, "and you were right to stop before suggesting it. The Pit would have you believe that the colour of a tennis ball is too trivial a matter to affect whether or not one plays tennis at all, but it is not trivial. Not in the least.

"A fluorescent tennis ball is not just an object, it is a *statement*; an ideological expression; an ideogram of the whole rotten, deracinated, filthy, ugly post-culture of the Pit. The Pit tries to tell one that these æsthetic matters are of no real importance, while sparing no effort or expense to corrupt them thoroughly and totally down to the last detail. The point about fluorescent tennis balls is that no activity shall be untainted, unmarked by the stamp of the Beast and his garish vileness; not even a simple game of tennis. That is a thing with which we can never compromise. Perhaps we can find sources of real tennis balls or a means of bleaching them, but if not, and it means never playing a game of tennis again, then so be it. Who, in any case, could *enjoy* playing tennis with a foul object like that signalling at every stroke one's capitulation to ugliness and impoverishment of soul?"

"It is all connected with type-3s and their horrid cult of the body that seems to affect women so terribly," said Alice Trent.

"What are type-3s?" asked Sinta, and simultaneously:

"But *is* it wrong to want to keep fit?" asked Lehnya.

"Lehnya's question first," said Emma Kadrina, "and then we can talk about type-3s, though really the two fit together like a pair of gloves. Who is going to try?"

"May I?" said Maria. The Hostess was not here tonight, leaving the club in the capable hands of Charmian and her new assistant.

"Please do."

"There is certainly nothing *wrong* with keeping fit, As so often the question turns on the *way* it is done. Bongo fit-keeping, with its hateful, garish clothes, is somehow deeply rooted in the directionless, rootless, atomised 'personal independence' of the Pit. It is the body-conscious-

ODEON

PARK PLACE

Presents

Direct from Trent,

**THE JUVENILE SINGING
SENSATION OF THE YEAR:**

Miss

DEANNA DURBIN

in

THREE
SMART
GIRLS

WITH FULL SUPPORTING
PROGRAMME

CIRCLE 6d   Ices 2½d   STALLS 9d

The management reserves the right to discipline patronettes
in accordance with the provisions of the Public Decorum Act.

ness of people who believe in nothing *but* the body. Somehow, that *particular* physical cult could *only* belong to people who thought marriage a temporary contract of no great importance, and sexual morality a thing of the past; who had no pride in their ancestry, no sense of *place*. It is all part of the same loose, garish, fragmented ethos. Insofar as it involves discipline, it is a *substitute* for any other form of order, a substitute for morality and ordinary restraint.—And one which, somehow, justifies and adds further superciliousness to their rejection of all normal values.

"The Nazis were keen on keeping fit, too. They too had a cult of the body; and by comparing the two, we can see how the same cult (outwardly speaking) can have entirely different meanings and implications. For the Nazis, the implication of keeping fit was all bound up with ferocious heterosexuality and Puritanism and the devotion of the individual to the State. In many superficial respects the values are quite the opposite of the bongo ones. But in every thread of clothing, in every jerk of the arm or leg, you can read the *meanings*, the built-in *ideologies* of the two different body-cults."

"And then," put in Annalinde, "there is the keep-fit craze in Trent or Quirinelle."

"Indeed," said Maria, "and there again, the craze speaks its own *language*, has its own *implications*. It speaks of home-life and feminine beauty and of sane, settled, healthy things."

"Yes," said Emma Kadrina, "and when we think of that, we realise that it is rather different from the Nazi or bongo fitness cults, and that they, for all their superficial differences, are much closer to each other than it might seem. The Quirinelle keep-fit craze is precisely that, a *craze*, not a *cult*. It has nothing of the feverishness or the holier-than-thou quality of the other two. It is compatible with dignity and charm."

"Charm, oh *yes*," said Lehnya. "I must admit that has always puzzled me. I suppose bongo-women go in for this sort of thing to keep themselves attractive, but the sight of a bongo-female in bongo sports clothes strikes me as just about the ugliest thing on God's earth."

. "All their unvarnished, un-made-up, raw health is just about as attractive as their raw 'sex' They seem like people who prefer dough to bread."

"To look at these smug, uncombed, antivirginal monstrosities in horrible baggy socks without feet, and realise that, had they been born a few decades earlier, they might have been fresh-faced Quirrie sweethearts doing bicycles-in-the-air at the local keep-fit class in the village hall, is enough to make you feel ill."

"It makes you want to get your hands round the throat of whoever has done it to them."

"Anyway, Lehnya," said Maria, "You see why one despises bongo keep-fittism—not because it is keep-fittism, but because it is bongo. It speaks very clearly in a particular language, a particular accent, a particular ideology. Bongo keep-fittism is just as much a statement of the bongo creed as Nazi keep-fittism was a statement of the Nazi creed. Its entire *look* and *manner* belongs utterly to the fragmented consciousness of the post-Eclipse world."

"Exercise is propaganda, what?"

"I am very much afraid it is."

"Why do you say 'exercise is propaganda' like that," asked Sinta. "It sounds as if you are referring to something else."

"She was," said Emma Kadrina. "She was referring to the old Aristasian adage: *design is propaganda*."

"And what does it mean?"

"I thought you wanted to know about type-3s."

"I do, but I want to know about this first."

"Well, you're just one jolly bundle of intellectual curiosity tonight, aren't you?"

"Tonight and every night. What about a cocktail before you start?"

"Thank you."

"Here, girl!"

"I say, you'd better not start hailing Charmian like that!"

"I shan't, but this one likes it, don't you, girl?"

"What were you wanting, miss?—Ow!"

"Susan, go home!" said Alice Trent. "You are too young to be here."

"Fountains of Youth all round, waitress," said Sinta politely.

"Yes, miss," said Angeline ruefully, but with thrilling submission. Her upper thighs had already been very sore.

"Coffee for me," said Lehnya.

"Design is Propaganda," said Sinta.

"There isn't an awful lot to explain," said Emma Kadrina, "and I expect you have gathered much of it already. The expression *design is propaganda* refers to the fact that the form of the made objects that surround us is never morally or ideologically neutral. They all *say* something. Ugly aluminium telephone kiosks, garish tennis balls, plastic jug-kettles, bongo motor cars are all making a *point*. They are surrounding every one in the Pit, day by day, hour by hour, with a barrage of visual propaganda. They are saying things about the world and life and the nature of reality, all the time. Design *is* propaganda.

"Take the motor car as an example. A real car is upright and digni-fied. It treats those who travel in it as ladies—or gentlemen. One steps up into it, and everything about even the cheapest family car from Trent, or even Quirinelle, has about it a certain stateliness.

"The bongo-car, by contrast, is made for consumer-serfs. One steps *down* into it and the seats encourage a posture characteristic of the loutish casualness of the Pit. The colours are garish and proletarian. The shape is slick and moulded, with an inbuilt hatred of clarity and form. Every attempt is made to eliminate each individual external feature in an amorphous whole, reminiscent of the obliteration of the individual in a mass-society; head-lamps are integrated into the body-work, their form mutates from the perfect round, reminiscent of the celestial orbs, to indeterminate oblongs which are moulded round the corners (the continual subjugation of form to contingency). Bumpers change from gleaming chrome fixtures to matt black plastic lumps. Windows are vast, like the hideous picture-windows in the worst sort of bongo house, and bent like the head-lamps. Instruments are changed from chrome-plated works of art to blobby plastic insults. In short, the bongo motor car is made to express haste, casualness, vulgarity and the trumpery gaudiness of pop-capitalism. More importantly, it is made to deny human dignity, uprightness, superiority, the sense of tradition, the sense of form and archetype.

"The design of the bongo-car is before all else a piece of propaganda. It is atomised proletarianism in tin; late-capitalism on four wheels."

"But aren't these dreadful designs dictated by the need for cheapness and efficiency?" asked Sinta.

"That is what the Pit likes to pretend, but it is simply not true. *Some* of these features have gone hand in hand with cheaper or more efficient methods. *None* of them would have taken the forms they did if the ideology of the late 20th century had been different. The æsthetic solution to technical problems depends *entirely* on the mentality with which one approaches the problem. Art Deco is the art of the machine age *par excellence*. It evolved a language of design for mass-produced efficiency which nevertheless retained decorum, *panache,* beauty and form. These principles—or ones developed from them—could be applied to the problems of late-20th-century design with beautiful results. The bongo car looks as it does because that is the *language* its designers choose to speak—because they are atomised, deracinated bongos.

"And what is true of motor-cars is true of just about every other manufactured object that surrounds the Pit-dweller. And each of these objects reinforces her Pit-mentality and helps to make her what she is. *Design is propaganda.*"

"So take things like—excuse the phrase—personal computers———"

"Ordinators, they are called in Aristasia."

"Yes, ordinators. Are you saying they could be works of art? That they don't *have* to be deracinated objects?"

"Absolutely. Ordinators would have come about whether the Eclipse had happened or not. The Octopus can take no credit for them. If they had come a little earlier—in the historical 1920s or '30s—we should see Art-Deco ordinators in antique shops, as beautiful as radiograms of the same period. If the Eclipse had not happened, their design would be completely different. They would do the same job, but their appearance and form would speak a completely different *language*.

"Remember, *every* design, whether bongo or real, carries a message: one that is all the deeper and more powerful because the designer was unaware of it—because it was in the bedrock of her consciousness as she made the design. Golem-objects break down our psychic integrity, they rupture and cheapen our consciousness. Real, up-to-date objects have the opposite effect. They help to re-build the shattered *psyche,* replace fragmentation with wholeness, create an ambience of harmony and solid value in place of the shifting, disjointed, neurotic cheapness of modern design."

"And when you say *cheapness*——"

"It has nothing to do with money. A thing can be made inexpensively without being morally *cheap*. And a thing can have money lavished on it and still be completely impoverished in every important sense, which is true of most of the 'luxury items' of the Pit, including its most expensive motor cars, which are pervaded by the same air of proletarian nastiness as its least expensive. Put a bongo Rolls Royce beside the humblest Trentish family saloon—both in perfectly good, shiny condition—and you will see what I mean. In an ugly world, the richest man can buy nothing but ugliness."

"Yes," said Annalinde. "One gleams and the other merely glitters. One has a heart and soul and the other is a flashy box of gadgets."

"Yes, but more to the point, they are *saying* different things. They are each flashing their subliminal message into our minds every moment we are seeing them, even when they merely sail by us on the road. They are each promulgating a different and utterly opposed view of the universe. One is subtly building up our sane, healthy human consciousness, and the other is subtly poisoning it and breaking it down.

"The consciousness of the Pit is an organic whole. It is a disease, and everything that comes from it is a microcosm of that disease, latching onto all it touches and reproducing itself. It is a disease of the mind, that battens on everything mental, everything visual, everything emotional and twists it to its own diseased shape. Everything that gained its form in the Pit has a Pit-form, and that form is part of a language. It is

telling us things, subtly, insistently, silently, over and over again. It is re-
galing us with its diseased view of the cosmos; insinuating it into our
very pores. Design is propaganda.

"The clothes, the music, the cars, the telephones, the wireless and
gramophone sets, the advertisement hoardings, the magazine covers. the
shop-fronts—everything from the Pit carries the disease of the Pit. It
could not be otherwise, because that disease is an organic whole.
Nothing it touches remains undiseased.

"And conversely, everything healthy is part of another organic
whole. That is why up-to-date films are so wonderful for us—because
everything in them, the cars, the telephones, the policemen, the little
girls, the magazine covers, the music, the clothes, the vowels, the shops,
the chocolate-wrapers and washing-powder boxes—*everything* is healing
and good. So long as we do not neutralise them by thinking of them as
'old films'. So long as we see that they represent *normality,* and the Pit
an aberration, they can do us the most wonderful amount of good. And
the organic whole of health and harmony which they show us, we re-
build in our own lives, surrounding ourselves with real objects and root-
ing out diseased ones as far as we can. Because design is propaganda and
more than propaganda. Design is an incantation that can profoundly
affect our lives for better or for worse."

"So when you said 'exercise is propaganda', you were really saying
much the same thing as 'design is propaganda'."

"In a more limited context, yes. Every form produced by the Pit par-
takes of its disease and, having partaken of it, spreads it; and its form of
exercise is no more an exception to the rule than anything else."

"Last orders please, ladies," cried Charmian. A flurry of drink-
arrangements. Doris Day was singing *Que Sera Sera* The atmosphere was
warm and happy, and Annalinde was pleased to note that Angeline
seemed to be enjoying it. She whispered to Sinta, suggesting that she
buy the waitresses a drink, and both accepted.

"Tell us about type-3s," said the insatiable Sinta.

"Does any one mind our going over all this elementary business?"
asked Emma Kadrina of the assembled company.

"Not at all," said Lehnya. "One needs to keep familiarising oneself
with the concepts, and you pettes seem to do it better every time."

"Oh, *thank* you. Well, in that case, type-3s are type-3 mutants. All
Pit-dwellers are mutants because they have all been strangely changed
from the human beings they would have been if the Eclipse had not
happened. They are deracinated, in short. But they differ in how *far* they
are mutated; and, for convenience we divide them into three types,
named, rather originally, Type-1, Type-2 and Type-3.

"Now the type-2 mutant is the average, no-frills bongo. The ordinary television watcher who has taken in all the nonsense of the Pit, dresses the way the Pit tells her to, but all in an average sort of way. She is not super-Pittish, just a passive receiver of all the propaganda.

"The type-2 is, as it were, the central mutant. The ordinary Pit-product, and the other two types are measured against her. The type-1 mutant is the mutant who has really not mutated very well at all. She *is* affected by the Pit, of course, as she has no intellectual protection against it, but as far as she can be, she is quite a lot the same person she would have been if the Eclipse had not happened. Older people often come into this category, and some less intelligent people, who really have not the brains to take in the propaganda. But there are a few young, intelligent type-1s who really just don't get on with the Pit and haven't ingested it very well. Type-1s tend to be rather passive, and not to have a conscious analysis of the Pit, only a sort of stolid, half-conscious refusal to accept its values. Many ordinary, decent well-educated people, especially those who retain a strong sense of family, are type-1s. But some type-1s are the sort of people most of us were before they entered Aristasia—very intelligent people with a real dislike of the ugliness and anti-romanticism of the Pit, who are looking for an answer to it. It is quite possible that people like us would have become type-3s if we were just a little less intelligent, and could not see through the falseness of the Pit's internal oppositions.

"Type-3s are at the opposite extreme to type-1s. They are the super-bongos. The ones who collaborate in their own mutation more than they need to, and adopt, willingly, the more extreme manifestations of the Pit disease. Obvious examples are the sort of people who tattoo themselves or pierce their bodies, radical 'feminists', hairy 'ecology' types, shaven-headed 'dykes', campaigners for bongo causes of all sorts, New Age types, people who attend Silly Monkey clubs, bongo-pop 'musicians', television producers, practitioners of alternative therapies, and in general, all those specimens who look, think and sound just a bit more like people who could never have existed before the Eclipse than their neighbours.

"The thing to bear in mind here is that a certain number of these type-3s actually dislike the Pit quite a lot. They become what they are because they are falling into the trap of reacting against one tentacle of the Octopus by clinging more tightly to another. The whole point about the tentacles is that many of them are in phoney opposition to one another, and whatever aspect of the Pit you dislike, there is always another tentacle 'opposing' it: and the more 'rebellious' the tentacle, the more bongo and mutated it makes its victims. So type-3 girls can be potential Aristasians if one can unglue them from the particular Pit sub-cult they are involved in."

"Julie Leaver was like that in *The Feminine Régime*," said Lehnya.

"Yes, that's right. She was a typical type-3 who was so because she disliked the Pit and who turned into a very good Aristasian quite quick-ly. Janet was similar, only I suspect she was a bit of a mixture of type-1 and type-3, which sounds odd, but it happens. People who are funda-mentally type-1 often latch onto some particular Pit-cult or tentacle for protection, or to find some sort of identity in their reaction against cer-tain aspects of the Pit, and become type-3s, in most exterior respects, while still being type-1 at heart."

"Time now, ladies," cried Charmian.

"It seems strange," mused Lehnya, "that the more a girl rebels against the Pit the more Pittish she becomes."

"That," said Emma Kadrina, "is because the whole of the Pit is based on a sort of false rebellion. Setting oneself against authority brings about exactly the sort of atomised, anarchic mentality that the Pit is trying to induce. Because every rebellion against order is symbolically a rebellion against the Golden Order."

"But when the authority is a false authority, the 'authority' of the Pit itself——"

"Exactly. It is a double-bind of the most brilliant devising. Obey the Pit and you are obviously Pittish. Rebel against the Pit and you end up even more Pittish. You turn into a type-3, which is *exactly* the sort of person the Pit is trying to create. Type-3s are much better than type-2s from the Pit point of view. Much more complete Pit-creatures."

"So what *is* the answer?"

"The *only* answer is to have a true Order, a real authority, as we have. A reflection of the Golden Order."

"And then one can rebel against the Pit without being co-opted?"

"Yes, in a way. But 'rebel' is no longer the salient word. We do not 'rebel' against the Pit because we no longer recognise its authority. So we no more see ourselves as 'rebelling' against the Pit when we do not act according to its will than we regard ourselves as 'rebelling' against the girl next door when we do not act according to hers. The Pit is an invalid authority, and therefore no authority at all. It is not recognised by Aristasian law, which is the *only* law. 'Taxes', for example, paid to the Pit, have no legal validity in Aristasia and are regarded as simple ex-tortion, or as enforced tribute paid to an enemy power.

"A parallel sometimes employed, is that if a powerful gangster, like Mr. Al Capone, ruled a city and extorted protection money from all persons and businesses, the prudent maid would probably pay it, if the

On the Service of Her Imperial Majesty

IMPERIAL COMMITTEE FOR GATEWAYS & BOUNDARIES

Immigration and Naturalisation

K N O W L E D G E   L E C T U R E   No. 7
<u>First Grade</u>
I M P E R I A L   M O N E Y

Imperial money comes in three units, <u>viz</u>. Pounds
(£), Shillings (s) and Pence (d). This system was
common to all Europe before the materialist
Napoleonic tyranny and can be traced back to
3,000 years b.c. It is, of course, far older.

Since the collapse of Tellurian civilisation,
the issue and control of this only real and
legitimate form of money is the exclusive prerog-
ative of her Imperial Aristasian Majesty. Real
money has a profound esoteric significance which
cannot be divulged to you at this stage, but the
following things you must learn if you are to
become an Aristasian subject:

1) There are 12 pennies to a shilling and 20
shillings to a pound.

2) An oblique stroke is often used to separate
shillings and pence, so 1/6 = 1 shilling and six-
pence (note the spoken stress falls on "six", not
"pence") 2/6 = 2s 6d, 2/- = two shillings.

3) The coins of the realm, are (silver): 6d

Part of instructional course followed by girls entering Aristasia

only alternative was having her premises dynamited. But this would not imply any recognition of Mr. Capone as a legal tax-collector. Furthermore, the term 'protection' is not entirely a fiction. It is in Mr. Capone's interest to protect his clients against other gangsters, and even against each other; and, because the Golden Order is inborn in humanity, insofar as he is not specifically violating that Order, he will tend to uphold it—in other words, for example, to make theft and murder 'illegal', except when he is perpetrating them. This is precisely the position of the Pit 'authorities' and 'police' in Aristasian law."

"So in cases like that—avoiding theft and murder and so forth—we obey the law not because it is Pit-law, but because it is *the* Law."

"Precisely, and in the case of things like tax-laws, we obey, if we do obey, for the same reason that we run away from a wild bull—not because we grant the bull any moral right to displace us, but solely because it is the prudent course."

"And that, of course, is the answer to any one who should say we were hypocritical to accept the protection of bongo-law while denying its validity. We do *not* accept the protection of bongo-law, we accept the protection of *the* Law, and if the Pit-powers happen, vestigially, to enforce *the* Law, we are right both to obey and accept protection without prejudice to our complete rejection of those powers."

"Yes, just as if Mr. Capone were in power."

"Except that the Pit is a lot worse than Mr. Capone in many respects."

"Oh, of course. He only wants to enrich himself. He isn't trying to undermine the very fabric of human decency."

"Please, ladies, it's past time," cried Charmian.

"But would you say," asked Lehnya, "that the Pit *government* is trying to subvert human decency? Or isn't that the work more of its mass-media and advertising industries?"

"Oh, the governments play their part wherever they are called upon to do so, but the whole of the Pit is a continuum. At the highest level, politics and finance are not really separate powers. The power-structure of the Pit must be regarded as an interlocking whole."

"And *should* we pay bongo-taxes? Isn't it really better not to? Shouldn't we deny resources to the tyrant wherever possible?"

"Not necessarily. After all, it is not actually within our power to deny resources to the tyrant. Money is only a means to an end, and the financial power of the Pit ultimately controls every bongo-cent in existence. Whether we pay taxes or spend our money on lollipops it all goes back to the Pit. Money is a means of organising resources, and as far as possible we should organise our own people and things without recourse to Pit-money."

"Like voluntary bonded service, and using our own currency?" asked Lehnya.

"Yes——"

"But even more, by creating our own scale of value, as you were saying last time we were here, by making ourselves *psychically* independent of the whole Pit value-structure," said Maria.

"Exactly. And as for such things as paying bongo-taxes, of *course* there cannot possibly be any *moral* obligation to pay them, but the Empire actually prefers that its subjects avoid unnecessary risks—not from lack of conviction or from cowardice, but because our job is to lay intellectual and spiritual dynamite, to build the world that shall become the Pit's final Nemesis; not to get ourselves incapacitated in petty individual skirmishes with the tyrant's myrmidons."

"I say," said Annalinde, "can I slip back a splot and say something about design?"

"But of course, fair Annalinde."

"Well, you said that charming designs could be made using the cheap-and-nasty methods of Pit production: but isn't the *depth* of cheapness and nastiness part of the bongo mentality? I mean a Trentish radiogram is pro-portionately more expensive (in Trent, I mean) than the latest Pit Home-Sound-Headquarters-in-a-Plastic-Box because a radiogram is a piece of *furniture*. It is an æsthetic object of real value. It is *sold* not only for what it *does* but for what it *is*. Just about the *only* 'selling points' of bongo phonographic equipment are what are vulgarly called its 'features', in other words the gadgets and technical 'improvements', whether genuine or just showy gimmicks. A word may be spared in the sales leaflet for the 'design', but really æsthetics are very much a secondary question, if a question at all. Bongos do not seem to care very much what ugliness they put into their drawing-rooms provided it has plenty of 'features'. So what I am asking is this: *could* one have racinated design with cheap-and-nasty bongo methods, or are those methods not in themselves part of deracination? A racinated people would *want* walnut cabinets and would be prepared to pay for them, instead of wanting the greatest num-ber of gimcrack 'features' at the cheapest possible price?"

"Yes," Sinta, "isn't it analogous to clothes? People who will put contemptible forms on their bodies will put contemptible forms in their drawing rooms. They have lost the *self respect* that makes such things un-thinkable."

"You are quite right, of course," said Emma Kadrina. "There are *two* questions here. One is that a people that had not been deracinated would, as you say, demand higher æsthetic standards and be prepared to pay for them. Only the poorest people would want the cheapest possible casing, and most people would be happy to exchange a little technical advancement for a degree of human dignity. Of course, their choices are largely forced by the propaganda of the 'market'. We are not assigning blame here, only noting phenomena.

"And, of course, Sinta's point is very important. Ultimately this ques-tion devolves upon the issue of what a *home* is. A real racinated home is, even in the historical 1950s, vestigially a Temple of Hestia: a place that is treated with a special respect and even a reverence as a mystical and indispensable thing that only the feminine can create. The Mistress of the House is still vestigially a Priestess, a keeper of something sacred and profound, a Hierophant of the *mysteria domestica* that goes back to the most ancient times and still keeps the heart nourished with the rich, symbolic reality that is Home. In a real home, only sound, dignified *furniture* is felt to be proper to the honour of the place. In a deracinated home, garish, ugly, essentially *cheap* things—for, like bongo cars, even the most expensive bongo phonograph looks cheap and *is* cheap in its æsthetic surface—as I say, garish, ugly, essentially *cheap* things are not felt to be out of place in a deracinated home, because a deracinated home is not seen as having any special dignity or honour *as* a home. It is just a dormitory for consumers.

"But even having said all this: even if, for whatever reason, the cheapest forms of casing were used in a relatively sane civilisation, it is indisputably true that reasonable forms could be created with no extra expenditure. The casing that is seen on a bongo phonograph is *not* the raw technics, it is a box that has been designed in a particular shape and could have equally easily and cheaply been designed in a hundred other ways. It *expresses,* in the algebra of design, the soul-impoverishing message of the Pit. It could express a quite different *message*. Even granted the need for cheapness; even granted the scale of values that relegates the æsthetic to the bottom, and negates the importance of solidity and dignity, and will not spend an extra penny on making things beautiful; equipment is still housed in cases, cases must still be designed and design is still language, still propaganda;—and a good propaganda can be made as easily as a bad one. Just as, even if we were restricted to only using one-syllable words, we could still say good things or bad things with those words."

There was a rattle in the background as Charmian rolled her dice. Then she made her way quietly over to Emma Kadrina and whispered something in her ear. Emma Kadrina left the room, taking Maria with her, and a troubled silence fell. In a moment Maria returned and after a minute or two the door opened again and some one new entered. She was a no-nonsense brunette wearing a neat dark mackintosh, a sensible hat and leather gloves. Every one knew, of course, what she had come for, but even had they not been prepared for such a visit, she had District Authority written all over her.

"Well, ladies," she said, "we seem to be out and drinking rather past closing time, do we not?" Her voice was crisp and clear, one might have called it somewhat affected, though that would not be a term of disapproval in this country. "Who is in charge of this club?"

Charmian put up her hand. "I am for tonight, miss."

"And have you requested these ladies to leave?"

"Oh, yes, miss."

"Did they refuse?"

"No, miss."

"Then why are they still here?"

"Well, they didn't refuse but they didn't take much *notice,* miss."

"Oh, didn't they? Well, perhaps they will take more notice of *this*." The District Official opened her neat bag and took out a three-tailed leather strap, about twenty inches long and one-and-a-half inches wide, quite dark and stiff.

"Throw your dice, please, girl." Charmian rolled her dice again. The District Official looked at it.

"Oh dear," she said. "Line up along here girls, and all hold out your right hands." The patronettes formed a line, each extending her hand as instructed. The District Official stood in front of the first girl.

"Name?"

"Maria Milchford, miss."

The strap descended with a hissing slap. Maria's face, despite her best efforts, contorted with pain. The Official did not wait to see her clasp her hand to herself, but passed briskly on to the next in line.

"Name?"

"Sinta Serendra, miss."

The strap hissed again and Sinta was enveloped in a wave of pain. She heard the Official passing down the line calling out names and dealing out strokes, calmly, briskly, inexorably. When she had finished she said smartly.

"Now your left hands, please."

"Oh, not again," thought Sinta. "I can't *stand* it. I just *can't.*"

Maria was holding out her hand beside her. The strap fell and a tiny sob escaped her. The Official placed herself in front of Sinta. The strap fell, and Sinta did the unimaginable. She withdrew her hand. The strap caught her fingertips, with a nasty sting, but without much force. The Official raised her eyebrows.

"Very well," she said, and passed on.

The strap fell again. The girl beside her (Lehnya) gasped in pain. The Official passed on. The strap hissed. Sinta could almost feel the horrid strokes. Her stomach felt leaden within her. What would happen to her now?

The Official completed her second passage down the line.

"I shall now give you a choice, ladies. You may accept a third stroke of the strap, or you may write one hundred and fifty lines." She pointed to each girl in turn. Only Sinta was left out.

"Lines, please miss."

"Lines, please miss."

"Lines, please miss."

So said they all.

"Dear me, you do not seem to like my strap, do you? She will be quite offended. I should have to put her away if it were not for this girl here. Sinda, was it?"

"Sinta, miss."

"Sinta. Clear that table, ladies. Sinta, position yourself over it. Now, I want all of you to hold her down. This is a girl who likes to avoid punishment by physical movement, so you are to hold her so she cannot move at all. That is right, you and you pin her shoulders to the table. You two hold her legs so she cannot move them. Good girls. If she manages to move I shall thrash you all and quadruple your lines."

Sinta could feel her lovely swirly Kadorian skirt being raised, her dark seamed stockings and her silk French knickers were exposed to the room. She felt embarrassed and hoped the girls were too preoccupied with holding her to look. Then the first stroke drove all other considerations from her mind. A searing lash across her bared thighs above the tops of her stockings. The Official whipped her with the strap, positively *whipped* her. The strokes fell rapidly, criss-crossing her thin, dark thighs, stinging the cheeks of her bottom through their loose silk covering as if it had not been there. She was an independent sort of girl. She did not cry in front of others, but now she found herself crying. She hardly knew it was happening until she had been crying for some little time. She suddenly tried to struggle free, but the girls held her so tightly that she could not move an inch. As she struggled they tightened about her, afraid of the promised punishments and afraid lest Sinta get herself into more trouble. Sinta was smothered beneath warm, pressing, scented femininity. Cocooned, swaddled, embraced, protected from everything except that relentless strap and the rising, exploding pain.

Suddenly it stopped. The strap stopped, that is, but the pain went on burning through her. She was pushed, lifted, floated to her feet. Her face was streaked with tears. Her dignity was gone. "Thank you, miss," she said. That much was instinctive.

"Well, dear. Do you want another stroke on your hand, or one hundred and fifty lines?"

"Lines, please miss."

"Very well. Now, Miss Charmian, was there any other girl drinking after hours tonight."

"Yes, miss. A girl called Emma Kadrina, miss."

"She is to receive the same punishment as the others. And here is a warning to you all. If I have to deal with this offence again I shall thrash you all as I thrashed Miss Serendra here, and I shall set enough lines to keep you amused during all your leisure hours for a month. Good evening, ladies."

"Good evening, miss."

"What a *beast*," said Annalinde as soon as she was gone.

"Are you all right, Sinta?" asked several voices.

"Oh, yes," said Sinta in a far-away sort of tone.

"She really laid into you, didn't she?"

"Mmm-mmm."

"Look, come on pettes. I think we should get out of here before she comes back or something."

With general assent the girls began putting on their coats, brunettes helping blondes. They went out the back way, into Park Place, where Emma Kadrina joined them.

"Would you like to come back to our house for a quick coffee?" asked Maria, for all the girls seemed a little shaky.

"Should we?" asked Lehnya nervously, "we don't want to get into any *more* trouble."

"Don't be silly. There isn't a *curfew,* just a law against drinking after time in public houses."

"All right then."

The company proceeded along Park Place and down Bottle Alley in their smart coats, hats and gloves. The door was opened by the maid and the order for coffee given. Armchairs were pulled round.

"What have I missed?" asked Emma Kadrina. "You all seem very full of something."

"A District Inspectorette or something came in after you went out. We all got two on the hands for drinking after hours and a hundred and fifty lines."

"Real stingers," put in Lehnya.

"Lucky for me," said Emma Kadrina.

"Not awfully," said Annalinde, "she asked after you and you're going to get it too."

"You pettes are just *too* kind."

"Couldn't be helped, the waitress reported you. She was asked point-blank who else had been there."

"You can have three on the hand and no lines if you want."

"But you get the two first, and you won't want," said Lehnya, shaking her hands.

"Not unless you get some one a bit less handy with the strap than that one."

"I hope I do."

"You won't. Not when it's a formal District punishment."

"And look at the lines," said Annalinde. "'I must obey the waitress at my club and leave when she tells me to do so.' How dreadful—I mean, writing about obeying Betty—I mean, Charmian."

"We have to obey *any one* who is acting with the authority of the Empire," said Maria piously.

"And we've also to hand them in to Charmian," said Alice Trent, "and you need not think just because she is a servant she will accept any old scribble. She is a very conscientious girl and expects others to be the same."

"Once she rejected my lines three times," said Emma Kadrina. "I was *so* tired of writing out the same thing by the time she decided to accept them."

"Imagine working like that for a little uniformed maid," said Annalinde.

"Yes, *do* imagine it. It's good for you," said Maria.

"And you won't just imagine it, you'll *do* it."

"No, I shan't. I'll get them right first time."

"Then you'll have to be jolly careful; she picks on every little thing."

Annalinde made a face. The idea of the neat, self-contained little maidservant exercising a prim power over her rankled.

"But how are you, Sinta?" asked Alice Trent. "You haven't said a thing."

"Oh, I *am* all right. Really I am."

"That inspector really thrashed her because she withdrew her hand," explained Alice Trent to Emma Kadrina.

"I don't mind," said Sinta.

"You seemed to mind a bit at the time," said Annalinde.

"Yes, but I don't now. I needed it. I feel grateful to her."

"For the whipping?"

"Well—well, because she didn't make me hold my hand out again at the end. I felt sure she was going to, and she probably should have; but I just couldn't have *borne* it. I was so grateful that she didn't."

"You don't like it on the hands, do you?"

"No—but who does? I'm unlucky, though. My new drawing mistress canes on the hands. It's only a little cane, or a sort of switch-thing really, but it hurts *terribly*. She gave me a sample just so I'd know what to expect."

"How will you *bear* it?"

"I shan't, I hope. I shall do everything she says, and do my practice diligently every week and hope to avoid it altogether."

"Yes, and I shall leave the Constant Nymph when Charmian tells us to, even if you other pettes stay," said Lehnya.

"Don't worry, we shan't." said Annalinde "Not for a few weeks, anyway."

"Talk about hard edges," said Lehnya.

"The edge of that strap was a touch too hard for me," said Annalinde.

"But I wasn't only grateful for not getting the stroke on the hand," said Sinta suddenly. "I was grateful for the whipping—and I still am."

MORE GOSSIP

Careless with her Kisses?
Who kissed *whom* in Saddler's Yard last Tuesday? This little birdie isn't telling—but if you *don't* know you must be the only pette in Maryhill who doesn't. Go to the bottom of the class.

Blessed Event
Not long ago the Milchford household of Honey Lane acquired a new member. A blessed event? Well yes, but not quite the sort you were thinking of. Miss Milchford has taken on a punitive maidservant from Foreign Parts. What's black and white and red all over? A uniformed maid with a smacked bottom!

She Knows, You Know
Who slipped out just before the Constant Nymph was raided (in the genteelest possible manner, of course) for after-hours drinking? Why, none other than local genius and noted cocktail-toper Miss Emma Kadrina. Did she have inside information? We shouldn't be surprised. And did it do her any good? None at all. The bar-maid snitched and she gets her hands strapped just like the other naughties. Ouch!

Setting a Record?
At the last three Odeons *no one* has been strapped. Are the pettes setting a new record for goodness? Or does the new usherette need a strapping for negligence?

WHY *SUFFER FROM THIRST?* WHEN YOU CAN *ENJOY IT* AT THE MARYHILL

SODA FOUNTAIN

GAUMONT
CINEMA, SADDLER'S YARD
THE PERFECT WOMAN
☆ Miss Patricia Roc ☆
PLAYS A ROBOT!
CARTOONS! NEWSREEL!
ALL SEATS ONLY 5d!!

ODEON
PARK PLACE
The Velvet Touch
Kadoria's Superior Lady, *Miss Rosalind Russell* in a story of romance and murder
With Full Supporting Programme
CIRCLE 6d STALLS 9d

STRICT DRAWING MISTRESS required for young lady aspiring to be artist. Please telephone RIVerton 4579

She was quite red, though she rarely blushed. It was true and she had forced herself to say it.

"Sinta was sweet, wasn't she?" said Annalinde.

"Oh, yes, she *was*," said Maria. "I do think she is coming along well."

"They are all sweet, really. Aren't we lucky to have such dear friends and live in such a lovely District?"

"I thought the District was too severe for you earlier."

"Well, one moans, of course, but it *is* right about hard edges, isn't it? They aren't exactly pleasant, especially when one bumps into them, but none of this would work without them, would it? We'd just be on the edge of the Pit, instead of inside our own walls. I don't even *quite* understand how it works, but I could see we should be in a completely different psychic *territory* without them."

"Well, really no psychic territory at all, except the Pit."

"Because nothing would be marked-off."

"Exactly."

"Is there any more coffee in the pot?"

Maria picked up the chrome Art-Neo electric percolator. "It feels heavy, but we must go to bed after this."

There was a knock on the door in the correct pattern.

"Some one from the District?" asked Annalinde nervously.

"Not at this time, I shouldn't think."

She went to the door and Annalinde heard Lehnya's voice.

"I'm sorry, Maria—I seem to have a flat tyre. I've tried pumping it, but it won't stay up."

"Well, come in."

Lehnya and Maria appeared in the room.

"Lehnya has got a flat tyre."

"Yes, I heard. We can run her home in Hilda, can't we?"

"Not really. Hilda is having trouble with her headlights. I was going to take her in tomorrow to get her ready for going to the Brace of Pheasants."

"It's all right. I can mend the tyre if you'll lend me a bowl of water."

"You don't want to start doing that at this time of night. Why don't you sleep here?" said Maria.

"Oh, *can* I?"

"Of course you may."

"Sit down and have a cup of coffee," said Annalinde.

"I say," said Lehnya, "can I just mention something I was wondering about?"

"But of course."

"Well, when Emma Kadrina was saying about type-3s—it all made perfect sense, but then I started thinking, as I was trying to pump my tyre up—I mean, what *about* ' hairy ecology types ', for example. I mean, they *are* ghastly, you couldn't see them and think them anything but ghastly, but what they say isn't entirely wrong, is it?"

"Of course it isn't," said Maria, " it isn't what they *say* that makes them ghastly, it is what they *are*. It is the fact that they are type-3s. Before the war, the English Essentialist, Lord Northbourne, wrote a book called *Look to the Land* in which he set out many of the dangers to the earth long before they had come to the point of crisis, and *long* before most people were aware of them. He was not wrong, he was right, and the substance of the bongo ' ecology ' movement is not wrong. The whole point is that it has become culturally corrupted. What was essentially a revolt against the Pit has been co-opted by the Pit, and the *manner* in which people adhere to that revolt glues them to the Pit closer than ever. They become muesli-eating type-3s, far more a specific product of the Pit than the average television-watcher. The only way they can react against certain aspects of the Pit is to cling to another tentacle; to express themselves by a vocabulary and a style of life and thought that belongs absolutely to the Pit and turns them into ultra-bongos, into one of the 57 varieties of type-3. And that is *just* what the Pit wants. It doesn't care whether you are for or against certain chemicals or the building of roads or anything else. What it *really* wants is that you should be as mutated as possible from a normal, pre-Eclipse human being. And the ' ecology ' movement is one of the hundreds of Pit sub-cults—many of them in apparent opposition to one another—that produce that effect and help to create a new type of deracinated person: the type-3.

"Many of these people are in *genuine* opposition to the Pit, or to the parts of it they can see through. But they cannot find any way of opposing it except through the ' alternative ' channels the Pit provides. The same is true of Pit ' feminism ' and all the other sub-cults. Many of them began as genuine, healthy reactions, but all of them have been co-opted and turned into mind-mills, sucking in type-1s and type-2s and churning out type-3s."

"And thus pursuing the most important cultural aim of the Pit."

"Exactly."

"Yes, of course. It all makes sense. It's sort of obvious really, isn't it? You feel you've known it all along, really, but couldn't *quite* see it. Does that make sense?"

"Yes, perfect sense. These things *are* obvious. We *do* see them even before we learn about them. But we lack the vocabulary to express them.

That is how the Pit works—denying us the conceptual apparatus to see what it is. Once we start to develop it, as we are doing now, the whole structure of mind-manipulation begins to fall to pieces. But the Pit's ultimate defence is that we cannot make this apparatus, this vocabulary, this understanding, general, and so, to most people the Pit continues to seem normal, if hateful, and *we* seem odd and hard to understand."

"But what can we do about it?"

"Do? In terms of outward action there is very little we can do. Outward action is what the Pit expects.It has every avenue tied up and co-opted, and it has the machinery of the mass-media to falsify and co-opt any new initiative. If our ideas became at all popular they would immediately be swamped by a massive, worthless type-3 counterfeit of them which would have all the advantages of mass-media recognition behind it—like bongo 'ecologism' and bongo 'feminism'. Of course, it would pretend to be a rebellion just as they do, and the mass-media would treat it subtly, half-attacking it, half-promoting it, just as it does with them. But it would be a teeth-drawn fake, just as they are and its sum effect would be to produce another brand of type-3, just as they have.

"So what can we do? We can build our own world from within. We can win the war on our home ground, casting their mind-tentacles out of our lives and producing the first real psychic setback the Pit has suffered since the Eclipse. Of course, to the masculine, externalist perspective this seems like nothing of importance. But the home, and the psychic reality we inhabit, is the centre of the world. We are creating the antidote to the Pit, and it does not matter how small it is in quantitative terms. The Pit is ultimately unreal, ultimately founded on falsehood and distortion. It contains within it the seeds of its own collapse. So long as the flame of truth and reality is burning *anywhere,* it may ultimately prevail. The millions on millions who are taken in by the Pit are of no account. The type-3s, even the cleverest, are just Pit-ponies working for their masters as they would work for *any* master (or mistress) who controlled their culture. They are just baggage that belongs to whoever wins the game. The only *players* in the game are the tiny handful who retain minds of their own. And however little we may outwardly do—indeed, partly *because* we know when to refrain from outward action—we are players, and who knows what turn the game may ultimately take?"

"It is rather thrilling, isn't it? And so fascinating I could go on talking about it all night."

"Not tonight, I am afraid, fair Lehnya. Little girls must get some sleep."

12. *Putting a Blonde in her Place*

"**I** MUST post these letters and get some shopping. Will you two be all right?"

"Yes, Mummie."

"Yes, Miss Milchford."

"I am taking Angeline with me—or would you rather I left her?"

"It's all right, Mummie, you won't be long and Lehnya will look after me."

"Very well. Kiss me goodbye, darling." Mummie looked so very real when she went out shopping, her coat so neat, her hat and her basket, her gloves, and just the right scent. How awful that she had to shop in the Pit.

"Is she taking Angeline with her in that uniform?"

"Of course, why not?"

"Well, what will the Pit-wallahs think?"

"They'll think Mummie has her maid with her to carry the shopping, if they are capable of thinking anything. But who cares what they think or whether they think?"

Lehnya laughed, but it felt like a bit of a bad start. What a weak thing to have said. But she was going to do it anyway.

"Annalinde, I want a word with you."

"Really, what sort of a word?"

"A serious word."

"What do you mean?"

"I'll tell you what I mean. I didn't like the way Susan was kissing you that day."

"What day?"

"You know what day."

"Well, it really isn't any business of yours, Lehnya. I understand you were upset——"

"Does your mother know how she was kissing you?"

"Of course Mummie knows about it."

"I said does she know *how* you were being kissed?"

"Well, I didn't give her a second-by-second account if that's what you mean."

"I'll bet you didn't."

"You've no right to talk to me like this, Lehnya."

"I'm not going to stand for it, Annalinde."

"How *dare* you——"

"Do you remember that long paddle-thing that prefect Julia Clarke punished us with a few months ago?"

"Yes, I remember."

"Go and get it."

"Lehnya, I am not going to be bullied by you just because you are a brunette."

"And twice as strong as the strongest blonde, which you aren't because you are a rather delicate fetching little flower of a blonde for all your cheek."

"Well, I may be——"

"Go and get it, Annalinde."

"All right, but don't think——"

"Now, Annalinde."

"Yes, Lehnya."

Annalinde returned with the 'paddle-thing'. It was a curious implement, shaped from light-coloured wood, some two feet long and widening to about two inches at the end. It was most like a long, narrow spatula, or perhaps a flat lengthwise cross-section from a rather slender baseball bat. She gave it meekly to Lehnya who swung it in her hand, enjoying the feel of it.

"Yes, I thought and thought, Annalinde, and I finally decided this is what you need. I don't really think I can cane you, but the girls use this——"

"Prefects, Lehnya."

"The girls use this, and it's rather painful, isn't it? Used with sufficient force."

"Yes, it is."

"Bend over the table, then."

"Lehnya, you *can't*——"

"You know you've been a naughty girl, now don't you?"

"Well, so was Susan."

"I don't care about Susan. I care about you."

"She *did* it, you know. I didn't take *her* by force."

"Brunettes have strong instincts. Blondes must be responsible."

"That isn't *fair*."

"I didn't say it is. It's just the way things are."

"But I couldn't *stop* her."

"Don't pretend you couldn't have pulled away, or slapped her face, or cried out when we were just round the corner."

"You don't know what it is *like* being a blonde. When some one overpowers us we become weak and submissive."

"Then you won't be able to resist me, will you, little blonde?"

"No, Lehnya."

"Bend over the table."

Annalinde positioned herself. "But you mustn't look at my under-things."

"I shan't lift up your petticoat," said Lehnya.

"Can't I have it over my skirt?"

"No. Now if you answer me back one more time I shall punish you for that."

"Yes, Lehnya."

Lehnya lifted Annalinde's neat, pleated pastel-tartan skirt. Her petticoat was a pleasing pale pink. So pale that it could almost be taken for white, with tiny lacy pleats an inch and a half deep round the hem. The outline of her nearly-matching pale pink cotton knickers could be seen through the thin nylon and one could tell that the flesh of her upper thighs was gathered into quite noticeable swellings above the pressure of her stocking-tops. Lehnya stood back and swung the long paddle, getting the feel of it. It was the first stroke she had ever given to any one, but she had seen and felt several punishments in her short time in Maryhill. She wanted her first stroke to be a good one; to impress this delectable blonde whom she had so successfully overawed.

She swung the paddle with all her force against the widest part of the petticoated thighs. The noise was startling, and the force jarred her own hand considerably. She watched the pink-covered flesh flatten and wobble back to its normal shape and she heard a gasping cry from Annalinde who had not expected anything quite so forceful. The cry was half-distressed and half-indignant and Lehnya felt afraid the girl would jump up and refuse further punishment, but she held her position like a well-trained Aristasian.

Lehnya felt herself smile. She felt powerful and very brunette. How delightful to be able to inflict another stroke. She swung again, feeling the satisfying crack of hard-on-soft, watching the well-filled knickers compress and quiver. She thought of that dreadful kiss—the brunette knee thrust between the all-too-yielding blonde thighs. Well, let those thighs yield now! Let them suffer! Blondes must learn to be modest and demure. She began to beat her rapidly. The strokes could not be each as hard as those premeditated single blows, but they were surprisingly hard for one so new to the art, and fell in furious succession. Annalinde began to wriggle.

"Lehnya—no———"

"Be quiet, blonde."

The pace of the strokes slowed, but each one became harder, and each one forced a little high, blonde squeaking breath from Annalinde.

The punishment continued for several minutes. Lehnya was tiring, and she was certain that Annelinde must be very hot and sore by now.

"A dozen *really* hard ones," she announced.

"Oh, Lehnya!"

"And I think I had better lift your petticoat so that you can feel the full benefit." Lehnya raised the pink slip and took the opportunity to admire her own handiwork. The helpless thighs, swelling above the dark nylon welt of the stocking-tops were a livid red, almost uniform in colour as the flesh disappeared into the pale pink cotton knickers. The suspenders were wide and strong, in a serviceable elastic, paler pink than the high-waisted knickers, and clearly made in the 1950s but not used until very recently. The clasps were of bright metal and one could see the nipples of dark nylon drawn over the white rubber suspender-buttons. She looked so very proper and well-appointed, the very everyday, self-contained femininity of the good, up-to-date undergarments somehow setting off the angry colour of the punished thighs. Those dozen strokes were going to hurt quite a lot on that warm and tender skin.

She drew back the paddle and struck with all her force across the very highest part of the naked thighs, just below the modestly frilled hem of pink cotton. The noise was very different from the other strokes, sharper and higher, and she knew from her own experience of punishment that the pain was sharper too. It is remarkable how much difference the protection of a wispy nylon petticoat can make. When one has that protection it seems as nothing as a heavy implement bites through its diaphanous impotency; but when it is removed, one cannot but notice that the sharper edge of direct contact brings a new and intensified immediacy to the punishment. Annalinde cried aloud with fresh distress as Lehnya watched the rise and swell of her pink-clad cheeks as the flesh directly beneath them was forced upwards.

She measured out the twelve strokes slowly and hard, working her way from that highest point of exposed flesh down to the tops of the stockings, each stroke overlapping the last and then working back up again. The last three she laid across the delectable roundness of the knickers themselves. Harder than ever and all exactly in the same place. Annalinde had remained fairly quiet throughout most of her chastisement, but Lehnya judged that she needed a moment to recover herself. She wanted to run her hand gently over the burning thighs and cheeks, as mistresses sometimes did and even prefects; but something would not let her. She was a brunette with a blonde, and it seemed wrong to indulge in such a familiarity. The very intensity of her desire made her feel that it would be wrong. She thought of folding down the petticoat and skirt and restoring Annalinde's modesty. But even this she felt unable to do. To touch a blonde's intimate garments, or even her skirt, that covered her private world, would be improper. True, she had raised them before ; but that was in pursuance of legitimate discipline—for despite the fact that she had no specific mandate, and could probably have been punished herself for thus taking the law into her unofficial hands, neither of the girls doubted for a moment that it was, in its own way, legitimate. That was over now, and a blonde's private places and lower garments must be her own inviolable domain, even though such a prohibition left Lehnya gazing in considerable fascination at—perhaps she should avert her eyes. Perhaps, in any case, Annalinde was sufficiently recovered by now.

"You may stand up, Annalinde."

Annalinde came to her feet as self-contained and blondely-dignified as ever. She was not flushed and crying as Sinta had been last night. She showed few signs of a girl who has undergone severe punishment. Perhaps Lehnya had been too gentle—but she had done the best she was capable of. These were her first thoughts. But then she began to perceive that Annalinde *was* changed.

Annalinde was a girl not unused to sound punishment and not given to demonstrations of her suffering. But quite unmistakably, she was changed. Her eyes were softer and wider, her stance more yielding, her entire manner suffused with a gentle, chastened warmth.

"Thank you, Lehnya," she said.

Lehnya felt the weight of the paddle in her hands. She had certainly given her a good beating. A beating *she* might have found hard to bear with as little sound as Annalinde.

"You were a good girl," she said.

"That makes up for being a naughty girl before, doesn't it, Lehnya ? "

"Yes, it does. We'll forget all about that."

She wanted to take the blonde in her arms. Whenever she was near Annalinde she wanted to take her in her arms, but now, so much more than ever. Would it be taking advantage ?

"Kiss better ? " said Annalinde. What was the delightful creature ? Infant or vamp ? She took her in her arms. The strange, sweet scent of whipped blonde-hood was in her nostrils as strongly as if it had been a physical smell. Annalinde was very warm, and somehow, she felt hardly physical in her embrace. Melting, almost, like buttery shortcake in the mouth : æthereal, yet almost animal at the same time. Her lips were moistly rouged in baby pink, her breath seemed literally scented pressed against Lehnya's own. She pressed her own red mouth against Annalinde's pink one, feeling the soft cling of heavily-applied lipstick. She held her body to her—her blonde body that a brunette might easily break like a matchstick, but that she was made to guard and protect always and to revere it as a sacred temple.

"I shan't be naughty again," said Annalinde.

"Aren't you being naughty now?"

Her eyes were full of childlike simplicity and she shook her head.

Here ends the story entitled **Children of the Void**, *but not the story of the Maryhill District which,* **Dea Volente**, *will continue in another book.*

AFTERWORD

To the One Girl in a Thousand

The rest of this book has been addressed to every one. For these fi-nal two pages we crave the indulgence of nine hundred and nine-ty-nine in every thousand readers. This is a private message ad-dressed to the one girl in a thousand.

THE STORY of this book is scarcely fiction. The life it depicts—*personae*, discipline, blondes and brunettes, District authorities, cinemas and cocktail bars—all of it is entirely real. Life as it is de-picted in *Children of the Void* is going on day by day, even as you read these words.

At this very moment Aristasian girls may be in school, they may be talking philosophy at an Art-Neo nightclub or having uproarious fun at a Soda Fountain. Some one, perhaps, is bending over a chair, awaiting the stinging kiss of the strap. A maid is washing clothes or brushing her mistress's hair. A mother and daughter are listening to a programme on the wireless (yes, we have up-to-date wireless programmes here). A blonde and brunette are dancing cheek-to-cheek to the strains of a Trentish dance band.

There *is* another world. A real alternative to the garish drabness and dreary madness of the Pit. A world of femininity and decency and charm.

And now that you have read this book, you know something about that world. You know what its life is like. You know something of the philosophy that underlies it. And you know something else. You know that if that world is *right*, then the Pit is *wrong*. But then, you have known all your life that the Pit was wrong, haven't you?

Yes. It is *you* I am talking to. Not the hundreds of other readers to whom this is just a book. But *you*: the girl in a thousand who have known all your life that the late 20th century does not and cannot offer you what you want from life. Who have always wanted to enter a mag-ical feminine world of kindness and strictness and goodness.

Were you about to shut the book and feel it was a lovely fantasy that is over now? It isn't you know. It isn't a fantasy, and it isn't over. It isn't over for the other girls who live in Aristasia, and it need not be over for you. For you it could be the beginning.

So think it over. If you *are* that one girl in a thousand, this is the turning point of your life. Either way. Whether you decide to take the next step or whether you put the book aside and forget it, you will have made the most important decision you are ever going to make.

Whether you come forward to meet your fate: to look through the golden doorway into another world, or whether you leave the door of opportunity closed and decide to continue in the Pit, you will have taken a fateful step. Which way you step depends on your courage and on whether you *are* that one girl in a thousand. I think you are starting to know by now.

If you know, or strongly suspect, that you are one of us, one of the Children of the Void, please write to this address:

Miss Marianne Martindale
C/O The Wildfire Club, B.M. Elegance, London W.C.1.

That is the full address. After you have written you will probably speak to some one over the telephone and then have a personal interview. Don't worry. You won't be swept into Aristasia all at once. We want to be sure of you just as much as you want to be sure of us. There is lots to learn and the process of becoming an Aristasian takes time.

But if you *are* that girl in a thousand, you will never be happy in the Pit, any more than Annalinde would, or Lehnya, or I. If you are that girl in a thousand, your true friends, your life's adventure and your heart's fulfillment lie here, and we are longing to welcome you.

And if you *think* you are, you probably are.

See you at the Odeon!

Soon.